mrs poole

CW00793331

Jacqueline Webb spent two years as a student nurse at Guy's Hospital in London, and worked at a school in France and as a nanny in Monaco before returning to the UK and training as a teacher at Bath University. After more travels through India, south-east Asia and Australia, she now lives on the Wirral with her husband, Shane, and their two children, Alex and Joe.

DRAGONSHEART

When Isabella Wyndham-Brown returns to London to celebrate her twenty-first birthday, she anticipates being able to direct her own life away from the restraints of her interfering relatives. But events conspire against her: she discovers that she cannot take control of her fortune until she is twenty-five, and then finds disturbing evidence that her father had a mistress . . . Nevertheless, there are compensations, including meeting her handsome French cousin, and being reunited with Peter Bennett, who saved her life in Egypt. However, when she discovers that her father may have found the lost family treasure, the Dragonsheart diamond, Bella's problems really begin . . .

Books by Jacqueline Webb
Published by The House of Ulverscroft:

THE SCARLET QUEEN

JACQUELINE WEBB

◆

DRAGONSHEART

Complete and Unabridged

ULVERSCROFT
Leicester

First published in Great Britain in 2007 by
Robert Hale Limited
London

First Large Print Edition
published 2008
by arrangement with
Robert Hale Limited
London

British Library CIP Data

Webb, Jacqueline
Dragonsheart.—Large print ed.—
Ulverscroft large print series: romance
1. Family—Fiction 2. Adultery—Fiction
3. Inheritance and succession—Fiction 4. Diamonds
—Fiction 5. Cousins—Fiction 6. London (England)
—Social life and customs—Fiction 7. Romantic
suspense novels 8. Large type books
I. Title
823.9'2 [F]

ISBN 978–1–84782–102–7

Published by
F. A. Thorpe (Publishing)
Anstey, Leicestershire

Set by Words & Graphics Ltd.
Anstey, Leicestershire
Printed and bound in Great Britain by
T. J. International Ltd., Padstow, Cornwall

This book is printed on acid-free paper

1

Hatfield, Hertfordshire, February 1910

The train finally pulled into the station at twenty past five, and I climbed down, barely noticing the great gouts of white steam that sailed away into the grey sky. I pulled the collar of my fur coat tighter around my neck. Aunt Augusta climbed down behind me, her own cape coat buttoned up tightly. She and Uncle George were even more unused to the cold than I was.

It was freezing in England of course. I had forgotten that after two years in the heat of Egypt. Two interesting years in which I had made some good friends and had some exciting adventures. But I was very glad to be home, particularly now. For in two weeks' time I was to celebrate my twenty-first birthday. An adult at last. No more having to accept someone else's decisions about what I could or couldn't do, or be packed off abroad every time someone thought I had misbehaved.

'Miss Bella! Yoo-hoo! Over here, Miss Bella!'

I looked up at the sound of the voice carolling my name and then smiled, ignoring Aunt Augusta's tut of disapproval. Seated on the top of the carriage was Marnie. She was dressed in her best black serge coat, her black hair streaked with more grey than I remembered, and more wrinkles on her face too. I ran over to her.

'Marnie!' I shouted as she struggled down from the top seat. For as long as I can remember I have loved Marnie. She might only have been an ageing nursemaid, but she was the one constant element in my life. Nannies and governesses came and went, but Marnie was always there to talk to me, play with me and comfort me when no one else was around. My numerous aunts and uncles did their best, but they all had large families of their own to see to and when one is the sole heir to a large fortune, people seem to assume the money makes up for lack of close family.

'Marnie, I missed you,' I whispered into her ear, so that Aunt Augusta wouldn't be too shocked at my over-familiarity with a servant.

'An' I missed you too, an' all, Miss Bella,' she said, her expression halfway between a scowl and a smile. 'I can't believe you're back safe and sound. I knew you shouldn'ta gone.'

'I didn't have much choice, if you recall,

Marnie,' I reminded her, as we watched the porters carry all our luggage from the platform out to the carriage. I frowned in the manner of Uncle Charles, the elder of my late mother's brothers and my guardian. ''You've got the choice, my gel. Either visit the Havershams out in Egypt, or spend the rest of the summer with Cousin Angus and his wife Morag in their castle in Arbroath. Now, which is it to be?' Really Marnie, what would you have done? I'm not sure I could find Arbroath on the map. And I have a sneaking suspicion Cousin Angus isn't even a cousin and their castle is a pile of stones on a hillside that they share with the goats.'

Marnie wasn't convinced however. 'It's still in England, miss,' she said darkly and erroneously. 'And they don't serve foreign muck. Or throw up murdering devils that try to kill you for a pile of heathen jewels.'

I grinned. Last year, I had been sent out to Egypt in disgrace by my uncle because of an embarrassing incident involving the married son of a powerful politician, and whilst there I had made friends with Kate Whitaker, the daughter of an archaeologist. We had gone out on a dig where Kate and her fiancé had found a pharaonic tomb packed full of treasures and we had all nearly been killed by a character called Richard Tillyard, the treasurer of the museum for whom she worked. It had been exciting, but I certainly wouldn't want to repeat the experience.

'My dear Marnie,' I said, taking her arm. 'Richard Tillyard was as English as cucumber sandwiches. And the food was delicious. You really should have come.'

I had been trying to persuade Marnie to accompany me on trips abroad since my first excursion to France at the age of sixteen, but Marnie steadfastly refuses to set foot beyond Dover. My parents had died abroad in Algeria in 1889 when I was six months old, leaving me alone in the desert with only Marnie to care for me. We had subsequently been rescued by foreign troops but the experience had scarred Marnie who had vowed never to travel abroad again.

'No, Miss Bella,' she said, shaking her head and making the fading artificial flowers on her best hat wobble. 'You do the travellin'. I'm stayin' right 'ere in yer ma's 'ouse.'

By this time Uncle George had paid the porters and Aunt Augusta was already in the carriage, frowning and ready to be off. I climbed up beside her and we set off on the last few miles home to Woodruffe Manor. It's not as big as Bowood Hall, the ancestral home of the Wyndham-Browns, but it's still very impressive and since Mama had the

4

foresight to will it to her eldest surviving female heir (me), rather than allow it to become part of the Bowood inheritance, it's mine now rather than my cousin Bertie's. Perhaps I should explain that my parents were the tenth Viscount and Viscountess Bowood and, as their only surviving child and a girl, I lost out on the title, the hall and lands that my father inherited from his father, but not any of Mama's property, which is why I now have a large modern house and a thriving fortune, whilst the new Bowoods are struggling with a draughty, magnificent ruin in Shropshire. As Aunt Augusta often remarks, I have a lot to thank the Married Women's Property Act for.

We drew up outside the house and Uncle Charles stepped out of the front door. Uncle Charles was of middling height with greying hair and a huge handlebar moustache which he tended lovingly as though it were a prize orchid. His daughters, Harriet and Helen, found this as amusing as I did, and many a dull Sunday afternoon was whiled away inspecting his collection of combs and waxes and lotions. Uncle Charles was a decent, dutiful man, but he did not inspire great love in small children.

'Isabella, my dear,' he said, as I alighted from the carriage. 'How delightful to see you again. I hope you found Egypt to your liking?'

'Wonderful, Uncle Charles,' I said. 'I particularly enjoyed being knocked unconscious by a group of ruffians and left to die in an underground tomb.' Actually I had had a wonderful time in Luxor, but I wasn't about to let Uncle Charles know that. I still remember his words to me in his London house after Henry's father's visit.

Uncle Charle's complexion became a little flushed. 'Ah yes. Bad business all around. Still no harm done in the end. Augusta, how are you?' he blustered, as Aunt Augusta and Uncle George followed me from the carriage. They kissed rather frostily. It should be said there wasn't much love lost between Uncle Charles and Aunt Augusta. But today I could see Uncle Charles was glad to find a reason to change the subject. We went to the drawing-room where a huge fire was burning in the grate.

'Hortensia is discussing dinner with Cook,' said Uncle Charles, flicking back the tails of his black coat and seating himself on the horsehair sofa. 'She'll be in directly. By the way, we're expecting Helen and Edwin later on this afternoon.'

'How are they?' I was fond of my cousin and her new husband, although I fancied Edwin was a little less enamoured of me after the affair with Henry. Edwin was rather starchy.

'Very well, thank you. Edwin was selected to the Chelsea ward last week.' Uncle Charles spoke these words with quiet pride.

'Oh I say, well done, old man.' Uncle George clapped him on the back and Uncle Charles's smile widened a little.

'We're very pleased,' he said. 'Of course, it's early days yet and the chap has to be elected. Even so . . . '

'Even so — splendid news.'

'How's Harriet?' I asked mischievously. Uncle Charles glared at me.

'She's very well, thank you,' he muttered.

'Oh good. Is she still a suffragette?'

'Charles, do you think Hortensia needs some help with the dinner arrangements?' asked Aunt Augusta, glowering at me. 'Because if so, Isabella and I will be more than happy to go and assist her.'

'Good idea, Augusta,' said Uncle Charles with relief, but Aunt Hortensia arrived just then, closely followed by Lily and Ada, the two parlourmaids, who held tea-trays in their hands, on which were placed a silver teapot with matching milk jug and sugar bowl, plates of cucumber sandwiches and tiny cakes. The subtle fragrance of the bergamot-flavoured tea mingled with the crisp, fresh aroma of the cucumber reminded me how hungry I was and I forgot about heckling Uncle Charles.

'How lovely to see you all again,' said Aunt Hortensia, as she sat down. 'Now, would you like a sandwich, Charles dear — but wait — ?' She looked up. 'Bella dear, would you like to do this? After all it's your birthday in ten days' time. This will be your job for good then.'

'Yes, it will, won't it?' I said happily. 'Which reminds me, Uncle Charles, you must make an appointment for me to meet the rest of the trustees.' Uncle Charles glared at me again, still angry with me for bringing up the subject of Harriet.

'I *could* do that, if you really want to, but I don't see the point,' he said, as Aunt Hortensia handed me a tea-cup. I looked at him, puzzled.

'Well, of course, I need to see them, Uncle Charles,' I said. I was becoming aware of a tension in the room. None of my relatives appeared to want to look me in the eye. 'How else will I know what affairs I have to manage otherwise?'

'Good lord, you aren't going to have to bother with that, dear,' said Aunt Hortensia nervously. 'That's what your uncle is here for.'

I glanced from Uncle Charles to Aunt

Augusta and then to Uncle George. They all looked distinctly shifty.

'But of course I have to, Aunt Hetty,' I said. 'You've looked after me splendidly since I was a baby, managing my affairs and so forth, but it's time I started seeing to things myself.' There was a short silence, then Uncle Charles cleared his throat.

'Yes, well, I suppose it won't hurt to give you some idea of what's going on. Tell you what, my dear, I'll meet up with the rest of the board next week some time and we'll have a chat about — '

'Forgive me, Uncle Charles,' I interrupted, 'but since I am about to be responsible for a not inconsiderable fortune in less than two weeks' time, I think I need a little more educating than merely giving me 'some idea of what's going on'.'

'Ah yes, well — '

'You see, my dear, the thing is . . . we should have told you — '

'Bella darling — '

There was chaos for a few moments as both my uncles and Aunt Hortensia all tried to speak at the same time. Before I could make any sense of what they were saying, Aunt Augusta tapped her lorgnette forcefully on the tea-tray.

'*Attention. Il ne faut pas parler devant les*

domestiques,' she barked, glaring at Lily and Ada as though the whole charade were their fault. They did look extremely interested, but I could hardly blame them for that. I was too, and personally I couldn't really see why we shouldn't speak in front of them. Servants always found out everything that happened above stairs, often before their employers did. Sometimes I thought it would be much easier if we just invited the entire staff to come and sit down with us while we discussed our affairs. It would be less hypocritical and probably we'd learn quite a bit.

But not today. Today I wanted to know exactly what my aunts and uncles were keeping from me and I didn't have time for whimsies.

'Lily, Ada, thank you, that will be all,' I said. The two girls curtsied and walked out.

'So what is it?' I asked in the ensuing silence. 'What haven't I been told?'

Uncle Charles harrumphed a bit more and began to fiddle with his moustache, but before he could speak, Uncle George held up a hand.

'Well, Bella, the situation is this: your mother's will stipulates that you are not to be given full power over your fortune until you are twenty-five.'

I stared at him silence for a few seconds.

'Twenty-five?' I echoed incredulously. That was another four years away. All four relatives nodded in unison.

'Just as an added precaution,' said Uncle Charles. I turned to glare at him.

'An added precaution? To what, pray?'

'To make sure you have enough maturity to be able to manage your affairs, my dear,' he said grimly and I knew he was thinking about Henry Fitzroy again.

'I see,' I said coldly. 'Is that it? Or is there more?'

Uncle George and Aunt Hortensia looked embarrassed and were clearly wishing they were anywhere but here. Uncle Charles and Aunt Augusta, however, were made of sterner stuff.

'You may not marry without the consent of the trustees during that time, if you wish to attain the bulk of your fortune,' said Uncle Charles crisply. 'In the event of a dispute between the two parties, Woodruffe Manor and all its estates will become forfeit and liable to be distributed to various other parties stipulated in the will.'

'Of course, you do get a dress allowance, dear,' said Aunt Hortensia nervously. 'Fifty pounds a month to spend as you will. Isn't that nice?'

I stood up and walked to the fire, my

11

appetite suddenly gone. I couldn't believe what I had just heard. After all this time of being pushed around from pillar to post, never mistress of my own life, I had believed I would at last have my independence, only to have it snatched away from me for another four years.

'I see,' I said again. 'So tell me if I've understood this correctly. If I'm a good little girl and do as I'm told and don't try to make any decisions of my own, I get fifty pounds a month to spend on frocks. Is that it? Is that the length and breadth of my new independence?'

'Really, Bella, don't be so melodramatic,' said Aunt Augusta. 'Of course, you have more independence than before. Your dear mama, God rest her soul, was simply trying to avoid putting an old head on young shoulders. You should be grateful for her prudence. This way you learn how to manage your fortune gradually.'

'Forgive me if I don't start singing hallelujahs to her memory, Aunt Augusta,' I snapped. 'I was expecting that being an adult meant I was going to be treated like one.'

'Bella, your mama knew what she was doing when she made that will,' said Aunt Augusta severely. 'And, I might add, your father agreed with her completely.'

'Hmph. Not that he had much choice,' muttered Uncle Charles, drawing Aunt Augusta's disapproval away from me and towards him.

'I object to that comment, Charles. Robert may have made a few unfortunate decisions in his life — '

'A few!'

' — as any young man might make, but he paid for them and they were all behind him. He and Amelia were in complete harmony over their arrangements for their children and I'll thank you not to sully his memory in my presence.'

'He got my sister to pay for them, you mean,' said Uncle Charles angrily. 'He'd have been penniless if not for Amelia. It was thanks to her, not him, that they had the money to go on that damn — '

'Now now, dear,' admonished Hortensia. Uncle Charles barely glanced at her as he edited his language.

' — blasted silly journey to that wretched, dangerous land of heathens and — '

'Now come on, old chap,' said Uncle George, ever the peacemaker in this never-ending feud between Uncle Charles and Aunt Augusta. 'Amelia was just as keen as Robert to go. You know that.'

'Yes, that is true, dear,' said Aunt

Hortensia. 'In fact, if anything, even keener. Do you know, Bella darling, I well remember two days before the ship was due to depart, it seemed there might be a delay and poor dear Amelia was almost beside herself with pique because — oh! Where is Bella?'

'She's gone,' Uncle George said, with a trace of amusement. 'I think she got fed up listening to a bunch of old duffers treading the same old path.'

*　*　*

I heard Uncle George's last words as I sped up the stairs angrily. He was only partly right. I had heard that argument many times before, but usually I found it mildly diverting. This time I was so incensed by the news of the will that I had used the ensuing clash of personalities to leave the room before I said something I might have cause to regret.

As I walked up the stairs to my bedroom I saw again the portrait my grandfather, Lindsay Wyndham-Brown, had had painted of himself and his family. It had been executed by an artist who had been popular about the time Queen Victoria was first widowed and since he obviously favoured greys and blacks, like the old lady herself, the resulting painting was a sombre family group,

14

almost puritan in its outlook. My two paternal aunts, Augusta as a serious child of ten and Phyllis, six, were standing next to my grandmother, with my father, at three the youngest and most important, being the only son and heir, seated on his father's knee. Actually it was hard to tell he was a boy because, in accordance with the fashion of the day, he had long hair and was dressed in a jacket with frilled drawers just showing under his knee-length skirt. Unlike his sisters and parents he looked neither sombre nor dutiful and until today I had always enjoyed lingering at this painting, revelling in the mischief in his eyes. Even the way he leant nonchalantly against the arm of the chair was endearing, one hand cradling his head with a hint of boredom.

However, today was different. Today I didn't feel quite so affectionate towards him. In fact, if it hadn't been pointed out so baldly to me that I still didn't exercise real dominion over any of my property, I think I might have ordered the painting to be destroyed, so angry was I with my dead parents' plans to keep me in enforced immaturity. I scowled at the 3-year-old Robert Wyndham-Brown. How could he and my mother have put me in this position? Twenty-one, and all I could do was spend money on dresses and trinkets.

Another four years before I had any say over my life. I picked up a fold of my hobble skirt and ran as best I could up the stairs to my bedroom.

My room is large, lately with its own bathroom installed, a marvellous luxury, and the maids had already lit a fire in the grate so it was warm and welcoming. As I sank on to the pink quilt on my bed I saw the tiny photograph next to my bed, the only one of me and my parents. It had been taken only days after my birth and I was little more than a bundle of white woollen blankets, held tight in my mother's arms. She was sitting on a chair, with my father behind her, one hand draped on her shoulder. The picture was typical of its era and they were serious and unsmiling. My mother had a long, thin face and large dark eyes and she looked rather strained, as did my father. I glared at them both for a few seconds more before turning the photograph to the wall in a fit of childish pique.

Just then I heard the sound of a horse and carriage. My bedroom overlooks the drive, so I walked over to the window and watched as the driver slowed the horses down to a halt in front of the house. A footman appeared and opened the carriage door and Edwin stepped out, closely followed by Helen, my cousin.

I walked away from the window. I loved Helen, but since she had married Edwin, she had evolved into the wife of a solid, Conservative MP with such incredible ease, it was sometimes almost impossible to remember the girl I had once giggled with over Uncle Charles's moustache combs. So I turned away and began sorting through my luggage. I knew the business over the will was not the fault of my aunts and uncles, and soon I would have to go back downstairs and make my peace with them. But just at the moment, I wasn't feeling too amenable, so instead I bent over the valises and examined the fragile Muski glassware, luminous in turquoise, green and purple, that I had bought from the bazaars in Egypt, determined not to let my English relatives spoil my reminiscences.

Suddenly there was a knock on the door. 'I'm busy,' I said disagreeably, hoping to scare the servants away.

'Too bad,' came the answer. The door suddenly burst open and there stood my cousin Harriet, her plump face glowing with cold and her dark-brown hair slightly frizzy from the damp. She was wearing a harem skirt, not really a skirt at all, but a pair of wide trousers. I began to understand why Uncle Charles had been so frosty.

'Harry!' I shouted, delighted to see her. I ran to the door, laughing as we hugged. 'How long have you been here?'

'Barely ten minutes, you goose,' she replied. 'Didn't you hear the carriage pulling up?'

'I did,' I said, drawing her into my room. 'But I thought it was just Helen and Edwin. I didn't realize you were here too.'

'Now what made you think I'd miss the return of my scandalous, rich, heiress cousin?'

'If there's any scandalous female here, it's you, my dear.' We sat down on my bed. 'Uncle Charles barely managed to acknowledge you existed, earlier on this afternoon.'

She laughed. 'Papa finds it hard to believe I can want to do anything as unladylike as vote in a general election. Last week at dinner he told me that Mrs Pankhurst deserved to be force-fed while in prison and Edwin laughed. Laughed! They had no answer though when I started demanding to know why prisoners and madmen could vote but not women. Mama and Helen practically had to drag me away from the table when the port and cigars were announced.'

I laughed. 'I wish I'd been there. Shall we refuse to leave this evening when Aunt Hetty invites us ladies to retire?'

18

'Yes, do let's. How I've missed you, Bella. There's been no one on my side since Nell married Edwin. She's so staid now I sometimes want to scream. Anyway, it is your house now, isn't it? Or practically. Papa can hardly order your own servants to escort you from the dining-room.'

At her words I frowned, my pleasure at seeing her diminishing somewhat. 'Actually Harry, I've a horrible feeling he can. It turns out I'm not going to be mistress of all I survey in two weeks after all.'

'Really?' She said, lying back on the bed and putting her hands behind her head in a most unladylike manner. 'Do tell.'

'My darling mama put an extra codicil in the will. Apparently she knew I wasn't going to be mature enough to spend the Woodruffe fortune wisely at the age of twenty-one and stipulated I have to wait until I'm twenty-five.'

'Oh, so that's what Mama and Papa were discussing the other night,' she said rolling over on to her side. 'I overheard them talking before dinner and Mama sounded worried then. 'Bella is going to be so disappointed, Charles', she said. You know how Mama hates arguments.'

'I'm sure Uncle Charles was heartbroken,' I said rather disagreeably, as I put a silver *sheesha* waterpipe on my bureau.

'Actually, darling, he said something that puzzled me enormously at the time, but now it makes perfect sense.' She sat up and harrumphed in exactly the same manner as I had done earlier with Marnie. ''Hmph, my dear. Just tell the girl to be grateful she's not a boy. She'd've had to wait until she's thirty if she was. Frankly, if I'd been Amelia, I'd have insisted on fifty'.'

'Really? Thirty if I'd been a boy?' I sat down beside her. 'I suppose being a girl isn't all bad then.'

'Of course it isn't,' said Harriet robustly, examining a traditional caftan in deep reds and purples and greens. 'This is gorgeous, Bella.'

'I know. I thought I might wear it to Charlotte Talbot's fancy dress ball in the summer. If I'm brave enough.'

'Oh yes, good idea. Listen.' She turned to face me suddenly. 'All this talk has made me forget why I came up here in the first place. Since you didn't see me get out of the carriage, I suppose you didn't see who was with me, did you?'

'I thought you said you came with Nell and Edwin.'

'Yes, but we brought someone else too. Do you remember the name Marivaux?'

I frowned. It sounded familiar, but I couldn't think why for the moment, and I said as much to Harriet.

'They're the French branch of our family. You remember Grandfather Woodruffe's sister Evangeline?'

'Didn't she marry badly?'

'That's right, darling. She fell in love with the French dance tutor and eloped to Brittany.'

'Of course. Now I remember. But wasn't there a terrible argument between Uncle Charles and one of the sons? I thought they'd refused ever to speak to any of us again?'

'They did. Or at least that's what Cousin Eugenie told me two years ago. Apparently they never forgave us for cousin Agnes being killed in Algeria with your parents.'

I nodded. I'd heard about the French companion who'd died alongside my parents. Since the Marivaux family was a great deal poorer than we were, Great Aunt Evangeline had swallowed her pride and used whatever influence she had with Grandfather to help improve her own children's lot. Consequently impoverished French cousins were despatched across the channel regularly at one time, working as glorified servants in the positions of governess or companion to elderly aunts or, in the case of boys, to be

21

humiliated at awful English boarding-schools. Cousin Agnes had been sent as a companion to Mama and had died along with my parents of typhoid, in the tiny Algerian village they had unwisely elected to visit. I have to say I'd never been very interested in her: faceless French girls were much less important to me than my own exciting part in the adventure. Apparently when it had become clear to Papa that they were in dire straits he had sent Marnie to find help, but she had been unable to do so and had returned to find me alone in my cot, wrapped only in my christening shawl, Mama already dead and Papa breathing his last. Marnie had fled the village and wandered extremely rashly into the desert, where we would both have died if it had not been for a passing platoon of French soldiers who found us and took us back to Algiers. I know I should probably be grateful that I was only a baby when it happened, but honestly, Marnie made it sound so exciting to a little girl, sometimes I wish I had been old enough to enjoy it.

'Well it was hardly our fault,' I said indignantly. 'I'm sure if Papa and Mama had known they were all going to catch typhoid, they would have left a lot sooner.'

'Of course not, darling. Anyway, the point is, last month we had a letter from Agnes's mother asking if her youngest son could visit. It was her husband, Sebastien, who blamed us for Agnes's death, but apparently he died a couple of years ago and the rest of the family wanted to get in touch with us again.'

'Oh. So what did Uncle Charles say?'

'He wasn't very happy, but Mama said she hated thinking that there were people in the world who blamed the Woodruffes for the death of an innocent girl, so Papa had a meeting with Uncle Geoffrey and Aunt Abigail and they decided in the interests of family harmony to welcome Cousin Laurent on a strictly limited basis.'

Harriet and I both burst into laughter simultaneously. I could just imagine my pompous Woodruffe relations sitting down and discussing such an emotive matter in this dry, business-like way.

'So anyway,' said Harriet, after we had calmed down, 'two weeks ago we had a telegram from Dover saying that Laurent had crossed the channel and was looking forward to seeing us. He only arrived last night.'

'Oh lord,' I said. 'Didn't he have enough money for the train? Did he have to walk from Dover? The Marivauxes must be hating us all over again.'

'Not at all, darling,' said Harriet, looking a bit smug. 'Papa sent a telegram back of course, enquiring if he needed help and got a rather stiff letter in reply. It turns out that over the last twenty years or so, the Marivaux family has become very prosperous. Uncle Sebastien and his three brothers all became successful dairy farmers and the family is quite well off.'

'Really?' I said. 'So what's he like then, this new cousin?'

Here Harriet really did look smug. 'Come and see for yourself, darling,' she said, getting up and walking back over to the door. 'And wear your turquoise silk Lucile design tonight. I guarantee you'll thank me for such advice.'

Before I could say anything else she had gone, leaving me intrigued as I dressed for dinner.

$$\star \quad \star \quad \star$$

The lamps were all lit as I walked down the great staircase later on and since I had taken Harriet's advice to wear the Lucile I was feeling elegant and sophisticated and just a little bit pleased with myself.

I walked into the drawing-room to find that I was one of the first to arrive. The only other person present was Uncle George.

'Hello, Bella. You look lovely, my dear,' he

said as he handed me a small glass of sherry.

'Thank you, Uncle George,' I said. 'Are you and I the only two punctual people in the house? The dinner gong went five minutes ago.'

Uncle George sat down in a buttoned upholstered armchair. 'Charles and Edwin are in the study. Edwin brought some papers for him to sign.'

'Oh. But what about Helen and Harriet? And Aunt Augusta and Aunt Hetty?'

'Hmph. Probably primping themselves in order to impress that frog who turned up this afternoon.'

I looked at Uncle George, surprised at the disapproving tone of his voice, but before I could say anything someone else beat me to it.

'Good evening, Sir George,' said a voice, with a distinct French accent.

I turned. Standing in the doorway was possibly the most handsome man I had ever seen in my life. He was in his early thirties, tall and dark-haired, his black tailcoat and white piqué waistcoat fitting him perfectly. Judging from the mischievous smile on his face, I gathered he had heard Uncle George's less than flattering remark.

Uncle George stood up. 'Good evening, Marivaux. Don't believe you've met my niece yet. Bella, this is Laurent Marivaux. Some sort of cousin of yours. Can't quite work out how many times removed, although Nell did try to explain it to me. Whisky, Marivaux?'

'Thank you, Sir George.' Laurent Marivaux nodded amiably to Uncle George, before turning large, dark eyes on me. He seemed to examine me with great interest as he took my hand in his and kissed it.

'*Enchanté, mademoiselle,*' he said. I could feel myself blushing. Behind me, Uncle George gave a disapproving cough.

'Monsieur Marivaux,' I said. Sadly this was all I could remember of the French that I had been forced to learn at school. 'How lovely to meet you.'

'The pleasure is all mine, *mademoiselle.*' He still had hold of my hand; that is until Uncle George thrust a whisky glass at him, somewhat closer to his face than I would have thought necessary.

'Here you are, Marivaux. Sit down, the ladies shouldn't be long. Ah, Charles, there you are. Everything shipshape?'

'Fine, thank you, George.'

Uncle Charles had returned with Edwin and, as I turned to them, I had to fight the urge to burst into laughter. At his wedding, I had thought Edwin a pleasant enough looking fellow, but he appeared to be

26

modelling himself on Uncle Charles, with a junior version of the ridiculous moustache growing under his nose.

'Edwin, darling,' I said. 'How lovely to see you. I hear congratulations are in order.'

'Well, we shall see,' he said gruffly, but I could tell he was feeling pleased with himself. He preened his moustache in just the same way Uncle Charles did. As I turned I saw M. Marivaux look away, the beginnings of a smile sparkling in his eyes.

'Bella, here you are. We looked for you in your room,' said Harriet, as she and Helen entered.

'I was being punctual like a good little girl,' I said, as I kissed Helen. 'How are you, Nell?'

'Very well, Bella. We're so glad you're back safe from that ghastly country, aren't we, Edwin? I couldn't believe it when we got Aunt Augusta's letter. Mama all but fainted and had to spend the day in bed.'

'Dreadful business,' said Edwin, accepting a glass of whisky from Uncle Charles. 'You can't trust foreigners.'

There was the tiniest of pauses whilst M. Marivaux studied his whisky glass intently, the mischievous glint in his eyes still there.

'Edwin, darling,' I said. 'Richard Tillyard was English.'

'Laurent, have these barbarians introduced

you and Bella yet?' said Harriet, sitting down next to him.

'We have met,' he said, turning to Harriet. 'I am enchanted. Mademoiselle Wyndham-Brown reminds me of my grandmother.'

'Really?' said Harriet. 'Do you mean Evangeline? How wonderful if you do, Bella. Laurent showed me a picture of her just before she died. Even at eighty she looked beautiful. Not at all like Grandfather.'

'Well she didn't have his nose,' said Helen, laughing. 'Not like us.'

Edwin smiled. 'Nothing wrong with your nose, my dear,' he said gruffly.

'That's very sweet, Edwin, but unfortunately it's not true.' Harriet rubbed her own admittedly rather large nose. 'We Woodruffes are cursed that way whilst Bella, luckily for her, isn't.'

Laurent Maricaux smiled. 'Your nose is perfect, Harriet, as is your sister's. But no, I think it is more something about your eyes.'

Before I could reply, Lily came into the room and bobbed a curtsy in the direction of Uncle Charles.

'Lady Faversham sends 'er compliments, sir, and says to tell you that dinner is served.'

Uncle George laughed. 'There's our marching orders, Charles. Come m'dears,' he added, holding out an arm to both myself and

Harriet. I would have quite liked to have gone in with M. Marivaux and so, I suspected, would Harriet, but we were both fond of Uncle George, so we took an arm apiece and let him lead us into dinner. As we walked out of the room, I glanced back and saw M. Marivaux was talking to Helen. He looked up briefly, caught me staring and winked.

I turned back to Uncle George, who was talking about Christobel Pankhurst's latest escapade with Harriet. I could feel myself blushing. I'd never met a man who'd done that to me before and I was discombobulated, to say the least. Nevertheless, I began to look forward to becoming better acquainted with my new French cousin.

★   ★   ★

Dinner was a pleasant and civilized affair that night. Aunt Augusta and Aunt Hortensia were clearly worried that I might still be sulking about the terms of the will and did everything they could to keep me happy. They were also very relieved when both Harriet and I stood up to leave the gentlemen to their port and cigars without a murmur.

We chatted for a while in the drawing-room, then I remembered a *baladi* shawl I had bought Helen from Egypt. I went to my room to fetch it and, as I came down the stairs again, I saw Laurent Marivaux examining the portrait of the Wyndham-Browns.

'Monsieur Marivaux,' I said, as I walked down to meet him. He turned.

'Mademoiselle. These are relatives of yours, no?'

'My father,' I said, stroking his dark ringlets on the canvas gently. It felt cool under my fingers as I traced the delicate swirls of the paintbrush. 'And, believe it or not, this serious young miss is Aunt Augusta.'

He raised an eyebrow as I pointed to the slim, unsmiling young girl standing next to Papa. 'Lady Faversham? This is true? But wait, I can see a similarity; yes, the eyes again. They are very . . .'

He waved a hand, trying to think of a description that was honest, yet polite.

'Disapproving?' I suggested, and he turned to me again with the expression of laughter in his eyes.

'I could not say, *mademoiselle*. It would not be correct, I think.'

'Please, call me Bella. After all, we are cousins, are we not? And may I call you Laurent?'

'I would be honoured. But tell me, Bella — this little boy, your father' — he tapped a

30

long finger on the picture — 'he would be the Robert Wyndham-Brown who went to Algeria, is that correct?'

'Ah. Yes. Sorry about that,' I said. He turned to face me, puzzled.

'Why are you apologizing?'

'Well, you know, your sister dying . . . '

'It was not your fault, Bella, nor even your father's. I doubt he was expecting to die either.'

'Oh.' I frowned again. 'But I thought — Harriet said — your father . . . '

Now Laurent frowned. 'My father adored my sister. She was his only daughter. When we received the news that she had died, a little piece of him died too.'

'Still, I'm sorry. I'm sure Agnes was a lovely girl and it must have been — ' I stopped. He was looking at me intently, trying to appear serious and yet I could see the same expression of suppressed laughter on his face that he had worn earlier on, with Edwin and Uncle George. 'I'm sorry. Have I said something funny?'

The smile spread from his eyes to the rest of his face now. 'You must forgive me, Bella. It is just the way you all say my sister's name.'

'Her name?' I was confused. 'I *am* sorry. I was sure Harriet said her name was Agnes. What — ?'

31

'It is. But — *Anyes*, not *Agnes*,' he corrected. 'You see? *Agnès*.'

'Oh! Yes, that's much prettier.' It was, too. Frankly I had been having some trouble matching a young girl to what I'd always considered an old lady's name. The way he said it made it sound much more flattering. He nodded.

'Yes, she was very pretty.'

'You miss her too.'

'We were very close. She was the eldest, and my three older brothers did not have much time for me, since I was the baby. We were together a lot until she left. I was nine when she died.'

'I'm sorry,' I said. 'You must have been devastated.'

'It is twenty-one years since she died. Life moves on, does it not?' He shrugged. 'And the painting of this very beautiful woman — who is she?'

I looked at the huge painting, that hung next to Papa and his family, of a Carolean beauty resplendent in her low-cut gown, the basque bodice a waterfall of lace. 'That's Arabella Wyndham-Brown, wife of the third Viscount Bowood. She is gorgeous, isn't she? I think she was my great great great grandmother. These two paintings were originally from Bowood Hall, but the present owners were having cash problems so Uncle Charles bought them for me.'

'I see.' He smiled. 'And what does she wear around her neck, this very attractive ancestor of yours?' He pointed to a huge, pale-blue diamond that dangled rather provocatively just above Arabella's scandalous *décolletage*. As he lifted up his hand I saw a long white scar running from the palm right up under the sleeve of his jacket.

'That's the Dragonsheart. It's the Wyndham diamond. Arabella was reputedly the last person to have seen it. It was lost during the Civil War.'

'Lost?' He lifted both eyebrows in surprise.

'Lost, stolen, sold in secret to keep the family afloat. No one is quite sure exactly what happened to it. I doubt we ever will now, but the Wyndham-Brown fortune never really recovered after its loss.'

Laurent leaned forward to take a closer look at the diamond. 'It was very precious?'

'Very.'

'Why is it called the Dragonsheart?'

'Apparently if you caught it in the right light, you could see an image of a winged creature right in the centre. Someone called it that and it stuck. Anyway, it's gone now.'

We both studied the pale-blue stone glinting from the sun that the artist had painted shining through the window. It seemed almost too heavy for the delicate silver chain threaded through it.

'I console you on the loss of such a magnificent stone. But your fortunes do not seem so poor to me,' said Laurent after a moment. 'This house is magnificent.'

'Thank you. But in fact, that was Mama's doing. She was the one with the money; Papa brought the title, although of course we don't actually have it any more, since I wasn't born a boy.'

'I'm sorry?'

I smiled. 'I'm only an 'honourable', Laurent. If I'd been a boy, we'd have kept the title, Viscount Bowood, and Bowood Hall too. As it is, when Papa died without a male heir, the title went to distant cousins.'

'That is regrettable,' said Laurent politely, and I laughed.

'Not nearly as regrettable for me as it is for my cousin Bertie. Thanks to Mama's will I get all the money and this lovely house, and all he got was a distinguished name and a pile of ruins in the country. You've no idea how annoyed his parents were when they first found out that I inherited the money. It's one of the few things that actually unite Uncle Charles and Aunt Augusta. She's never really got over seeing her childhood home go to my

Aunt Mary, whom she's never liked, and Uncle Charles was furious when they tried to take Mama's will through the courts.'

'Here you both are!' Suddenly Harriet's voice called us back to the present. 'Whatever were you doing, Bella? Nell's losing faith in ever seeing that shawl.'

'I was just telling Laurent about the Dragonsheart,' I said, as we began to walk back down the stairs towards Harriet and the others in the drawing-room. 'And he was telling me about his sister. Do you know we've all been pronouncing her name wrong. It should be Agnès. Is that right, Laurent?'

'*Parfait.*'

'Agnès.' Harriet put her head to one side. 'That's much prettier than Agnes.'

'Isn't it?' I put a hand through her arm. 'Harriet, have you told Laurent about my birthday party?'

She grinned. 'Of course, darling. It was the first thing we discussed when he arrived. He's looking forward to it immensely, aren't you, Laurent?'

'Immensely,' he repeated gravely and I laughed. As we walked back into the drawing-room where everyone had reassembled, I realized how pleased I was to have met this new cousin.

2

The music of the waltz reached its climax and ended on a flourish for which I have to say I was grateful. I steered Laurent across to the window and sat down with a sigh on an empty seat.

'You are tired, *mon ange?*'

'Exhausted. But isn't it wonderful?'

I looked around with some satisfaction. Woodruffe Manor had been spruced up for the occasion of my twenty-first birthday and it looked magnificent. The floors had been polished until they shone, there were fresh flowers everywhere and above us the chandeliers sparkled. As I listened to the music from the ballroom and watched all my friends dancing, I couldn't help feeling the tiniest bit smug.

Laurent nodded. 'Wonderful. As you are, *ma belle.*'

I had become very fond of Laurent in the three weeks since we had first met. Uncle George and Aunt Augusta had left after a few days to visit their daughter Julia and her family, and Uncle Charles and Edwin had returned to London before my party, but

36

Laurent, Harriet and Helen had stayed on with Aunt Hetty and we had had a great deal of fun, riding in the countryside, taking walks in the grounds and visiting various neighbours. During the second week, he had left us to our own devices for a whole day, refusing to tell us where he was going or what he was doing, merely insisting he would have a surprise for us on his return. We had spent the time wandering about the house, frightened to leave in case we missed him and becoming increasingly more irritable with each other, until at last he had returned just as dusk was falling, seated proudly behind the wheel of a motor car, with a crowd of children running behind him. No one had seen anything like it in the village; it was a Rolls-Royce Silver Ghost, its metal body gleaming, the red leather upholstery still shiny. It attracted a crowd wherever we went. All of us, apart from Aunt Hetty, had lessons in driving it, although Helen had rather lost her nerve after she steered it into the vicar's hedge and buckled the wheel. It lived behind the potting shed since Henderson refused to let it anywhere near the horses, and he became very cross with the stable-boy who cooed over it constantly. All in all, the last few days of my minority had passed very pleasantly.

I stood up. 'Come along. We mustn't sit here. It simply isn't done on one's birthday to sit and watch others dancing. Either one must dance oneself or one must mingle. And I think my feet would thank me for some gentle mingling at the moment.'

We passed through the hallway slowly, with me shaking hands and thanking everyone for their congratulations and presents until finally we found ourselves in the drawing-room, where my older relatives and friends had gathered as it was quieter. Aunt Augusta was sitting talking to Great Aunt Evadne who was 91 and had insisted on being present, to the irritation of her daughter Daphne, who was 67 herself. Great Aunt Evadne could be difficult at times; she suffered from intermittent deafness and I had heard Uncle Geoffrey say she was overfond of the sherry bottle, but I had a soft spot for her myself. She always used to thrust threepenny bits into my hand when I was small. However, Laurent steered me away from them towards a sofa near the window.

'We should go and sit with the aunts,' I reproved him gently.

'Are they Wyndham-Browns or Woodruffes?'

'My lot,' I replied, sinking into the soft pile of the elegant green damask couch.

'Then I cannot be bothered,' he answered with the arrogance of the French. I smiled. 'Thank you so much. Now I'll get into trouble.'

'It is your birthday, *ma chère*. Your twenty-first birthday. On such a day, one is allowed to be selfish. Here.' As he sat down beside me, he felt into the pocket of his tailcoat and took out a small box. 'I forgot. This is a present from my mother. She and all my family wish you *félicitations*.'

'Laurent, how kind.' Inside the box was a silver chain with a tiny blue diamond nestling in a filigree silver heart. It was exquisite.

'It's beautiful,' I whispered, taking it out as gently as I dared, and examining the sparkling blue stone.

'Not as impressive as the Dragonsheart, but my mother saw it in Paris and since I had told her about the diamond she thought it might amuse you.'

'What a lovely present. She really shouldn't have done, especially since we've never met.'

He shrugged. 'I have written to her about you.'

I looked at him in surprise. 'Really? What have you been saying?'

He shrugged again, picking an invisible piece of lint from his sleeve. 'Only that if your parents were as charming as you are, Agnès would have been very happy with them whilst she was here. That is very important to my mother. She always worried that Agnès went away too young.'

I put the necklace back in the box for a moment as I reached up and felt for the clasp of the pendant I was wearing.

'Did your father hate us terribly for her death?' I asked, struggling with the clip.

'Outwardly he cursed your father, but of course really he blamed himself for letting her go. *En effet*, Agnès gave him no choice. She was desperate to leave Lisieux. It was too dull for her. Even though I was only eight when she left, I remember how excited she was to be travelling abroad for the first time.' He leaned over and pulled my fingers gently away from the clasp, fastening it round my throat, the thin silver chain a delicate trickle of cold water against my skin. 'Let me see. Yes, it suits you. It matches your eyes.' He looked at me intensely for a moment before bending forward and kissing me lightly on the cheek. 'Happy birthday, *chèrie.*'

The warmth of his kiss tingled against my cheek and I felt flustered, something that had never happened to me before.

'How kind of you to say so, Laurent,' I babbled stupidly. 'Agnès's leaving must have been very sad for you since you were so attached to her.'

He leaned back on the sofa again, looking relaxed and slightly amused.

'I was desolate, inconsolable. Until my uncle bought a pony and taught me to ride.' He shrugged. 'Such is the cruelty of the child. Only when we heard of Agnès's death did I remember how much I loved her. Now all we have are photographs.'

'I would love to see one.'

'*Hélas*, I have neglected to bring any with me,' he said, holding up his hands. Once again I saw the long white scar that ran down his palm.

'Laurent, may I ask you something?'

'Anything, *mon ange*.'

'Where did you get that fearsome-looking scar?'

He looked down at his hand and laughed. 'A riding accident — from the same horse my uncle bought for me. Perhaps it was divine justice.'

Just then Aunt Augusta bustled up to us. 'Isabella, my dear, I hate to intrude on your special day, but go and sit with Aunt Evadne for a moment, would you? She seems to be getting tired and I must go and find Daphne and I don't want to leave her alone.' Aunt Augusta frowned. 'She might take it into her

41

head to wander off.'

'Is she capable of doing that?' I asked. These days one tended to think of Great Aunt Evadne as being glued into her bath-chair.

'Well she's certainly capable of trying. Really, Daphne should have been firmer with her,' she added crossly.

'If you will permit me, I shall help you look for her,' said Laurent standing up, but Aunt Augusta shook her head.

'Not at all M. Marivaux. I wouldn't dream of it. Besides, I'm sure Aunt Evadne will enjoy the company of a young man. I'll be back as soon as I can,' she said, pushing us in the direction of Great Aunt Evadne who was staring rather wistfully at the empty sherry glass in her hand. I looked at Laurent, one eyebrow raised.

'Thank you for attempting to abandon me,' I said, as we walked over. 'I thought we were friends.'

'We are, *ma chère*,' he said good-naturedly. 'But she is your elderly relative, not mine. I have plenty of them at home.'

'Then you can give me the benefit of all your experience in dealing with them.'

'Certainly. For example, I think the lady would like another glass of sherry,' he said smoothly. 'Let me just go and fetch — '

'Oh no you don't,' I said catching his hand. With a smile he gave in and followed me across to the sofa next to Aunt Evadne.

'Hello, Aunt Evadne,' I shouted in her rather whiskery ear. She had an ear-trumpet, but the vain old lady rarely used it. She looked up and smiled, her wrinkles giving her face a concertina effect.

'Ursula! Where have you been? I told Gussie to fetch you twenty minutes ago.'

'No, I'm not Ursula, Aunt Evadne. Ursula is in India with her husband. I'm Isabella, Robert's daughter.'

'Eh? Robert? Who's Robert?'

'Robert, Aunt Evadne,' I said. 'You remember — Lindsay's son.' Aunt Evadne's toothless smile grew impish.

'Robert, I remember him. A little devil he was; too clever by half except when it really counted. And, of course, Phoebe always spoilt him. I told her, a rod to his breeches, that's what he needs, but she wouldn't listen. They never do. And later on he wouldn't leave the chambermaids alone. Lindsay despaired of him. I remember when he lost the carriage at faro, Phoebe had to stop Lindsay from — '

'Yes, he married my mother Amelia,' I said quickly. I wasn't sure I wanted Laurent to hear about Papa's less than illustrious early life. 'It's my birthday party. Isabella,' I added.

Evadne leaned a little closer to me, making the wicker of her bath-chair creak.

'Isabella, eh? Can't say I recognize you, but you look like a nice gel. Who's he?' she added, pointing a bony finger at Laurent.

'This is Laurent Marivaux. He's my cousin on my mother's side. Amelia Woodruffe.'

'Amelia? She's dead.'

'Yes I know, Aunt Evadne,' I yelled. 'She was my mother.' I looked at Laurent helplessly, but it was obvious he was going to be of no use. The grin on his face was growing. Meanwhile Aunt Evadne's unreliable memory was throwing up disconnected threads of family history.

'Woodruffe? Woodruffe? I know the name, don't tell me now. There was some scandal with the Woodruffes.' Her face screwed up with effort.

'No, no, Aunt Evadne,' I said desperately, trying to throw her off track, but it was no good. She suddenly held up a hand.

'I remember now: Evangeline Woodruffe, dreadful hussy, ran off with a Frenchie. Her poor mama was distraught and her father was furious, even — '

'Yes, Aunt Evadne, but that was a long time ago.' I could feel my face flushing with embarrassment, but I don't know why; Laurent had turned away and I could see his shoulders shaking with laughter. 'Evangeline had five children and this is her grandson, Laurent.' I poked him and he turned back and bowed slightly.

'*Madame*, I am pleased to make your acquaintance,' he said gravely. Aunt Evadne glared at him.

'You're a Frenchie, too.'

'Aunt Evadne, you mustn't say things like that. It's rude,' I shouted, but Aunt Evadne just huffed.

'Rude? Stuff and nonsense, my gel. You have to be careful with these Frenchies. They can't be trusted. All that rolling the words round on their tongues, disgusting it is, not decent. Evangeline Woodruffe ran away with one and look what happened to her.'

'Yes, I know, Aunt Evadne. This is her — oh, it's no use,' I said, turning back to Laurent. 'She's getting worse. Poor Aunt Daphne must be driven to distraction.'

'It is of no moment,' said Laurent, patting my hand. 'She is an old lady. Be assured I will not take offence.'

'Then I will on your behalf,' I muttered, but Aunt Evadne was well away by now. She leaned forward again, a wicked little smile on her face.

'Of course, some of our young men were no better — '

'She's completely demented now, the poor old thing.'

'Take Robert, for example; terrible trouble Lindsay and Phoebe had — '

'One day you will be like this, *ma chère* Bella.'

'Although when he married Amelia it seemed he put all his naughty ways behind him.'

'In that case, dear Laurent, I shall instruct my grandchildren to put me out of my misery.'

'*And* he still owes me thirty pounds. I never got that back. They kept telling me he was dead, but I said to them, 'That's no excuse. Thirty pounds is thirty pounds'.'

'Who owes you thirty pounds, Aunt Evadne?' I asked gently. She squinted at me through eyes that were surrounded by myriad wrinkles.

'Why Robert, of course. He needed it for the trip.'

I sighed and looked at Laurent who raised an eyebrow.

'I think you must be mistaken, Aunt Evadne,' I said patiently. 'Papa had plenty of money.'

'Hah!' the old lady cackled triumphantly. 'That's all you know, miss. Amelia wouldn't pay for it, you see. I liked Amelia, even

46

though she was a Woodruffe. She had fire in her belly, not like these namby-pamby gels nowadays. They wave a few banners around in Trafalgar Square and think they're the first ones to talk about emancipation. I remember seeing Mrs Shelley once at an assembly in Kensington. Dreadful woman, of course, and heaven knows the fuss that was made of that awful little book, but her mother had the right idea. The married Women's Property Act was a blessing we should have had a long time ago. When Daisy Armstrong got married she lost all — Ah Daphne, there you are,' she said, and I turned to see Aunt Daphne with Aunt Augusta and a woman dressed in a nurse's uniform. 'Tell this gel Robert owes me thirty pounds. Where is he, anyway? Why hasn't he come to see me? He was quick enough — '

Daphne sighed. 'Mama, it's very late. You must be tired. Perhaps you'd like Powell to take you to bed?'

'Bed? Is it time for bed? We've only just got here.'

'No Mama, it's eleven o'clock.'

'Nonsense. I only had dinner a little while ago. And I've hurt my ankle. That boy was very rough getting me up the steps. He didn't look where he was — '

'No, Mrs Winthrop,' we heard the nurse say

47

wearily, as she unlocked the brake on the chair. 'You hurt your ankle last week when you got out of your chair without waiting for me to help you — '

As the nurse wheeled Aunt Evadne away, I turned to Aunt Daphne. 'Did Papa really owe Aunt Evadne thirty pounds? Because if so, you know I'd be pleased to — '

'Good lord dear, don't be silly,' said Aunt Daphne as she pushed a stray lock of grey hair back. 'She's very old, and she gets confused about the oddest things these days. Why only yesterday she thought the boot-boy was my uncle Alfred's stepson. We had to give her a sedative in the end.'

'She seemed very sure,' I said.

'Don't be ridiculous, Isabella,' said Aunt Augusta crisply, her lorgnette out as she peered disapprovingly at a crowd of my friends who were laughing loudly by the door. 'Aunt Evadne is sure of nothing these days. Come, Daphne. We had better make sure Powell has taken care of your dear mama. Young people can be so slipshod these days and one simply cannot find the right sort of . . . ' She took Aunt Daphne by the arm and together they sailed out.

'She is a formidable woman, your aunt,' Laurent mused, as we watched them go.

'That's one word for her, certainly,' I said

48

with a grin. He smiled back.

'Come, let us forget old ladies and dance. It is your birthday, after all, *ma chère* and we must make the most of your day.'

He held out his hand and after a moment's hesitation, I took it. I no longer felt tired and the prospect of dancing with Laurent was irresistible. I smiled and he led me out on to the dance floor.

★ ★ ★

I was kneeling on the floor surrounded by a sea of yellowed crumbling documents when Lily brought in the morning post with a pot of hot coffee.

''Ere you are, miss.'

'Thank you, Lily. Oh, all the way from Persia. It must be from Mrs Ellis.' I got up and sat down by the desk, opening the letter with the paper-knife Lily handed me. 'I wish I was with her.'

'So do I, miss,' said Lily wistfully.

It was a week after my party and I was alone in my house with only the servants for company for the first time ever. As yet I had had no time to feel bored. Uncle Charles had given me the keys to various drawers and cupboards in the study and told me that if I was so interested in learning how to take care

49

of my fortune I could start by going through all Mama and Papa's papers. I think he had expected me to give up after a couple of hours, but on the contrary I was fascinated.

Since I had spent a lot of time in the kitchen with Marnie and the other servants as a little girl, I had always known from the things that were said that Mama and Papa's marriage was less a romantic love match than a shrewd business contract on my mother's part, but from the letters she kept it was clear that she had a head for business that my father could only have dreamed of. Their prenuptial correspondence consisted mostly of my mother demanding facts and figures about the estates and how much they grossed a year and what Papa intended to do about various business assets, until I think he just capitulated in the end and let her speak to the lawyers on any subjects she chose. Certainly it was possible to see in the two years before I was born that Mama had a beneficial effect on his income, with new stocks and shares being bought and sold at an alarmingly lucrative rate. Mama clearly had a flair for that kind of thing and I could see why Papa let her have her way. I think I must have taken after him, because after a while I became mesmerized with all the figures and had to put them to one side and concentrate instead on Papa's letters.

He was clearly the more frivolous of the two as his diaries made clear. Papa, it transpired, had kept diaries since the age of about ten, but only for about two months of the year before getting bored and finding lots of other things to do. The New Year must have had some kind of effect on him though, or perhaps some well-meaning, if misguided, older relative, always bought him the same present because every January a new journal would be started with all sorts of promises to keep a rigid report of his daily adventures, before tailing off around the middle of February. I learnt an awful lot about how mischievous he was, and how he enjoyed tormenting his older sisters, and how he loved riding and hunting but loathed being forced to spend time in the old schoolroom with a succession of unfortunate tutors. He must have had a new one each year until the age of thirteen, when grandfather Lindsay eventually gave up and sent him away to school. He did not enjoy school either. Also, it appeared that every year Papa seemed to think he had discovered the hiding place of the Dragons-heart only to be disappointed with a never ending succession of rusting farm implements or decomposing mouse corpses

51

— which he nevertheless found interesting in that dreadful way boys do. In fact, as Lily had come in I had just finished reading his diary for the year 1876, when the Dragonsheart had turned out to be a pig's trotter. Papa, apparently, had had plans for the pig's trotter which included, to my shameful delight, Aunt Augusta's bed.

I put the diary down for a moment and poured myself a cup of coffee before opening Kate's letter. She and Adam Ellis had married soon after finding the pharoah's treasures and had left Egypt for Persia to try to find out more about the remains of a boat that was supposed to exist on some mountain. It had sounded dreadfully dull to me, but both Kate and Adam had been very excited about it.

The letter was dated six weeks ago.

My dear Bella

Thank you for your last letter which reached us yesterday. I imagine that by the time you get this letter your birthday will have come and gone, so I can only hope you enjoyed yourself and being a mature adult at last is everything you hoped it would be.

She went on to give a description of the countryside through which they had travelled on their way to Mount Ararat and how difficult progress had been due to bureaucracy. It struck me as quaint somehow that a country as exotic-sounding as Persia would suffer from bureaucracy. However, as I read the following sentence I had to fight down the urge to shout with joy:

You may have noticed that I haven't enclosed a present. This is not, dear Bella, because I have forgotten, or taken notice of your ridiculous suggestion that I should not bother, but rather that I hope to be seeing you in the very near future in person and so do not wish to chance a gift to the rather uncertain safety of the post. You will not believe this, darling, but Papa is getting married.

Married! She was right. It was hard to believe. Her father, Professor Whitaker, was an old man in his fifties who seemed to like nothing more than scrabbling around dirt pits, surrounded by dusty, broken pots. So when I read the next sentence, I nearly dropped my cup of coffee.

. . . and the most amazing thing is, he is marrying Alice Faulkner!

I could hardly believe it. Alice Faulkner was Adam's cousin, a sophisticated socialite who loved being surrounded by luxury and beauty. The idea of her marrying Kate's father was just incredible.

I'm sure you are as shocked as I am by this, although Adam says he is not surprised at all. Apparently he had worked it out when Alice remained in Egypt so much longer than she need have done. I pointed out, of course, that she wanted to be at the wedding of her beloved cousin, but Adam seems to think I am just being petty, which I am most certainly not.

I couldn't help grinning. Kate is the most kind-hearted of people, but she never really did trust Lady Faulkner much where Adam was concerned, and to be honest she had some justification for her attitude. I myself sometimes wondered exactly what Alice Faulkner felt for her handsome cousin.

However, Adam insists that it was obvious from the start that Papa and

Alice were more than just old friends and he could tell at our wedding that they were, as he phrases it, 'enjoying a special new bond'. I asked why he didn't feel he had to share this amazing intuition with me, but he just muttered he thought I knew as well, which means of course, he had no idea really and just can't bring himself to admit it. Anyway, the wedding will take place as soon as we can return. Indeed, I hope by the time you receive this we will back in England, or nearly there.

I resolved to get in touch with Lady Faulkner as soon as possible. She had not been able to come to my birthday celebrations due to a prior engagement, she had said. Now, as I perused the rest of the letter, I wondered exactly what that prior engagement was.

While I think of it, Bella darling, could I ask you to do your best to help out Peter Bennett? I know he's not a favourite of yours and you know I agree with you that his behaviour at our wedding was unforgivable but really he does mean well and he did save our lives, darling, you must admit that.

I frowned as I read this. Peter Bennett was the private detective who had eventually rescued us from the tomb in which we had been trapped, and although, as Kate said, we had a lot to thank him for, gratitude can only go so far. And he certainly *wasn't* a favourite of mine. He had masqueraded as a local inspector of antiquities, although he was, in fact, employed by the Egyptian Antiquities Service to try to find out who was stealing so many of their most valuable treasures. Apparently this charade involved him behaving like a complete boor in my company, flushing an unbecoming shade of red (not at all attractive with red hair and sunburn), stuttering every time he spoke and constantly dropping spoons during tea. I admit that perhaps I wasn't as sympathetic as I might have been, but it was very hot out there and, quite frankly, one becomes irritable and bored very quickly with awkward boys. And how was I supposed to know it was only a charade? Indeed when you think about it, I was actually helping him. He was pretending to be clumsy and shy and I had given him plenty of opportunity to do both. Some people have no gratitude.

Anyway, after we had been rescued from the dreadful tomb, I had tried to thank him on more than one occasion and each time he had been extremely abrupt. At Kate's wedding he had called me a spoilt brat, for heaven's sake. If I had a penny for every time I had heard that, I'd be — well, not rich all over again, but I'd certainly have plenty of loose change. And now here was Kate trying to persuade me to help the unmannerly brute. I knew she liked him, but this was ridiculous. I frowned even more deeply as I read on.

Although he doesn't say anything, it's obvious the business isn't going well and the commission he made from his work in Egypt is practically gone and he is so good at his job, Bella, he just needs a little extra help.

I sniffed. I knew, because Kate insisted on keeping me up to date constantly with the daily business of Mr Peter Bennett, that after he had left Egypt he had opened his own detective agency somewhere south of the River Thames in London. It sounded rather squalid to me but Kate, as I have pointed out, is rather fond of the ill-bred lout and up until now has always been at pains to point out how well he'd been doing since I last had the pleasure of his company. His luck must have changed since her last letter.

And frankly, as much as I liked Kate, I wondered what on earth she expected me to do. What would I need a detective for of all things? And even if I were inclined to help the wretch, how could I possibly introduce the subject to my friends? 'My dear, if you ever need someone to poke about in your private affairs, I know just the man.' Really, it simply wouldn't do.

The letter ended saying she looked forward to seeing me very soon and as I put it to one side I knocked over an old tin which I had found in a wooden box right at the back of a drawer. The box had apparently been Papa's and contained what I assumed were nostalgic knick-knacks. There were a couple of battered lead soldiers, an old, chewed puppy collar and a collection of rusty keys. I hadn't been able to open the tin, but I'd shaken it and had heard the dry feathery sound of papers knocking against the sides. I had assumed they were old cigars or something like that, because I'd found enough butts around to realize Papa had a habit of leaving them in the oddest of places. But, as I knocked the tin, it fell on to the floor and the force finally caused the lid to come off.

Several small ticket-like objects fluttered to

the ground. I knelt down to pick them up, turned them over and looked at the writing on them.

Since I was unfamiliar with the wording it took me several seconds before I realized I was looking at pawn tickets. And not pawn tickets for the same place but for several different establishments. There were ten altogether and three of them did not have any address on them at all, just names or letters. There was also an envelope with 'F and H' written on it. I opened it and found a sturdy key inside.

I sat down in my chair once more and stared at the tickets in amazement. Poor Papa — I had known he was not exactly rich in the years before Mama came along and wrenched his affairs into order, but what on earth had made him so desperate he had had to go to some dreadful pawnshop to make money? Also, I wondered why he had not gone back afterwards and reclaimed his goods. Probably he was too ashamed, or the items were simply not important enough to him. Even so, there were quite a few tickets here. I wondered idly what exactly it was he had let go.

As I sat turning over the rather musty, grubby little tickets in my hands, I caught sight of Kate's letter again — '*he is so good at his job, Bella, he just needs a little extra help'* and then a deliciously wicked idea came to me. Suddenly I knew exactly why I needed a detective.

3

Three hours later I was pinning on my favourite ostrich-feather hat. I had telephoned Aunt Hortensia and arranged to stay with her and Uncle Charles for a few days: I had also made an appointment with Saunders and Todd, the family solicitor, and I had, after a great deal of searching, managed to find Laurent. He had told me he was staying with one of the many cousins we share, but this had not been entirely true, as it turned out.

'Not with me, old thing,' Hugh had informed me, when I telephoned him at his club. 'Damned — uh — blasted chap tootled off about four days ago in that little tin can of his and hasn't been seen since. Oh, wait a minute.' I'd heard some murmurings and muted laughter then he came back on the phone. 'He's just walked in, m'dear. Would you and Aunt Hetty be available for dinner tonight? Mother would love to see you, and Harry too, if she's not too busy banner waving and plotting the downfall of the government with Mrs P?' There was the sound of manly guffawing at this, as I thanked him and put the phone down. A little

61

of Hugh goes a long way.

As I waited in the hall for Henderson to bring the carriage round to the front, I pulled on my gloves and frowned. Marnie had yet to appear. I was just about to ask Nicholls, the butler, who was waiting to open the door, to find her, when she arrived in the hall, her third best hat on and a decidely grumpy expression on her face.

'Oh, do cheer up, Marnie,' I said somewhat crossly. 'After all, how often do I make you leave Woodruffe?'

'It ain't the leaving what's gettin' me nerves all in a state, Miss Bella,' she sulked, 'it's where we're goin' what's the problem.'

The carriage had drawn up and, as she followed me down the steps, she kept up her litany of complaints.

'Me back's playin' me up again, Miss Bella. I should be in bed wiv a nice warm bottle against me sciatics. An' I told Cook I'd 'elp 'er rearrange the jams an' now she's going ter be stuck wiv just young Ethel to do the donkey work and there'll be 'ell ter pay. An' 'e won't like it, will 'e?' she added darkly. I sighed, knowing immediately to whom she was referring.

'Darling, you know Uncle Charles has the utmost . . . ' I tried to think of a word that was both truthful and complimentary to describe Uncle Charles's opinion of Marnie, but at the last moment had to admit failure.

''E 'as the utmost 'ump when 'e sees me, darlin', and you know it.'

I patted her hand. Unfortunately this was true. Uncle Charles always unfairly associated Marnie with the accident in Algeria, and took out his ire on her whenever he saw her. Over the years he had tried everything to get rid of her and only Aunt Augusta's insistence that she remain as my nursemaid had kept her on. Aunt Augusta had a soft spot for Marnie, although she kept it well buried.

'Never mind, Marnie,' I said, as we climbed into the carriage and it set off for the railway station. 'We'll keep you away from Uncle Charles. And you can go and see your sister in Bermondsey. Surely you'd like that?' I was wheedling now, but I knew I had her interest.

'Well, I s'ppose a coupla days in the Smoke ain't so bad. An' I ain't seen Eileen in a while,' she conceded grudgingly.

I patted her hand again and settled back to enjoy the journey.

★　★　★

We arrived at Uncle Charles's town house just after four o'clock and in between taking tea and dressing for dinner there was hardly

63

any time to chat, which was just as well. I was also pleased to hear that Uncle Charles was away on business for a few days and was not expected back until the following Wednesday which gave me ample time to conclude my own affairs. Not that Uncle Charles had any right to interfere in my comings and goings any more, but after twenty years he had got into the habit and I knew he would be a lot harder to throw off the scent than Aunt Hortensia.

We dined that night at Carter's, a fashionable new restaurant in Chelsea. Laurent arrived last, just as we were about to sit down, amidst lots of jokes from Hugh as to where he had been, although we all lost interest very quickly when it appeared he had had to visit a farm in Yorkshire to inspect some cows for his brothers. Aunt Hermione, Hugh's mother, seemed to feel we should take more interest in our new cousin's business and for her pains condemned the entire table to a lecture on different strains of producers until Harriet managed to divert her attention with news about the latest scandal over the Cat and Mouse Act, during which both Emmeline and Christobel Pankhurst had been in and out of Holloway, so thankfully no more was said about cows. All in all the dinner was very noisy and it was only afterwards as we were leaving that I managed to get Laurent to one side for a few moments.

'So where have you been these last few days, Laurent? Apparently, I'm not the only one you abandon.'

He took my hand. 'Always you accuse me of abandoning you, *ma chère*, but in truth I have only been attending to business.'

'Ah yes, the cows. You do realize poor Aunt Hermione was only being polite when she asked you to explain the relative merits of Friesian versus Jerseys, don't you?'

He gave a rather wicked smile. 'But she seemed so interested. You all did.'

'Darling, you know perfectly well everyone was hoping to hear you'd disappeared because of some scandalous reason like visiting a mistress or something.'

He put my hand to his lips and kissed it. 'And do you think if that was the case I would have admitted it in the company of a group of such respectable ladies?'

'Certainly,' I said, as a servant held out my coat. 'This is the twentieth century. We ladies don't just want to be treated like decorative toys any longer. Weren't you listening to Harry at all?'

'Unfortunately since I was next to her, I heard every word she said. The cows, I think, were more interesting.'

I smiled. As much as I love Harriet, she can go on a bit sometimes. 'So, are you back in London for good, or do you have to rush off and look at more flocks of cows?'

'The word you search for is herds, *ma petite* and alas, I must be away early tomorrow morning. My oldest brother is not happy with me. He thinks I have been wasting my time here in England, instead of working on behalf of the family as I was sent to do.'

'Oh just ignore him,' I said with the casual ease of the only child. 'Why should you have to run around the country looking at boring farmyard animals when there are so many more exciting things you can do here in London?'

'Sadly Guillaume would not agree with you.'

'And do you always do as Guillaume says?' I asked. Laurent smiled.

'When one is the youngest of three brothers one learns at an early age to obey orders. But what is wrong, my dear Bella? You seem perturbed by something.'

'Well actually, I was rather hoping you could help me in a small personal matter, Laurent. Can you come to Aunt Hetty's tomorrow?'

66

He frowned and looked thoughtful. 'I have a meeting I cannot, in courtesy, cancel and it will last most of the day. But I could be back by five o'clock. Will that help you, *ma chère*?'

I beamed. 'Perfect. Thank you, Laurent. Yes, I'm coming Aunt Hetty.'

I gave him one last smile and followed Harriet out into the damp March evening.

★   ★   ★

I had barely returned to Aunt Hortensia's myself by five o'clock the next day when Laurent arrived.

'Bella, *ma chère*,' said Laurent, as he walked into the drawing room. 'I trust I find you well?'

'Yes thank you, Laurent. Will you have some tea?'

'No,' he said firmly, giving me the impression he'd been forced to drink far too much of it since he'd arrived in England. 'Now how can I help?' He paused and smiled. 'Is Charles being tedious?'

I bit back a smile. 'Of course not. What on earth makes you say that?'

He sat down on the sofa, looking as relaxed as a cat. 'I have observed that Charles can be pompous on occasions.'

'What a dreadful thing to say. Poor Uncle

Charles. I'm shocked, Laurent, appalled.'

He smiled lazily. 'No you are not. Admit it, *chère cousine*. Sometimes you wish you were free of his restraints.'

I forced myself not to smile back. 'This is a scandalous conversation. We must stop it immediately. Tell me, how have you found the weather during your stay?'

His grin grew. 'Do you know, we have a saying in France: never trust a man with more than three moustache combs.'

I put down my cup, unable to stop myself laughing now. 'You just made that up.'

He shrugged. '*Eh bien*, it should be true. But come, tell me what it is you wish me to do.'

'I want you to take me to Bermondsey tomorrow in your car. If you're not busy,' I said. He nodded, unconcerned, but then why should he be? He was French; he had no idea where Bermondsey was. And by the time we got there, it would be too late for him to worry about how perilous the surroundings might be for a lady.

'I am not busy tomorrow. I will take you with pleasure.'

I waited for the inevitable questioning to begin, but he said no more. I looked at him curiously.

'Don't you want to know why?'

He smiled again lazily. 'Bella, *mon ange*, you sound guilty. Is there some reason I should not do this?'

'No, of course not. It's just that usually people demand to know everything I'm doing. How refreshing you are, Laurent. But I will tell you anyway. I was looking through Papa's business papers the other day and I came across some rather unusual items.'

'Indeed? And what would they be?'

'I found some pawn tickets.'

'*Quoi?* Pawn, what is that?'

'Oh usually only very poor people do it. If you need money quickly and take something very valuable to a special shop, they give you some money for it, and if you don't return the money within a period of time they can sell it.'

'Oh.' His eyebrows shot up. '*Mettre en gage*. Yes I know it. But why would your father have done this?'

'Exactly my question, Laurent. That's what I want to know.'

'Very well. But how do you intend to find out? This must have happened a long time ago. The *prêteur sur gages* might not even exist anymore.'

'I'm going to hire a private detective,' I said.

'*Quoi?*'

'A private detective. You know, like Sherlock — '

'Yes, yes, I know what a private detective is,' he answered, for once slightly less urbane than usual. 'But I do not think this is a good idea, *ma cousine*. You have no experience of these things and you will only be — '

'Ah, but there you're wrong, my dear Laurent. I do know something about these things and I have a man in whom I have the utmost confidence.' Well, I was only stretching the truth a little.

'Really?' Laurent's lack of faith in my judgement was less than flattering. 'How do you know this man?'

'He saved my life in Egypt,' I declared dramatically, grateful to Kate for reminding me about this. 'And he comes highly recommended by other good friends too.'

'I see.' I noticed Laurent regarding me a little more shrewdly now, for which I was grateful. I think up to this point he had thought of me as one might consider a kitten, or a puppy, or a very small child; charming but not to be taken very seriously. 'But even if he can find out for you what your father sold, what good would it do? You will still never know why. And, in truth, I cannot see why you would care to know. All this happened a long time ago.'

I hesitated for a moment, before replying. 'I went to see the family solicitor this morning,' I said eventually. 'Mr Todd was reluctant to talk to me without Uncle Charles present, but in the end I managed to bully him into talking to me alone. He was adamant that he had never heard of Papa being so desperate that he would need to go to a pawnbroker.'

He shrugged. 'I still do not see why you want to know what was sold.'

I got up from the sofa and walked towards Harriet's piano. 'To be honest, Laurent, I always feel a little protective of Papa. Whenever the uncles and aunts get together, they make it clear that Mama was the saviour of the family fortune and Papa was the careless spendthrift who was lucky to have found her. I want to know what he had to sell to gain his little bit of independence.' I sighed. 'Heavens I know what that feels like.'

'I see.' He nodded. 'And you wish me to take you to see this excellent private detective because you know none of your English relatives would permit such a thing.'

'It's none of their business,' I said rather tartly. 'I just don't want them knowing about it.'

'And if I say no?'

'Well, of course, you must do as you think right, darling. I'll just have to go alone, with only Marnie to accompany me. She's very old and hardly robust, but she does know Bermondsey, so I'm sure we'll be all right. And if there is any — '

'Stop.' He laughed and held up a hand. 'Now I understand why your English relatives do not trust you. You win, my dear Bella. I will take you to see your private detective and we will see what he has to say.'

'Thank you,' I said gratefully. 'You're an absolute angel.'

There was a lot of muttering in French at this. I'm sure it was all complimentary.

* * *

The next morning Laurent arrived just after half past nine. I already had my hat and coat on and had prevailed on Marnie to be prompt too. As Laurent took off his long driving gloves I hustled Marnie out.

'Good morning. Here we both are, ready to go,' I said brightly.

'I am impressed. Usually one must wait hours before the ladies are ready to leave.'

'Oh, I'm always punctual,' I said, ignoring Marnie's snort of derision. 'Shall we get in? Don't worry about directions. Marnie knows the way.'

Laurent helped me into the front passenger

seat and we set off.

We arrived in Bermondsey some two hours later. Marnie hadn't been as much help as I thought she'd be, since she'd never been in a motor car before and kept losing track of street names. She insisted this was because the car was going too fast for her and she was losing her bearings, but since we couldn't go much faster than the horses and carriages that took up most of the road space, I strongly suspected she just wasn't paying much attention to street signs, being too interested in making sure she was being watched in the car.

But eventually, at about a quarter past eleven, we arrived in front of the address Kate had given me for Mr Bennett's offices and not a moment too soon as far as I was concerned. I felt as though I was covered in soot and the motor car could not be entirely blamed for this. Bermondsey was a dull grey muddle of crumbling houses and dilapidated shops, with huge ugly factories dotted here and there and hardly a blade of grass or tree in sight. In fact, there was no colour anywhere, at least than I could see, and the stalls that dragged along the street pavements seemed to be filled with the dreariest vegetables that no one in their right mind would want to eat.

But if the area seemed ugly and colourless, the same could not be said of its inhabitants. People of all ages, from tiny urchins up to ageing grandmothers surged in the streets, making the place seem like a living thing. They shouted and screamed and cackled as they went about their business, stall holders yelling at me to buy their wares and calling me 'sweet'eart' and 'darlin'' just like Marnie did when she was in a good mood with me. As Laurent helped me down from the car, I stood a moment trying to gain some equilibrium.

'Right. This is the place then, Miss Bella,' said Marnie, briskly, adding, 'git lorst,' to a gang of small boys who had appeared as if by magic to stare in awe at the car.

The building in front of us was no more elegant than its companions, with paint peeling off the walls and the door covered in soot. A sign next to a knocker confirmed this was indeed the office of Mr Peter Bennett, Private Investigator. I hesitated. If this was where Mr Bennett was working from then he certainly was having problems. For a moment, I wondered if I had made the right decision after all, but then remembered I was an adult now. It was time to make decisions on my own. I took a deep breath and immediately regretted it. The smell of smoke mixed with manure and rotting vegetables was overwhelming.

'Very well,' I said, in my most commanding voice. 'Let us speak with Mr Bennett.' I opened the grubby door and began to climb the rickety stairs somewhat cautiously, Marnie following behind me.

There was of course no carpet to muffle our footsteps, but I doubt our entrance would have been heard anyway above the sound of the argument going on just above us. Even before we reached the first floor we could hear every word that was being said.

' — ten bob, Mr Bennett, that's wot you said an' that's wot I want. An' it ain't no use you — '

' — my good Mabel, why on earth would I have said ten shillings? I don't even have tenpence. And even if I did, I can assure you I would not have offered you that much just for following a customer to his house and finding out the address for me. I could get one of the brats on the street to do that for tuppence and I — '

'Why dincha then?'

'Because I was hoping for a little finesse. Running down the street after him, throwing bottles and screaming obscenities is not my idea of finesse. And you lost him at Rosamund Street.'

There was a pause while Mabel considered this version of events. She must have decided to lower her sights because when she next spoke her tone was no longer shrill but lower and almost honeyed.

'Or right, then, maybe I was a little bit confused about the amount you said — '

'You certainly were.'

' — yeah, but I swear I can get 'is address if yer give me a bit more time. An' I'll be as — as finessfull as yer like. Only I'd need a bit ter keep me going — '

'Mabel, are you joking?'

'Aw come on, Mr Bennett, just a few coppers. On account like. You know I'll get 'is number sooner or later. I always do.'

There was a loud, weary sigh and the sound of a tin box being scraped. Intrigued, I walked round the corner just in time to see Mr Bennett hold up a half-crown, his hands encased in fingerless gloves.

'Here, but I expect some solid news by tomorrow,' he warned, pulling the coin away for a moment as Mabel attempted to snatch it from his grasp. She was a tall, thin creature, dressed in a hotch-potch of clothes, a bright green feather boa, a blue velvet riding jacket that was rather too small for her and in desperate need of a wash and a long mermaid skirt with high-heeled black boots just visible beneath the ragged hem. She was hatless and her blonde hair was scraped back in a bun from which curls kept escaping.

'Good morning Mr Bennett,' I said briskly, as he stared at me open mouthed. Mabel took advantage of his shock to grab the half-crown and slip it down her bodice.

'Fanks, Mr B,' she said, beaming at him as she walked out. 'I'll do you proud. 'E's all yours now, darlin',' she added, winking at me.

Her voice seemed to remind him he had a tongue. 'Mabel, god dammit — I mean — ' He looked at me with that familiar expression of distaste for a moment, before finally saying very disagreably, 'What are you doing here?'

'Is that how you greet all your potential customers? No wonder you're doing so badly.' I stepped into the tiny office, hardly bigger than the broom cupboard in Woodruffe Manor and wondered if it was safe to sit on the chair in front of the desk. This was possibly the most sturdy piece of furniture in the room, being huge and made of dark oak. The top was covered with bits of paper, which Mr Bennett suddenly seemed to notice. He began to sweep the sheets up into one pile.

'Potential customer? Is that what you are, Miss Wyndham-Brown? Have you lost your pet poodle or something then?' This was said in a most sneering manner.

I took out my handkerchief and dusted the chair before sitting in it. I know it was rude, but really, the man seemed to bring out the worst in me.

'Supposing I had, Mr Bennett,' I said, smiling at him cheerfully. 'Convince me you're the best fellow I could hire to find him.' I sat back and waited for his reply.

He didn't look his best. Since the room was freezing he had on his overcoat, which was worn and frayed around the cuffs. His face was thinner and paler than I remember and his red hair was much darker now it was no longer bleached by the burning Egyptian sun, and badly in need of a cut too. I couldn't help noticing the crack in the window which should have been repaired a long time ago.

Mr Bennett sat down in the chair on the opposite side of the huge desk. 'I'm afraid I don't have time for trivial cases, Miss Wyndham-Brown. If you like, I can give you the name of a couple of colleagues who specialize in service to the gentry.'

I smiled. 'Of course you're far too busy, Mr Bennett. I noticed that. No doubt that's why you need someone like Mabel to help you catch errant husbands.'

His eyes darkened. 'Why have you come

here, Miss Wyndham-Brown? Because if it was merely to gloat and make fun of me, I think we can assume you've achieved that aim and you may now leave.'

I stood up, amazed to find myself suddenly very angry. 'Mr Bennett, I really have no idea what I have done to make you despise me so much. I came here because Kate Ellis, for reasons beyond me, thinks you are a fine person who deserves some help and I happen to need someone who can act discreetly and competently on my behalf. Clearly we were both mistaken. Good day to you.'

To my utter horror I felt close to tears, although I had no idea why and I turned smartly on my heel so that the brute wouldn't have the pleasure of seeing me cry. Marnie, who had been waiting in the horrid, smelly corridor for me since the room was so cramped saw me though and took me in her arms.

''Ere, what's up, darlin'? What's 'e said? D'you want me ter go in there and give 'im a piece of my mind? 'Cos I will — '

I took a deep breath. Really, this was ridiculous. 'Don't be silly, Marnie — ' I began, but then there was the sound of someone clearing their throat behind me. I turned and saw Mr Bennett leaning against the doorway.

'Actually you're right, Miss Wyndham-Brown,' he said, with a sheepish expression on his face. 'I do need the money. How can I help you?'

I looked at him for a moment, before going back into the room and sitting down on the rickety chair again. Just then Laurent appeared.

'Ah there you are, darling. I was beginning to wonder where you'd got to.'

'There were many disreputable-looking children standing around my motor car,' he explained, his eyes widening as he took in the shabbiness of the room. 'I feared for its security.'

Mr Bennett peered down through the grubby window. 'That Silver Ghost is yours?' He sounded desperately envious.

'*Oui, monsieur.*'

'Four cylinder?'

Laurent smiled. 'Six.'

'Will it be safe?' I asked.

'I think so, *chèrie*,' he said, turning to me. 'I found three even more disreputable looking children and paid them sixpence to guard it. And I promised them another sixpence on my return if the car was unharmed.'

'How clever of you. I would never have thought of that.'

Mr Bennett nodded. 'Vinnie Watkins and

his little mob will see it's safe for you,' he agreed, walking back to the desk and sitting down again. 'Actually he'd have agreed to knife someone for you for half that.' As I shuddered, he grinned at me and I knew he wasn't that repentant. 'My name's Peter Bennett,' he said to Laurent, holding out a hand, without standing up. 'And you are . . . ?'

'Oh do forgive me, Mr Bennett, how rude of me. This is my cousin M. Laurent Marivaux. Laurent, this is Mr Bennett, of whom you've heard me speak. Mr Bennett saved my life in Egypt. He was an absolute hero.'

To my delight he blushed a deep red in that way I remembered from my time in Luxor. 'I wouldn't say that,' he began to mutter.

'Of course you were, Mr Bennett. And so machiavellian too. Kate and I were simply in awe of you. Do you know, Mr Bennett got one of the Egyptians to dress up as a ghost to frighten away the locals.'

'A ghost?' Laurent echoed, bewildered.

'Yes, and he left a scorpion in Kate's boot in order to get us out as well.'

Laurent looked at me, alarmed. 'He put a scorpion in your friend's boot?'

'Oh it was all right, it wasn't a deadly one and it stung Uncle George by mistake anyway.' Laurent's eyes were growing rounder and Mr Bennett was looking more uncomfortable by the second, I noticed.

'You must mention it to him,' I continued. 'He loves to tell people all about it. And then Mr Bennett didn't arrest the dreadful villain who he was actually searching for straight away. He decided to wait until the middle of the night when Kate and Adam and Ruby and I were left for dead in a simply appalling tomb — '

'Exactly how can I help you, Miss Wyndham-Brown?' Mr Bennett interrupted loudly.

'Of course. You're very busy, Mr Bennett. I forgot that. I have some pawn tickets I would like you to trace for me.'

'Pawn tickets?' He looked surprised. 'Forgive me, Miss Wyndham-Brown, but you're the last person I would have expected to be in possession of pawn tickets.'

'Oh they're not mine, Mr Bennett. At least, I suppose they are legally. I found them when I was sorting out some papers belonging to my parents and I was curious to know exactly what they pawned. I took the tickets and the envelope with the key in it out of my Dorothy bag and handed them to him.

'These are very old,' he said, after examining them.

'I know. Does that mean you can't find out where they're from?'

'I could try.' He scrabbled around in a desk drawer and found a battered old magnifying glass to examine them more closely. 'Some of them are probably traceable. This looks like a key to a bank security box,' he added holding up the key. 'I'll see what I can do.'

'So you think it's possible to find out what was sold?' I asked.

He frowned. 'I'm not so sure about that, but I think I could certainly find out where they originally came from. At least some of them.' He put them down and smiled at me, rather nastily I thought. 'So which parent do you suspect of visiting the Shylocks then, Miss Wyndham-Brown?'

'I don't think that's any of your business, Mr Bennett,' I replied. 'Perhaps you could tell me what your terms are and we could agree a price for your services.'

'Certainly.' He became very businesslike and pulled out a sheaf of papers from yet another battered drawer. 'I charge two pounds a week, plus any expenses incurred. Is that agreeable to you?'

'Two pounds a week?' I echoed, looking round at the shabby offices.

'I base my rates on ability to pay,' he said cheerfully. 'However, if that's too much for you, Miss Wyndham-Brown, I'd be happy to negotiate a lower rate. I don't see why an old client shouldn't benefit from a discount.'

I gave him a brittle smile back. 'Not at all, Mr Bennett. Clearly you need all the patronage you can get and I did promise Mrs Ellis that I would — '

'Patronage?' he spluttered. 'I don't need patronage. Whatever Kate told you about my circumstances is no concern of yours and if you think — '

'You certainly need some help, Mr Bennett. And quickly, before you die of exposure in this — '

'What I don't need is some spoilt little brat — '

'*Monsieur, soyez calme.*' Laurent's low voice cut across our increasingly shrill ones and we both turned towards him in surprise.

'Bella, you want someone to find out where these tickets came from and Mr Bennett has indicated he can help you. Equally, two pounds seems a reasonable request for such a service. I think if we all remain calm we will find that we can both be of service to each other, *n'est ce pas?*'

I glared at Mr Bennett. 'Yes, of course. Two pounds is perfectly acceptable. Here.' I took my purse out of my bag and placed two guineas on the desk.

'That's too much,' he said sulkily, but picked them up nevertheless.

'Consider it part of your expenses, Mr Bennett. When you have some information for me, I can be contacted here.' I wrote down Uncle Charles's address. 'Please be aware this is a private matter and I do not wish you to discuss this with anyone other than myself or my cousin, Mr Marivaux.'

'You are over twenty-one now, aren't you Miss Wyndham-Brown?' Mr Bennett asked disagreeably. 'Only I don't want to find myself up on a charge of defrauding a minor.'

I could feel my cheeks beginning to flush red with anger again at the fellow's impudence, but before I could reply, Laurent stood up.

'Do not worry, *monsieur*,' he answered calmly, taking my hand. 'You may rest assured Miss Wyndham-Brown is in charge of her own fate from now on. Shall we go, *ma chère*?'

I stood up, my equilibrium restored by Laurent's effortless grace. 'Of course. Good morning, Mr Bennett,' I said, and swept out of the room, noticing how put out Mr Bennet seemed by my composure.

★ ★ ★

We dropped Marnie off at her sister's for the afternoon, after I had managed to reassure her that my reputation would not suffer by spending an hour or so alone with Laurent in his car. As I pointed out, if Harriet could chain herself to railings in Parliament Square, then a short car journey back to Uncle Charles's house in broad daylight through crowded streets should be respectable enough. She muttered a bit at this, but the prospect of spending a couple of hours with Eileen was too good a chance for her to pass up and soon Laurent and I were motoring across London Bridge back into the more civilized area of the capital.

For a while, we did not talk. Laurent had to concentrate hard as he negotiated the other horse-drawn carriages and carts and stalls that spilled out into the streets and I was enjoying the sensation of the speeding car and the wind rushing over my new motoring hat and veil. But after a while I turned to him.

'Very well. What is it?'

He looked at me innocently. 'What is what, ma chère?'

'You've had a smug grin on your face ever since we left that awful place. What is it that has kept you so amused?'

He said nothing for a moment, obviously

trying to decide whether or not to tell me the truth. Eventually he shrugged.

'You like him, *ma petite*.'

'Like him? Mr Bennett? Don't be ridiculous!' I said. 'Did you see how rude and uncivilized he is? His manners are deplorable and — '

'You like him.' Laurent repeated, with an air of finality. He turned to look at me for a moment, the lazy smile back on his face. 'Almost as much, I think, as he likes you.'

'Now you're just being absurd.' I adjusted the cerise chiffon scarf holding my hat on.

Laurent held up a hand. 'Of course, he pretends to himself he hates you. I would too if I were him. You are young, rich and beautiful, *chèrie*, everything he is not. What hope has he of ever being a suitor?'

I considered this. The idea of Mr Bennett actually admiring me from afar — a great deal afar, if his behaviour was anything to go by — was not unattractive. And, of course, Laurent did have a point; socially he was so beneath me as to be almost invisible.

'I think you're being unfair, Laurent,' I said lightly, after a while. 'I don't believe Mr Bennett is very much older than me.'

Laurent slowed the car to let a cart full of coal cross in front of us. As he pulled on the brake and the various metals crunched in protest, he turned to face me.

'*Eh bien*, he is young. I will give you that. And beautiful — ' He smiled. 'That I will leave to your good judgement. But rich, that he most assuredly is not.'

I thought back to the shabby little office, with its scuffed, damaged furniture and freezing temperature. I knew Laurent was doing the same.

'No,' I said slowly. 'He is very poor, isn't he?'

'Not as poor as some, *ma chère*. But yes, he is poor. I would not expect too much from him. *Eh bien* here we are back at the house of your aunt. We should think of a story to tell her to explain your absence this morning, should we not?'

As he halted the car and helped me down, I found myself wondering if I would ever hear from Mr Bennett again. I hoped for Kate's sake I had done the right thing in engaging his services. She was so fond of him that I hated to think of him letting her down. Then as I saw Aunt Hortensia waving at us from a window I resolved to put him from my mind. I had done the best I could; now it was up to him to show me how good he really was.

4

A few days later I was sitting at breakfast with Aunt Hortensia and Harriet. As I spread some marmalade on to my toast, the maid brought in the post. She gave several items to Aunt Hortensia, a couple to Harriet, then put one by my plate. It was a thick white envelope in expensive vellum with the writing in mauve ink.

'It's from Lady Faulkner,' I said. 'Kate and Adam arrive in town on Friday and she hopes I will call on them at the earliest possible convenience.'

'How nice,' said Aunt Hortensia. 'Perhaps Harriet could accompany you.'

Harriet sighed and rolled her eyes as she put down her own toast. 'What Mama means, Bella, is that you are going to be forced to take me so that I don't go out to some dreadful suffragette meeting. Please feel free to refuse her.'

Aunt Hortensia scowled. 'Don't be absurd, Harriet, although you might consider how embarrasing your behaviour is for Papa and myself sometimes, particularly that disgrace-ful incident in Parliament Square. Do you

89

have any idea how difficult it was getting you released without you having to go to prison?'

'Mama, that was the whole point. I wanted to go to prison. If we are ever to — '

'Oh really, Harriet, you do make me cross. You wouldn't last five minutes in one of those dreadful places. And what about poor Papa — ?'

Just then the maid appeared again. 'A telephone call for Miss Wyndham-Brown,' she said, and I left Aunt Hortensia and Harriet to their argument.

I picked up the telephone in the hall. 'Hello, Isabella Wyndham-Brown.'

'Good morning, Miss Wyndham-Brown. Peter Bennett here.'

'Ah.' I glanced round rather guiltily but Aunt Hortensia and Harriet were still arguing in the breakfast-room. 'Do you have some news for me, Mr Bennett?'

'Well, er — I think you'd better get round here as quickly as you can, Miss Wyndham-Brown. Would this afternoon be convenient?' He sounded worried.

'I'll try, Mr Bennett. Is there — ?' I began, but the line went dead.

I stared at the receiver in confusion, then after a few minutes hurried thinking I rang Aunt Hermione, with whom Laurent was currently staying. Mr Bennett's request

90

sounded urgent: with any luck Laurent would be able to take me this afternoon.

★ ★ ★

The next day found us motoring slowly along the road towards Bermondsey again. Marnie was not with us this time. There hadn't seemed any point in keeping her at Uncle Charles's house, especially since he had returned home yesterday unexpectedly.

'This is so sweet of you,' I said, rather acidly as we swept across Tower Bridge. 'Are you sure you can spare the time?' He turned to me and gave me one of his lazy smiles.

'I believe you are angry with me, *ma chère*. Should I be apologizing?'

'Good heavens, of course not. How you spend your time is entirely your own affair.'

'Indeed?'

'Yes. Although I have to say sometimes you're very hard to track down. I seemed to spend all yesterday morning on the telephone trying to find you. How do you manage to keep all the aunts off your scent?'

'Off my scent?' He looked perplexed.

'Yes, you know, how do you manage to stop them prying into how and where you spend your time? I had to make up the most elaborate tale to keep Aunt Hetty satisfied

91

this morning. I can't keep saying I'm showing you around London.'

He smiled, as he negotiated a corner that was littered with market stalls. 'I just tell them I have business to attend to.'

I frowned. 'Of course. If you're a man no one thinks twice about that.'

'Yes. Especially if I start mentioning cows. That usually makes Hermione realize she has some important business of her own to attend to with the cook.'

I laughed then. Laurent had a way of turning conversations around that was very endearing and the rest of the journey passed quite agreeably.

We arrived at Mr Bennett's office much earlier this time and the neighbourhood seemed somewhat quieter, even subdued. I walked up the stairs to his tiny little office and gasped. The door was off its hinges.

Inside the place was even worse. The desk, hitherto the most sturdy item in the place, was now balancing precariously on some flimsy looking boxes, three of its legs completely broken off. There was a pile of wood in one corner of the room and only one chair left which also looked a lot worse for wear. Papers were strewn across the little room as though a tornado had hit the place.

But what was even worse was Mr Bennett

himself. He still wore his coat, but the lapel had been completely ripped off one side, and there no buttons left on it. He looked dreadful. There was a nasty-looking cut across his nose and a huge bruise under his right eye; I could see more on his knuckles. He smiled wanly at the horrified expression on my face.

'If you think I look bad, Miss Wyndham-Brown, you should see the other two fellows.'

'Mr Bennett, what happened? Good gracious, you look terrible.'

'I think I investigated the wrong errant husband, Miss Wyndham-Brown,' he said, as he lifted up a box from the floor and began slowly placing papers into it. Just then Laurent came in.

'*Mon Dieu*, what happened here?'

'Angry clients, sir, as I was just telling your cousin. They came here yesterday morning presumably with the purpose of destroying evidence. What they didn't know was that I was working late. Or early. I was here anyway.' As he said this he suddenly went a horrible shade of white and sat down on the last remaining chair.

'Mr Bennett, are you ill? What can we do?' I cried. 'Good heavens, this is dreadful. Where are the police? Have you informed them — ?'

He gave a short laugh. 'I don't think Bow Street's finest are going to be too concerned about this, Miss Wyndham-Brown. After all, I'm not dead and nothing of any value was taken.'

'Really?' Laurent walked round to where Mr Bennett was sitting and crouched down beside him. 'Then why does your office look like this?' As he spoke he touched Mr Bennett gently on the stomach. Mr Bennett winced.

'Oh they took most of my papers and notes, but they're only of value to me. Could I ask you not to do that again? I'm finding it hard enough to breathe as it is.'

'You have broken several ribs, *monsieur*.' Laurent got up and surveyed him dispassionately. 'You should really be in bed.'

'I'll be fine.' He winced again as he sat back in the chair. 'But I'm afraid I've got some bad news for you, Miss Wyndham-Brown. My visitors weren't very discriminatory about what documents they took and all your tickets have gone too with the rest of my ongoing cases.'

'Good heavens, Mr Bennett, don't worry about that.' I was becoming quite concerned about his pallor. He looked as though he might faint at any moment. 'Have you seen a doctor? I can't believe he would have said you could be here now.'

'Really, I'll be fine, Miss Wyndham-Brown. The thing is' — he looked at me briefly before turning away and I could see shame in his eyes — 'I won't be able to reimburse you straight away for the money you advanced me. You see I started to look into the case, but before I could — '

I frowned. 'Mr Bennett, do you honestly believe I care about two guineas? It doesn't matter to me that — '

'It matters to me,' he snapped, before wincing again.

'Well then, when you feel better you can continue, but for the moment — '

'Miss Wyndham-Brown I don't think you understand. I've lost all the tickets you gave me. There's nothing left. I'd only gone to one pawnbroker by the time these louts set on me and that visit had yielded nothing. And I hadn't examined the others in any detail because I didn't think it would be necessary and now . . . ' He tailed off, looking so dejected I almost wanted to cry.

'Dear Mr Bennett, I really don't care about the silly tickets. Or the money. If I never know what Papa pawned or why, it really won't make any difference to my life. As you keep pointing out, a spoilt brat like me doesn't have anything to worry about. Now the most important thing is to make sure you are all right. What does your doctor say?'

'Nothing.' He waved a hand vaguely in the air. I looked at Laurent who shrugged.

'Mr Bennett, have you seen a doctor since this happened?'

He shook his head. 'There's no need,' he said, a forced smile on his face. 'I'm just tidying up here then I'll go back to my rooms and — '

'*Monsieur*, you really should see a doctor,' said Laurent gently. Mr Bennett's smile became even more forced.

'What for? I know exactly what he'll say. 'Stay in bed, rest and eat well'. I can work that out for myself.'

'Oh for goodness' sake, Mr Bennett,' I said, becoming exasperated with his stubbornness. 'You must come with us immediately. Laurent, we must get him in the car. Guy's Hospital is just around the corner.'

'Of course. *Monsieur*?' Laurent gestured to the door, but Mr Bennett stayed where he was.

'No. Thank you, but no.'

'Mr Bennett, why are you being so ridiculous? You clearly need — '

'Because doctors cost money, you stupid woman, and I don't have any!' he said savagely, sitting up then slumping back down again.

'Well then, I'll pay for it. Do you really think I'm going to leave you here like this?'

'I don't need your charity,' he snapped, trying to sit up. I frowned.

'Very well. Come, Laurent, I need your assistance.'

'Really? To do what, *ma chère*?' Laurent had that irritating smile on his face again, but I ignored it this time.

'Since Mr Bennett is clearly not going to come with us to the hospital, then I shall have to engage a doctor to come out here privately. Of course, it will be much more expensive, but nevertheless if Mr Bennett insists on being so stubborn then he leaves us with no choice and he'll find himself in debt to me even further. I would instruct you to wait here, Mr Bennett, but why bother when you can hardly move?'

As I moved towards the door, Laurent crouched down beside the stupid man again.

'Monsieur Bennett?' he said gently. 'Which would you prefer? A trip to the hospital, or a visit out here? I would choose now because she will have her way in this matter.'

Mr Bennett looked up a wretched expression his face. 'This is completely unnecessary, you know,' he said at last, standing up rather shakily.

I sighed. 'Indulge me, Mr Bennett. It's

what we spoilt brats are most used to.'

'I *will* pay you back.'

'Of course you will,' I soothed, gesturing to Laurent. Between us we managed to get him down the stairs and into the car. As he lay back on the leather seats he fainted.

★ ★ ★

We took Mr Bennett to Guy's Hospital and a doctor saw him immediately, tutting and shaking his head as he examined the wounds and injuries.

'How long has he been like this?' he asked eventually. I glanced at Laurent.

'Since yesterday morning,' I said. 'Will he be all right?' The doctor, a balding, middle-aged man with a greying beard, tutted again.

'He's young. And generally healthy, although there's evidence of malnutrition. I should say he'll survive. Leave him here with us, Miss Wyndham-Brown. I'll let you know as soon as there's any progress.'

I looked down at Mr Bennett's wan face. 'Please do.'

'Bella, we should leave,' said Laurent. 'There is nothing more we can do here.'

I hesitated. 'I know,' I said reluctantly 'but —'

'And we would do more good returning to Mr Bennett's office to see that it is secure.'

I thought back to the ruined office with its shattered door and floor strewn with papers. 'You're right, Laurent. Let's do that immediately.'

I left my details with the nurse on duty and we returned to the horrid little office in Bermondsey. We were not a moment too soon. We drew up outside the tumbledown building as a crowd gathered, watching with great delight the argument that was going on between a gang of huge, rough-looking labourers and Mabel.

'Oi! Leave that alone! That ain't yours. Put it back. Put it back, I say, or I'll 'ave the law on yer!'

This shrill cry did not seem to worry any of the labourers, who grinned at her whilst they carried down various items of furniture from the building and placed them on a cart by the front door.

'Suit yerself, Mabel,' one of the men said, as he threw a box on to the cart. 'Go up there now if you like. I daresay you'll give Sergeant Hobson a good laugh. 'Ere, leave that alone,' he added, as Mabel attempted to wrest the box back. I gasped.

'Laurent,' I whispered. 'That's Mr Bennett's box. They're stealing from Mr Bennett's office. These must be the thieves he mentioned before. They've come back!'

Laurent surveyed the gang of workmen. 'I do not think they are engaged in theft, ma chère. Otherwise they would not be out in broad daylight. It would seem more likely that they are pursuing legitimate business.' He glanced back at me. 'Mr Bennett did mention he had no money after all.'

I frowned. 'You there,' I said, stepping out of the car and addressing the nearest pilferer. 'Stop that immediately. What's going on here?'

Being an heiress can be tedious, but one does learn quickly to develop a certain air of authority, especially with servants, and my words caused all the workmen to stop what they were doing and look up at me. The crowd around the doorway turned towards me too, anticipating fresh entertainment. Taking advantage of the situation, Mabel slipped free with the box still in her hands.

'They're fievin' Mr Bennett's stuff, thass what they're doin'. Daylight robbery, it is. Go on, miss, you call the p'leece. They'll listen to a lady like you.'

'Who is in charge here?' I asked. Mabel's tormentor nodded towards the door.

'Jenkins is the landlord. Oi! Jenkins!' he yelled. 'Someone down 'ere to see you.'

After a few seconds another man came down the stairs and out the peeling front door. He was considerably better dressed than his workmen, although he hadn't bothered to shave and dirty stubble dotted his cheeks.

'That's *Mr* Jenkins to you, Michaels. Watch your mouth. What do you want?'

Michaels leaned back on the cart and crossed his arms. 'All right, *Mr* Jenkins. This 'ere lady wants ter talk to you. Seems she's takin' exception to us nabbin' Bennett's stuff.'

'Oh, is she?' Jenkins turned round, an unpleasant leer on his face. 'An' what's it got to do wiv you?'

I drew myself up and stared as condescendingly at him as I knew how. But before I could say anything, Laurent had jumped down from the motor car and stood beside me.

'Well, Jenkins,' he asked, flicking contemptuous eyes up and down the landlord, as he drew off his gloves. 'We were considering paying you what you are owed on Mr Bennett's behalf. However, I think we will allow you and your comrades to carry on with your unofficial duties and return later with the police. *Madame*,' he said to Mabel. 'Here is sixpence. Go and fetch some paper and a pen. We will note down what these gentlemen remove and take restorative action at the proper time. Peter will not be needing these particular premises' — he looked up in disgust at the building — 'again, will he, my dear?'

'Certainly not, Laurent,' I said. 'But by all means let us allow the law to take its proper course.'

Mr Jenkins stared at us shrewdly. He might not have been a particularly pleasant person, but he recognized money when he saw it and it was obvious that Mr Bennett's pitiful collection of worldly goods was worth far less than the back rent he actually owed.

'Ah, now, let's not be too 'asty, sir, miss. Of course, if you 'appen to be friends of Mr Bennett's then I'm sure we can come to some agreement. I didn't realize Mr Bennett 'ad such important friends. Now then, lads,' he added to two men who had come out with the last remaining unbroken chair. ''Old on a minute. We may not 'ave ter take nothing after all, if this lady and gentlemen are prepared to help out.'

'Help out?' asked Laurent softly. 'Is that what you were doing, *monsieur*? It seemed more that you were helping yourself.'

There was general laughter from the crowd at this and someone called out, 'Yeah, yer good at that, ain't yer, Jenkins?' The landlord scowled, but mindful of his back rent, refused to allow himself to be sidetracked.

'Well now, sir, a man 'as to keep 'is finances in order. An' Mr Bennett owed five weeks' rent an' I let him stay on on credit — '

'Yeah, only 'cos 'e promised not to snoop on you, like yer old lady wanted,' someone else yelled, and the crowd roared with laughter. I frowned.

'Oh for heaven's sake, how much does he owe?' I asked. Mr Jenkins licked his lips and rolled his hat around in his hands, clearly wondering how much he might possibly get away with.

'Well, five weeks at — let me see, twenty-five shillings in all miss, if you'd be so kind.' I reached for my purse, but Laurent stayed my hand.

'Twenty-five shillings? You astound me. We have seen how poor the accommodation is, *monsieur*. Or perhaps I forgot to mention that?'

Mr Jenkins flicked a glance at me. 'Oh yeah? Professional visit like, was it?' he asked, considerably less deferentially. There was a blur of movement and then I realized Laurent had Mr Jenkins by the throat.

'Do not try my patience, *monsieur*,' he said, still in the same soft voice. The crowd, thrilled by this turn of events, all leaned a little closer.

'No, no, no, 'course not, sir. No offence meant,' Mr Jenkins croaked, trying to extricate himself from Laurent's grip. Laurent glared at him in disgust, then dropped him, as though he were somehow unclean.

'We will remunerate you to the order of one pound,' he announced. 'Providing you return all the goods immediately, replace the door and attach a good lock this time. *Madame*,' he added to Mabel, who was watching all this with something like awe. 'You may retain the sixpence I gave you. Now you will use it to make sure that Monsieur Jenkins and his men do as I say.'

'Yes, sir.' I got the distinct impression Mabel and the rest of the crowd would have done that for free anyway. Laurent nodded as he took a sovereign from his coat pocket and flicked it at Mr Jenkins. Then he helped me back into the car. We had barely got down the street before Mabel ran after us.

'Oi, 'old on a second, miss, sir. 'Old on!'

Laurent halted the motor car. '*Madame*, do you need more money? Here.' And he began to search in his pockets for another coin. Mabel, who had been panting with effort after her run, put her hands on her hips as she shook her head.

'No, it ain't that, sir, it's just — are you a friend of 'is, like?' she asked, turning to me.

'Yes,' I said.

Apparently this wasn't enough. 'A good friend?' she insisted. I frowned.

'Yes,' I said, ignoring the grin which was growing on Laurent's face. 'Why?'

Mabel shrugged. 'Well, if you really want to 'elp 'im, 'e's gonna lose his room over at Mrs Burman's too, if 'e don't turn up wiv the rent tonight. An'e ain't, is 'e? I saw you take 'im to the 'ospital.'

I bit my lip. How could I have been so stupid not to have realized how desperate Mr Bennett was? I opened my purse.

'How much does he owe Mrs Burman, Mabel?' I asked.

'Ten bob, miss. But she'll take five, 'cos 'e already paid 'er back fer the last month owin'.'

I took a ten shilling note out of my purse. 'Here's ten shillings, Mabel. Can I trust you to pay her?' Mabel was blinking at the sight of the note, but she took a deep breath and nodded.

'Yeah. I'll give it to 'er.'

'Good. And here's five shillings for you.' Mabel's face lit up.

'Fank you very much, miss,' she said fervently.

105

'But Mabel, you mustn't tell him it was me who paid his rent to Mrs Burman.'

Mabel nodded as she pocketed the note. 'Yeah, 'e gets dead funny about stuff like that. Keeps goin' on about 'ow 'e won't accept charity. I dunno why. 'E ain't been eating much fer the last few weeks. I'd take whatever was give to me, meself. Still there you are. See you, miss.' And she began to walk away.

'So, Mabel, you won't tell him it was me, will you?' I shouted after her.

'Oh I got to tell 'im, miss. Acherly I got to tell 'im you forced me to give the money to Mrs Burman.'

'Why?' I asked, as she backed down the street.

'Well, if 'e finks I asked fer money from you, 'e'll yell at me. 'E ain't gonna yell at you, is 'e?' She gave me one last grin as she disappeared around the corner.

'Well, of all the — ' I began, but Laurent roared with laughter as he started up the motor once more.

'Actually that is not quite true, is it, *ma belle*? He is just as likely to yell at you as to that *cocotte*.'

I glared at him. 'Laurent?'

'*Oui, ma chère?*'

'Just drive the car.'

Laurent did not stop laughing all the way back across the bridge.

★   ★   ★

The door of the smart London house opened and a maid bobbed a curtsy.

'Ruby! How are you?' I asked in delight. Ruby smiled back at me.

'Very well, thank you, miss.'

'You look a picture of health. But I thought you were with Mrs Ellis?'

'I'm just 'elpin' out whilst 'er ladyship and the professor get theirselves sorted out with the weddin', miss.'

'Oh, I see.' I entered the hallway, drawing off my gloves. 'And did you enjoy Persia?'

'It was lovely, miss.' She took off my coat. 'I'm 'oping Miss Katie and Mr Ellis will take me wiv 'em next time they go orf.'

'Ah, I knew they wouldn't be here for long.'

Ruby showed me into the morning-room. A tall figure was sitting in front of the window, going over what looked like a book of accounts.

'Kate do put that down,' I said. Kate looked up.

'Bella,' she said, leaping up and coming across to kiss me. 'How lovely to see you again. How have you been? I'm so sorry we missed your ball. How was it? And have you — ?'

Seeing Kate again after an absence of over a year was wonderful. I hadn't realized how much I missed her and we talked non-stop for most of the morning, hardly drawing breath through lunch. It wasn't until the clock struck three that I realized how long we'd been talking.

'Darling, I've monopolized you all day. And you must be so busy.'

She smiled. 'Well, Papa wanted a quiet wedding, but you know Alice. She loves any kind of society function and since she seems to know most of London, the whole affair grows by the day. Alice is in her element, of course. All she does is talk about silk and taffeta and menus and such like.'

I smiled at the slight increase in tension in her voice. 'And you are not in your element, I take it?' I said, pouring out tea from the tray Ruby had brought in a few minutes before and adding some lemon. The light citrus smell was very refreshing.

She grimaced. 'I love Alice, of course I do, but wearing elaborate dresses and discussing the relative merits of silk over satin really isn't my forte, Bella. Half the time I have very little idea of what she's talking about. And Papa and Adam are no help. They just rush off to

108

the museum as soon Alice gets her swatches out. It's like watching trained dogs. Really,' she insisted as I began to laugh. 'Besides, I can't, in all courtesy, leave poor Alice to sort out everything on her own, but I must be a sore trial to her. The other day she asked me to see the florists with a list of flowers she wanted to view and I must have got the order wrong because the next day a messenger appeared with a hysterical letter asking if Lady Faulkner really wanted five hundred white lilies on each table. Alice was very patient, but she hasn't asked me to help since.'

I patted her hand. 'Well then, how about coming to stay with me for a few days? I've still got lots of sorting out to do. Absolutely piles and piles of old documents to organize, Kate, and I'm useless at it.'

'Really?' Kate's face lit up. It was the sort of thing she was much more at home doing and I would certainly be grateful for the help. As fascinating as I was finding it to delve into my parents' lives before I was born, I just didn't seem to have the knack of organizing paperwork. Documents I'd had in my hands seconds before seemed to disappear almost before my very eyes.

'You'd be doing me a huge favour, darling, and think how much fun we could have.'

Kate looked thoughtful. 'I'd certainly be more useful than I am here — ' she began. Just then the door opened.

'Bella! I was hoping I hadn't missed you. How are you?' Adam smiled at me, taking my hands in his and kissing me lightly on the cheek. 'Has Kate been telling you all about Alice's wedding dress?'

Kate tutted. 'Ignore him, Bella. He thinks it's hilarious that Alice asks my opinion about clothes.'

'It's your duty as a loving daughter to do your best to support your future stepmother through this busy time,' he said smugly, sitting down on the sofa beside Kate. They both looked tanned and healthy from their time in Persia, unlike the rest of us Londoners who were still suffering from the effects of a cold and sunless winter.

'I've done lots of supporting already,' Kate said grumpily. 'But enough of us. Have you seen anything of Peter Bennett since he came home, Bella?'

I picked up my tea-cup. 'Once or twice,' I said airily, taking a sip. 'Have you?'

They both grinned. 'Hmm, let me see; I think we did visit him last week didn't we, Kate?' said Adam.

'In hospital, wasn't it? He wasn't very happy about being there, as I recall.' Kate looked at me briefly from over the teapot. 'What was it he called Bella, Adam?'

'Let me see. An interfering, condescending, insensitive — '

'Yes thank you,' I said, irritably. 'I'm well aware of what that ungrateful brute thinks of me. I went to see him in Guy's and all he could do was snap and shout at me. One would have thought I'd had him thrown on the streets myself rather than actually stopping that from happening. I wish I had left him to starve now. He's the most — '

Before I could finish, both Adam and Kate had burst into laughter.

'I'm sorry, Bella,' said Kate, after a few minutes. 'You're quite right. He was horribly ungrateful and we told him so, didn't we, Adam?'

'The idiot doesn't know when to thank his lucky stars,' Adam said. 'He'd probably be dead by now if it weren't for you. The doctor at the hospital said he was lucky to have lasted as long as he did without medical care.'

'To be fair, darling, I think he was prepared to forgive Bella for that,' said Kate happily.

I snorted. 'How gracious of him.'

'You're right,' Adam continued, as though I hadn't spoken. 'Apparently what really annoyed him was your overindulgence.'

'My what?'

'You were overindulging yourself by helping him with his rents,' said Adam helpfully. 'Apparently it's wallowing in the — now what did he say, Kate? — wallowing in the smug — '

' — smug pit of the spoilt, idle rich,' finished Kate. 'Although again, to be fair, darling, he didn't say any of that until Mabel arrived and started telling us what a nice lady you were. And she was terribly admiring of your French beau, wasn't she, Adam?'

'Terribly.' Adam fixed me with his eyes. 'Actually I could see why that annoyed Peter. The last thing a man wants to hear when he's lying ill in bed is how brave and resourceful and commanding another man is.'

'So do tell us, Bella. Who is this brave and commanding man?'

I put my cup down. 'He's my cousin. There was a rift in the family for many years which was resolved during my absence and Laurent came over to visit.'

'Oh, I see. Well, I shall look forward to meeting him. I need to practise my French, it's become rather rusty of late. Well, Adam, do you think Alice will agree to doing without me for a while? Bella's asked me to stay at her house in the country.'

Adam smiled. 'If it means not having to dispose of ten thousand lilies, I'm sure she'll get by. But why don't I get an invitation as well?'

As they bickered amiably together, I found my attention wandering. Mr Bennett was extremely annoying, but I did feel some responsibility for him. Perhaps I should go back to the hospital before leaving for the country. I was trying to work out how I could do this without involving Laurent, who was becoming far too amused by the whole affair, when Alice Faulkner arrived. I had to leave soon afterwards, as I had made arrangements to dine with Harriet and some of her rather hearty suffragette friends, but I did not leave without making firm plans for Kate to come to Woodruffe Manor. Also, I had an invitation to Lady Faulkner's wedding. And the knowledge that Mr Bennett was being invited as well. As I got into a hansom cab, I reflected that my stay in London, while not going entirely to plan, had been most productive.

5

Kate took off her spectacles and polished them with the striped blue and white tie she was wearing.

'You know Bella this is fascinating. Some of these documents date back to the Restoration. They're really quite valuable.'

I walked over to her and looked at the yellowing conveyances she was studying. They seemed very fragile and, frankly, rather dull.

'That's nice, Kate, but they're not really what I'm looking for. I'm much more interested in anything we can find about Mama or Papa.'

We had been going through the papers for three days now, ever since Kate had arrived and she had brought that same thoroughness to my familial memorabilia that she employed with the pharoah's treasures in Luxor. In no time at all everything was organized according to date, time and place and I had an even greater respect for Mama's business acumen than before. Papa's share, however, was much smaller. It comprised mainly of old letters and, rather alarmingly, unpaid bills. I began to suspect Great Aunt Evadne had been telling the truth when she had said Papa owed her thirty pounds and that she was not the only person who had never been repaid.

Kate looked at me for a second, then put the papers down carefully and took off her thin cotton gloves. Fine white powder floated away from her hands to the floor.

'Let's stop and go for a stroll around that little rose garden of yours, shall we, Bella? I think we both need some fresh air.'

It was a beautiful spring afternoon as we walked through the archway of the walled garden, stopping occasionally to admire the dahlias and hyacinths. The roses were actually only part of it; really Henderson had the run of the place because no one else knew enough about gardening to gainsay him. He had done a marvellous job, though. The garden was a positive rainbow of colour and the smell from the hyacinths and roses was heavenly.

As Kate and I strolled along the path we saw Henderson leaning on a hoe, taking a break from his work. He touched his cap politely when he saw us.

'Afternoon, Miss Bella, ma'am.'

'Good afternoon, Henderson. We were just admiring the roses.'

'Thank you, miss. I'm pleased with them meself. 'Course I'm going to have to make sure — '

He began to talk at some length about the garden then and my attention wandered a little. I like looking at flowers and smelling their delicate perfumes, but my interest in them wanes when it comes to actually having to do any work around them. Then he said something that did interest me, however.

''Er ladyship was very partial to roses too, Miss Bella. She used to come down 'ere practically every day when she was 'ere. Now 'is lordship, 'e preferred the summer'ouse. 'E often used to be down there, scribblin' away on rainy afternoons.'

'Really?' I remembered playing in the summerhouse once or twice with my dolls when I was a little girl, but it was under a large tree which made it rather dark and dingy and not the most alluring of play areas when one was alone. Then I remembered something else.

'Wasn't there a little cupboard in it, Henderson? It was always locked and Marnie wouldn't let me open it. She said it was private. Is it still there?'

'I believe so, miss. P'raps you'd like to see it now.'

Kate and I looked at each other. 'By all means,' I said, and Henderson took us down to another section of the garden. This part

116

was dominated by a large pond full of goldfish and with a magnificent statue of Neptune rising from the sea, the horses on his chariot spouting water. Over in a corner, shaded by a graceful willow tree was the little white gazebo. It was actually rather pretty in a somewhat forlorn, neglected way.

Henderson opened the door, which creaked a little and motes of dust danced along the stream of sunlight as we walked in. The place was very much as I remembered it. There were three wicker chairs covered over with dust sheets and a long, low table facing the doorway. In one corner of the room was a huge vase with red and gold Chinese dragons chasing each other around its length and breadth and in the other corner a small dark oak credenza.

''Ere we are now, ladies. I think a fox or summat got in 'ere once. Must 'ave 'eard a rat or a mouse inside.'

Henderson crouched down beside the credenza and gently stroked three long scratches raked deep into its locked cupboard. I cleared my throat.

'Actually I'm afraid that was my handiwork, Henderson. At least mine and Harriet's. We were rather bored one afternoon and convinced each other there was some treasure or another inside which we were determined to find. As you can see we didn't succeed.'

Kate took off her spectacles as she peered closely at the credenza. 'What stopped you?'

'Oh, we'd also convinced each other the place was haunted and I seem to remember hearing a crash and Harriet and I fleeing as if our lives depended on it. No doubt we knew we were doing something wrong in the first place.'

'Well, nobody's been in there from the last time your dad was 'ere to now. I mind I told Lady Faversham once about it and she said she'd come down and take a look but she never did.'

I nodded. Aunt Augusta wasn't really very keen on summerhouses. I think she thought them a little indulgent. I took an experimental tug at the door, but it was firmly locked.

'How annoying. I suppose I'll have to ask you to break it open, Henderson, although it seems a shame.'

'No, don't let's be hasty, Bella,' said Kate, standing up again. 'Have you forgotten that little box you showed me? There were several keys in that.'

I thought back to the box that had originally held the pawn tickets. 'None of them will fit, Kate. They were all far too small.'

'I'm not so sure. I think there was one that might just be the right size. Will you wait here for us, Henderson?'

'Of course, ma'am. I wouldn't want you ladies opening this on your own. You never know what you might find.'

'Yes, I know. It's terribly exciting, Henderson. There could be treasure in there after all.'

'I was thinkin' more in the line of rats and spiders, miss,' said Henderson soberly, and I grimaced.

'Well, I suppose so. We'll be back in no time.'

Kate and I left the summerhouse and went back to the study. We found the little box and, as she had said, there was one key in there that looked large enough to open the credenza. We went back to the summerhouse to find Henderson waiting for us. He had on a pair of huge workman's gloves. Clearly he did not share my romantic ideas of lost treasure, his own thoughts running more to dead and rotting rodents, possibly even live and disgruntled ones.

'Here we are Henderson,' said Kate, as I held out the key. He nodded.

'I've oiled the lock, Miss Bella. If you turn it slowly and it's the right one, it should open easy like.'

I put the key in the lock and slowly turned it. It creaked a bit, the tumblers protesting at being expected to move after all this time, but finally we heard a click.

'Well done, there, miss. Move back,' said Henderson. As he pulled the door slowly open we all peered in.

'Seems all right,' he said after prodding gingerly at the contents of the inside with one hand. He put both hands in and lifted out a large wooden box. It was beautifully inlaid with mother-of-pearl markings, but at the moment rather dingy with a thick layer of dust. As Henderson drew it out, a mouldy musty smell wafted out with it.

'Here you are, miss. Let me just give it a bit of a wipe down,' he said, and dislodged twenty years of dust with an old cloth. We all coughed.

'It is rather lovely, Bella. Indian, I'd say,' said Kate, as she tried to open it. Again it was locked tight, but this time it seemed more likely that one of the keys from Papa's box in the house would fit. Henderson, meanwhile, was still poking about in the cupboard.

'Nothing else in there, miss. I'd say that was your lot.'

'That's all we need, Henderson. Thank you so much for your help.'

'My pleasure, Miss Bella. Let me know if you find any buried treasure maps,' he chortled as I picked up the box.

'Of course,' I said. Kate and I looked at each other. We walked quickly back to the house.

★ ★ ★

Two hours later, we were still sitting in the study. A tray of tea and sandwiches lay untouched on the desk. Suddenly the door opened.

'Dr Ellis is here, Miss Bella. Shall I show him in?' Lily asked. I nodded.

'Here you two are. Didn't you hear the carriage draw up?' said Adam, walking into the room. 'I've come down here for the weekend specifically to save you two ungrateful wenches from boredom and you don't even have the decency to come running to greet me. Ah food,' he added, his eyes lighting up as he spied the sandwiches. 'Thank heavens. I'm starving, and I know I can't wait until dinner.' He grabbed at one as he sat down on a basket chair, then realized that neither of us had said a word.

'Whatever is the matter? You two look as if you've seen a ghost.'

Kate got up finally and went over to where

he was sitting and kissed him on the cheek absently.

'We've spent the afternoon going over some old letters and diaries of Bella's father that we found locked away. And it really is the most amazing thing, Adam, but it seems Viscount Bowood found the missing diamond.'

'Diamond? What diamond?' asked Adam, the sandwich still in his hand.

'The Bowood Diamond,' I said. 'The Dragonsheart. You remember, I told you about it.'

'Do you mean that one that went missing a couple of hundred years ago? I thought you said the Roundheads were supposed to have stolen it?'

'They were. At least that's what everyone in the family always supposed. The diamond went missing during the interregnum when the house was temporarily evacuated. But it appears, according to Papa's diary, that the third viscount, Francis, must have hidden it to keep it safe and then been killed in battle before he could tell his wife what he'd done. Anyway, Papa writes that he was in the eastern turret at Bowood one afternoon, when he happened to notice an old pen he'd lost behind a cupboard. He'd pulled it out to get the pen and it was then he noticed one of the bricks seemed looser than the rest. There was quite a bit of damp all over Bowood at the time and Mama had been on the warpath looking to see nothing was unsafe.' I grimaced. 'According to Papa's diary, he was rather fond of the turret, although it had a tendency to mould and he was worried Mama might insist the place was renovated, of which he would not have been in favour, so he'd deliberately not called any of the servants to help him move the cupboard in case they let slip anything to Mama. Anyway he poked at the brick for a bit, but it seemed so damp and loose that even he got a bit worried in the end and that was when he pulled it right out.'

'And this was what he found. Look,' said Kate, showing him the scrap of yellowed parchment we had found inside the box. Adam took it, holding it delicately.

My beloved Arabella
Keepe the Dragonsharte hydden untyl you are sure it is safe.
My lord Exeter, if he yet lyves, will advyse you on how best to use it. If

It ended abruptly, the torn paper hinting maddeningly at what other information the beleaguered viscount was trying to give to his wife.

'Exeter. I wonder who he was,' Adam said, as he examined the document.

'Probably the local sheriff and a family friend. Francis must have known there was a good chance he wouldn't survive the Civil War, but he thought he would at least have had a chance to speak to Arabella before he was killed,' said Kate.

'Papa was absolutely beside himself when he found it,' I said, showing him the diary we had found in the box. 'He was going to have it taken to a jeweller's to be verified and valued and then he wanted to have a ball to celebrate its discovery. He had it all worked out. He was going to insist Mama had a new dress made especially for the occasion and he was not going to take no for an answer.' I put the diary down. 'Apparently Mama did not approve of wasting money unnecessarily on clothes.'

'I see.' Gently, Adam placed the parchment down on the desk. 'Well come on then; don't keep me in suspense. Where is it?'

'Well that's the odd thing, Adam,' Kate said, glancing at me. 'It's not here.'

'Not here? But I thought you said — '

'We said Robert found the diamond, according to his diary; we didn't say it was here in the box. Believe me, my dear, we've looked. We've tried every little crevice that looks like it might be a secret hiding place but it's not here.'

'The diary is very patchy. Papa didn't write every day. In fact, there's a long gap between apparently finding the Dragonsheart and his last entry. Look.'

I pointed to the diary again. It was like Papa's other diaries in that he had written excitedly for a period of about three weeks on finding the diamond, at the end of February 1888, then nothing for about three months. The last entry ended abruptly:

14 August 1888

At last everything is ready. I managed to transfer the monies in time. A sick continuously. I fear for her during the voyage, but she refuses to even hear of postponing the journey and I know in my heart she is right to do this. I

'I take it A is your mother,' said Adam, flicking back through the pages, but finding nothing as we had done. I nodded.

'Aunt Augusta always said they didn't know she was carrying me at the time, but it appears they did.'

'Your mother was very adventurous, no doubt,' Kate said. She had settled down by

125

the desk and was examining the letter from Francis to Arabella once more. I knew it fascinated her.

'No doubt,' I replied. 'Although I must say it appears rather odd that she would have put herself in such a precarious position. According to Aunt Hortensia, she and Papa feared they would never have children. After all, they were married for two years before I came along. One would have thought Mama would have been more circumspect when she finally found out she was with child.'

'Perhaps they did not mean to be gone so long,' Kate said. 'Papa told me once that he and Mama intended I should be born in England.'

'Where were you born then?'

'India,' she replied. 'Look at this script, Adam. We must take it to the museum immediately. With your permission, of course, Bella.'

'Of course.' I got up and walked across to the window. 'How maddening that the tickets were stolen. The Dragonsheart must have been one of the things that Papa pawned.'

Adam picked up a document at random and began to examine it. 'I wonder what he spent the money on,' he said.

'Unpaid debts,' Kate replied crisply. Adam looked at her in some embarrassment.'

'Kate, isn't that rather rude — ' he began, but I just laughed.

'I have no secrets from Kate, I'm afraid,' I said getting up. 'Or at least the Wyndham-Browns don't. We found far too many bills that never seem to be paid. I suspect Mama had refused to pay them for him. I'll see you both at dinner,' I added, for a carriage had just drawn up outside the window. I had invited Helen and Edwin to dinner, along with Harriet. Laurent was due to arrive later. 'I must go and say hello to my cousins.'

And I left them in the study still examining the letter and the diary.

★ ★ ★

In the end Laurent did not have dinner with us. He had intended to travel with the others but he had been obliged to return to France at short notice that morning, due to some family crisis. He did not know when or if he would be able to return for some time.

'What a shame,' Kate said, as we waited for dinner to be served that evening. 'I was so looking forward to meeting him.'

Harriet sipped at her sherry. 'Our new cousin is rather difficult to pin down, isn't he, Bella? He seems to fly about the country in his motor car like one demented.'

127

'He's got a car?' Adam, who had seemed uninterested in the conversation up to this point suddenly perked up. Edwin nodded.

'A Rolls-Royce Silver Ghost. Six cylinder.'

'Really? Six?'

We women all looked at one another wearily. Every time the motor car was mentioned, the men in the room developed acquisitive sparkles in their eyes. Just then, fortunately, Lily announced dinner was served.

'By the way, darling,' Harriet whispered in my ear, as we walked into the dining-room. 'I'd better warn you Papa is not happy with you.'

'Really?' I tried to think of anything I might have done to annoy him over the past few weeks, but apart from billing the trustees for a pair of lilac kid leather boots which I simply had to have, making me go over my monthly dress allowance by ten pounds, I could not think of anything. I felt rather aggrieved to be honest. Uncle Charles had no right to be angry with me any more. Besides, the boots were absolutely adorable and it was only ten pounds.

'Yes, apparently you've brought the family into disrepute.' She grinned at me as she rolled her eyes. 'Lord, do you know how many times I've heard that? So who is Mr

128

Peter Bennett, my dear? He sounds deliciously mysterious.'

'Peter Bennett?' I said rather more loudly than I meant. 'How on earth did Uncle Charles hear about him?'

'You know Papa. Nothing gets past him. So — out with it, my girl. What have you been up to?'

I frowned, trying to think of how I could explain Mr Bennett away without having to mention Papa or his wretched pawn-shop adventures. I love my relatives, but really there are times when one wonders how long it will be before one is allowed any privacy. Happily, before I could stutter out some obviously made-up lie, Kate came to my rescue.

'Did I hear you mention Peter Bennett, Miss Woodruffe? He's a good friend of ours. He's the private detective who saved us when we were trapped in the tomb in Luxor.'

'Oh *that*'s the one,' Helen said. 'Of course, Bella told us about him.' A satisfied nod passed between her and Edwin and in spite of my relief that their curiosity had been sated, I couldn't help feeling annoyed, too. Clearly Uncle Charles had been discussing my behaviour with them and I had been found wanting.

'Yes, Kate gave me his address and I went

to see him the other day,' I said, as nonchalantly as I could. 'It was so nice to meet him again.'

'He's got some rooms over in Bermondsey, hasn't he?' Edwin said, a little too casually.

'Yes he has. Now how could you possibly know that, Edwin?'

Edwin coloured. 'One hears these things, my dear.'

'Does one? And how, may I ask?'

'We went to see him the other day, didn't we, darling?' Kate said to Adam, before Edwin could reply. 'He's doing so well. He hopes to be moving across the river soon.'

After a quick glance at me, Adam agreed with her and Edwin and Helen smiled, obviously relieved that Mr Bennett's address was going to become so much more acceptable in the near future. Then, before they could ask any more potentially awkward questions, Kate engaged Harriet on the latest news on women's suffrage and dinner continued smoothly.

I was content to let them talk for a while. The mention of both Mr Bennett and Laurent reminded me that I wasn't feeling too charitable towards either of them. As I had said to Adam and Kate, I had gone back to the hospital once more to see how Mr Bennett was, but neither time, medicine nor good food had improved his manners. He seemed to feel I had deeply insulted him by paying the rents on his office and rooms and in the end the nurses had asked me to leave because I 'was upsetting the patient'. I had left the hospital vowing never to have anything to do with the wretch ever again.

And Laurent was just as bad in his own way. After our meeting with the vile landlord he had taken me back to Uncle Charles's house and left me abruptly with tales of another meeting for which he was late. I had not seen him in the month since and frankly I was becoming a little weary of constantly calling him for so little reward. I had been amazed when Harriet had managed to pin him down to dinner this evening and I had not really been surprised when he did not arrive.

Dinner ended and we left Adam and Edwin to the port. As we walked into the drawing-room, Harriet took me to one side.

'I'm so sorry, darling. I didn't realize Papa had been discussing your comings and goings with Helen and Edwin. I would have waited until we were alone if I had known.'

I smiled as I took her arm. 'It doesn't matter, Harry.'

'Yes, it does. I know how annnoying it is to have one's every move watched and commented on and disapproved of. I promise to be more discreet in future.'

I patted her arm. 'I will too, I think. I would like to have some privacy.'

Harriet just laughed. 'If you ever manage it, let me know your secret.'

6

Lady Faulkner's wedding day was beautiful. It was late April, the sun was shining and the flowers were in bloom as though they felt her wedding was something to be celebrated in style as well. A few airs from the orchestra strayed across the perfectly manicured lawn, wafting delicious freesia scents with them. As I sat by the fountain in her magnificent Richmond garden, I adjusted the brim of my 'Merry Widow' hat. The leather kid boots were just visible beneath my lavender silk dress and since no one was around I decided it was safe to admire my own taste. It was then I heard a voice behind me.

'Good afternoon, Miss Wyndham-Brown.'

I turned round to see Mr Bennett standing in front of me, a slightly disgruntled expression on his face. I smiled and stood up.

'Good afternoon, Mr Bennett. You look well.'

And he did. Much better, in fact, than the last time I had seen him in hospital, when his face still had bruises all over it and he was thin and pale. He was also wearing a cutaway morning coat with a matching waistcoat and he looked quite smart for once.

'Thank you, Miss Wyndham-Brown.' There was a short silence, which I did nothing to break. Mr Bennett cleared his throat. 'Might I join you?'

'I thought you already had, Mr Bennett.'

He stared at me stonily, but I saw no reason to make anything easy for him. The man had been unbearable.

'It has been brought to my attention that I wasn't quite as grateful to you as I could have been the last time we met,' he said rather sullenly. I nodded.

'Which time was that, Mr Bennett?' I asked, walking along the path. 'Was that when I offered to pay for a doctor to attend you and you told me in no uncertain terms that you didn't need my charity and called me a stupid woman?'

'Erm . . .'

'Or do you mean the time I visited you in hospital and you told me I was a spoilt brat — which I have to say is becoming rather repetitive — and instead of interfering in other peoples' affairs I should mind my own business and you'd thank me to go and play Lady Bountiful somewhere else?' I was quite enjoying myself, but apparently Mr Bennett wasn't. He took hold of my arm and pulled me round towards him.

'Are you finished?' he asked, his eyes narrowing. I looked pointedly at the hand on my arm and he pulled it away.

'Actually no,' I said, continuing my leisurely stroll along the path. 'Whilst we're on the subject, perhaps you could explain to me why you felt it was perfectly acceptable to treat me like the worst kind of criminal that afternoon in Kate's house in Luxor? All I was trying to do was say thank you for saving our lives and you spoke to me as though I were a — a —'

'A spoilt brat?' he interrupted. 'Oh that's repetitive, isn't it? But then what else would you expect from a member of the lower classes who doesn't know how to behave in polite society? Did I get that right? Oh I forgot — I'm also a brute and a boor and I should be grateful you didn't insist the embassy arrest me for gross negligence and dereliction of duties and if you had —'

'You were behaving abominably!'

Heads began turning and I realized people were beginning to stare. I began walking quickly down the path to where a weeping willow tailed its delicate feathery branches in cool green water. It was quieter and more secluded here and Mr Bennett, who was clearly no gentleman, followed me.

'How else did you expect me to behave?

You'd spent the last five months making fun of me. I don't know how the aristocracy react to mockery, but where I come from, if a girl treats you like an idiot you don't take too kindly to it.'

'Perhaps if you hadn't behaved like an idiot I wouldn't have treated you like one,' I said.

'Oh I don't think so,' he sneered. 'You were definitely doing what came naturally. And correct me if I'm wrong, Miss Wyndham-Brown, but wasn't it such high-handed behaviour that got you sent out to Egypt in the first place? Only the last man you took for an idiot wasn't quite as stupid as you'd thought?'

I glared at him, feeling the blood rush to my cheeks. 'Mr Bennett, I thought you had come to apologize to me, but clearly the very concept is alien to your nature, so I'll save you the bother. Please don't approach me again. In fact, from now on, I think we'll do very well if we agree never to speak to each other in future. Good day to you.'

I left him standing by the pond and walked off angrily. It was a magnificent exit, even if I do say so myself, although I nearly slipped on a patch of mud by the water's edge and it left a nasty stain on my beautiful boots which I just knew was never going to come out.

I had decided that I needed a very

unladylike stiff drink and was about to speak to one of the servants when Aunt Augusta came out of the library opposite. She was wearing a royal-blue bombazine dress, new for the occasion, because she liked Lady Faulkner, even if she was now no longer Lady Faulkner, but plain Mrs Whitaker.

'Isabella dear, are you enjoying yourself?'

'Absolutely, Aunt Augusta,' I lied.

'I'm so glad, dear,' she said, taking me by the arm and leading me back to the library, which was empty. That was when I knew there was going to be trouble.

'Who were you talking to just now, Isabella?'

I glanced briefly out of the library window. The view was magnificent, looking out over the gardens and on to the pond. I turned back to Aunt Augusta but she was utterly shameless.

'You know perfectly well to whom I was talking, Aunt Augusta,' I said.

'Isabella, I thought Charles had already spoken to you about this matter.'

'And what matter would that be, Aunt Augusta?'

Aunt Augusta frowned and tutted. 'Don't play coy with me, miss. You — '

'Dear Aunt Augusta, perhaps I should remind you, as I reminded Uncle Charles last week, I am no longer a child and if I want to — '

'Exactly. You are no longer a child and it should not be for myself or Charles to point out what is or is not appropriate behaviour. We were appalled — the whole family was appalled to learn that you had gone to Bermondsey of all places to visit a common — '

'Tell me, dear Aunt, who was it that I have to thank for informing you all of my scandalous behaviour?' I know I was being rude, but Uncle Charles and I had already gone over this ground and I was still smarting from his comments. It was like the Henry Fitzroy affair all over again, the only difference being that this time he couldn't bundle me off to foreign parts, although it was obvious he would have dearly liked to.

'That is neither here not there, Isabella,' Aunt Augusta replied crisply. 'What I must insist on is that you now promise me you'll have no more to do with that man. Naturally one is grateful for all he did, but he was well paid for his services and that should be the end of it.'

I found myself staring at Aunt Augusta angrily, understanding for the first time why Mr Bennett found people of my class so repugnant.

'I shall do no such thing, Aunt Augusta. I'm sorry if my friendship with Mr Bennett upsets you, but I find him most agreeable and I'm afraid I cannot make any such promise.'

Before she could say anything else I swept out of the room back into the gardens, the cool air fanning my cheeks which were now flushed with anger.

As I marched down the path again, I almost had to stop myself from muttering under my breath like a lunatic. I took a deep breath to compose myself, then began walking at a more leisurely pace, stopping every now and again to admire the roses and compliment friends on their new gowns, or make small talk about how beautiful the ceremony had been. Eventually I felt calm again and I wandered back to the lawns where I could just see the new Professor and Mrs Whitaker still having photographs taken. I could also see Adam and Kate with them, Kate desperately trying to tame the long train on her wedding finery as the photographer ordered people about. Grateful that I wasn't a close enough relative to have to be part of this charade, I walked over towards to the conservatory. Mr Bennett was standing outside.

'Ah, there you are, Mr Bennett,' I said gaily. He was talking to Emily Parkinson and her older brother. Emily and I had known and loathed each other at school. 'Had you forgotten your promise?'

For a private detective who was presumably able to play any part at a moment's notice, he was exceptionally dense. However, since I had told Aunt Augusta I found him agreeable, I was determined to do just that for once, even if it killed me.

'What?' he said, frowning.

'I do believe you have,' I said, putting a hand on his arm and beaming at Emily and Oliver, who was slightly less objectionable than his sister. 'I'm afraid I'm going to have to take him away from you for a while, Emily. Mr Bennett promised to show me a book on Egyptian artefacts that he'd found in the library. Didn't you, Mr Bennett?'

'What?' he said again. Fortunately Emily was too busy glaring at me in her familiar sour way to notice his confusion.

'Really? I would have thought you would have had enough of Egypt, Isabella,' she said cattily. My smile widened.

'Not at all. Do excuse us, won't you, Emily, Oliver?'

'Of course,' said Oliver, with his usual good humour as I led Mr Bennett away. 'Let's go and get a drink, shall we, Em?' As they walked off in the opposite direction, Mr

Bennett stared at me.

'I thought you never wanted to speak to me again,' he said.

'I've changed my mind. It's a lady's prerogative,' I said, less pleasantly now the Parkinsons were gone. 'I decided to give you one more chance to show me you're not a complete scoundrel.'

'Did you really? How decent of you.' He shook his arm away from my hand. 'And did it occur to you, Miss Wyndham-Brown, that I might not care what you think of me?'

'Well, since you make that clear every time we meet, it could hardly fail not to occur to me, now could it, Mr Bennett?' I said. 'But since we last — Do forgive me,' I added, as I inadvertently bumped into one of the guests. Then I saw who it was.

'Hello, Henry,' I said, glaring at him. 'Are you enjoying the day?'

Mr Bennett looked confused again, an expression with which I was becoming very familiar. In contrast, the person I'd collided with, a young man of about thirty, but looking much older, turned beetroot red.

'Miss Wyndham-Brown,' he said, bowing awkwardly. My eyes narrowed.

'Oh come, Henry, surely we're on first-name terms, especially after all we've been through together,' I said, not bothering to lower my voice, because I could see this was embarrassing him. 'Surely after one has thrown oneself at the son of a Member of Parliament, some familiarity must be acceptable.'

He flushed an even deeper red, which I would not have thought possible if I hadn't seen it. 'For God's sake, Isabella,' he hissed in a voice hardly above a whisper. 'My wife is over there.'

'Is she?' I turned and saw Vanessa Fitzroy in the middle of a group of people staring at us, her gloved hands gripping the handles of her beaded reticule tightly. When she first came out four seasons ago, she had been considered the prettiest debutante of her year. Time, however, had laid its mark on her and today she looked somewhat careworn. I waved at her gaily and was rewarded by a scowl.

'Vanessa looks tired, Henry,' I said, turning back to him. 'You should take better care of her. No doubt coming home at night would help.'

His angry expression turned thunderous. 'Your — '

'Oh by the way, Henry, I haven't introduced you to Mr Bennett, have I? How remiss of me. Henry, this is Peter Bennett. Mr Bennett, Henry Fitzroy.'

Henry barely glanced at Mr Bennett. 'A pleasure,' he said curtly, ignoring Mr Bennett's outstretched hand. 'Isabella, I know you think — '

'Mr Bennett is a private investigator, Henry. Isn't that interesting?'

'I — what?' The thunderous expression, which really didn't sit well on his plump features, disappeared instantly, to be replaced by pallid fear. I wondered for a moment if he might faint. 'A private investigator? What is a private investigator doing at Alice Faulkner's wedding?'

'Tut, tut, Henry, it's Mrs Whitaker now, you know. And I believe Mr Bennett is a guest here, as you are. Although, of course, one should never assume a private investigator is off-duty. What sort of cases do you take, Mr Bennett?' I added looking at him innocently.

Mr Bennett raised an eyebrow at me, but finally he seemed to be entering into the spirit of things because he perched on a stone wall which separated the rose garden from the lawns and, crossing his arms, turned to Henry with a mischievous smile.

'Mos'ly errant 'usbands, Miss Wyndham-Brown,' he said, imitating Mabel's accent superbly. 'It's frivin' livli'ood. In fact, lookin' at all the toffs round 'ere, I'd say I could do quite a bit o' business. An' I rarely 'ave to bother goin' to court. You'd be amazed at 'ow generous some 'usbands are when they bin caught aht.'

'Really?' I beamed at Henry. 'Did you hear that, Henry? Perhaps I should introduce Mr Bennett to Vanessa. What do you think?'

Henry's face went a rather alarming shade of purple at this. 'If you dare to take this . . . this creature any where near my wife, I'll sue — '

'Oh yeah, I do a good bit a' that an' all,' Mr Bennett said, unper-turbed, as he examined Henry's expression. 'Suein', perjury, defamation o' character. An' I know all the beaks round 'ere — they give me quite a bit o' business one way and another.' Suddenly he winked at Henry, who looked ready to explode. 'Wouldn't be in their int'rests ter lock me up. Know what I mean?'

Henry stared at him for a moment longer. 'May I congratulate you on your choice of companion, Miss Wyndham-Brown? It's no more than I would have expected. Good day to you.' And he spun round and left us alone.

I sat down next to Mr Bennett, adjusting the brim of my hat to keep the sun off my face.

'I enjoyed that,' I said.

'I could tell,' he replied drily.

'And you were magnificent, Mr Bennett. I confess I didn't understand everything you said, but Henry obviously did and I was most impressed. Well done.'

'Thank you. Now are you going to tell me why I put the fear of God into him?'

'Revenge, Mr Bennett,' I said, smiling at him. 'He made life most unpleasant for me a while back and I have to tell you Byron was right — revenge is sweet.'

'Especially to women?' he enquired and I couldn't help looking surprised.

'Mr Bennett, you're a romantic. I would never have expected it of you.'

'I daresay there's a lot about me you wouldn't expect.' Then he frowned. 'Did you say Fitzroy? The name sounds familiar.'

'Henry's father is Jeremy Fitzroy, the MP. Edwin tells me he'll be a cabinet minister soon.'

But Mr Bennett shook his head. 'No, that's not it. Henry Fitzroy . . . Henry Fitzroy. I know I've heard that name somewhere before. I think it was back in Egypt.' He frowned, then his face cleared. 'I remember now. Henry Fitzroy — he was the one who — ' Suddenly he stopped, his face flushing slightly.

I nodded. 'People do love to gossip, don't they?' I said. 'And what exactly did they tell you about me?'

'Nothing.'

'Oh come, Mr Bennett. It was such a delicious piece of scandal. Come, indulge me.'

He sighed. 'Why don't you tell me what happened, instead?'

I stood up and began walking back towards the house.

'How tiresome you can be, Mr Bennett. But I can see I must provide the entertainment; so, very well. It was all so ridiculous really. I was at the Ramseys' country house for the weekend and in the afternoon a few of us decided to take a walk in the grounds before dinner. They have a maze there and we had decided it would be fun to go in groups and see who could get to the centre first. I was with Elizabeth Holt and her two brothers and Henry and Vanessa. We'd managed quite well at first, but then took a few wrong turns and it was clear we were going to be among the last to get to the centre. Of course, most of us couldn't have cared less — we'd probably drunk rather more than we should have done at lunch and we were finding the whole thing rather fun, but Elizabeth's wretched older brother Jonathan is an absolute bore when it comes to competitions and he was getting annoyed because Elizabeth and I were just laughing and making fun of him. Anyway, at some point I got a stone in my shoe and although I tried to hobble on for a bit it became too painful to walk so I told the others to go on ahead and I would catch them up.'

He nodded and I knew he'd already heard that part of the story. Henry and I apparently agree up to this point; it's the next part where our tales diverge wildly.

'Anyway, I'd just managed to remove the stone from my shoe and was buckling it back on again when I heard a noise and when I looked up I saw Henry standing there staring at me. I remember saying something stupid like, 'Hello, darling, could you just help me' and before I could finish, the brute had grabbed me and was kissing me. It was horrible.'

I could feel my frown deepening as I relived the scene again. Henry's awful little wispy moustache tickling me, his tongue, thick and slimy, yet surprisingly powerful, forcing my mouth open, the stink of whisky on his breath — I'd said we'd all drunk a little too much at lunch but Henry had clearly been in a class of his own.

'What did you do?' asked Mr Bennett.

'I kicked him,' I said. 'Very sharply on the

shins. I was wearing new shoes and Elizabeth told me later I drew blood, which I was very pleased about. I'm a good kicker.'

He smiled faintly. 'I'll make sure I remember that, Miss Wyndham-Brown.'

'Please do. Not that it did me much good in the long run. He jumped back, yelping and I shouted some nonsense at him and he began abusing me in the most vile manner, telling me I shouldn't flirt with men if I didn't know what I was doing and why had I deliberately hung behind if I hadn't wanted this.'

'Hmm,' said Mr Bennett. 'I suspect this would be where Mr Fitzroy's version differs from yours.'

'I imagine so,' I said. 'So what were you told?'

'That you were waiting for him in the maze and after he'd peeled you off and tried to explain that he was a happily married man — '

I felt myself flushing all over again at the sheer awfulness of the whole thing.

'He did no such thing! In fact, I have a horrible feeling that he would not have taken no for an answer and might have tried to kiss me again' — I shuddered — 'if we hadn't both noticed Vanessa at that moment, with the most awful expression on her face. She must have seen the whole thing and she looked dreadful, as well she might. Anyway she ran off and Henry ran after her and I just stood there like a fool for about five minutes wondering what on earth had happened. And when I finally did manage to catch up with the others, Henry and Vanessa were nowhere to be seen.'

'I'm sorry,' said Mr Bennett, after a few minutes.

'You know, what I really can't understand is why everyone believed him and not me. You would have thought that guileless *naïvete* would have counted for something over undoubted experience. But apparently not.'

He studied me for a moment. 'Do I take it Mr Fitzroy had a reputation even before your brush with him?'

'Indeed he did. Apparently, as I learned later, there are several chambermaids and parlourmaids at his school, for heaven's sake, as well as at Oxford, who can testify to what a busy little bee he was. But that didn't seem to matter at all. He was believed and not me. Life is very unfair, Mr Bennett.'

Mr Bennett gazed across the gardens to where we could just see Henry, with a large whisky in his hand. 'Would you like me to go over and punch him?' he asked.

I looked at him in surprise. 'Why, Mr

Bennett, I do believe you would.'

Mr Bennett smiled at me. 'I meet a lot of Henrys in my working life, Miss Wyndham-Brown and my sympathies tend to lie with the women who have to put up with them.' He looked back at Vanessa, who couldn't help sneaking hunted glances at me. 'Mrs Fitzroy does look rather tired, doesn't she?'

I nodded. 'She's lost three babies so far. In fact she was just getting over the first one on that wretched weekend. We'd all noticed how thin she was. The rumours about their marriage were starting even then.'

'I really will go and give him a sock on the nose if you like,' said Mr Bennett seriously, and I laughed.

'As much as I would enjoy that, I have to decline. Henry's father is very powerful you know. Not even your toffers would be able save you from his wrath.'

He looked shocked for a moment then grinned. 'Toffs.'

I frowned. 'Toffs, Mr Bennett?'

'Toffs, Miss Wyndham-Brown. It means rich men. Or 'beaks', which means magistrates. Toffers means something quite different.'

'Does it? Do tell me what.'

'No. So why did you change your mind and come back to speak to me again.'

The sun had burst out suddenly from behind a cloud and I took the opportunity to put up my parasol. I had seen it in a little shop in Kensington and had been dying to use it all day, especially after Harriet, who had been shopping with me, had laughed at me and told me it was a waste of money.

'I told you, it's a lady's prerogative, Mr Bennett,' I said, opening out the gorgeous cerise folds and admiring the lace trim along the seams. But Mr Bennett turned me back to face him.

'I really am grateful for what you did the other day. And I'm sorry for treating you so rudely. It was unpardonable.'

I looked up, surprised at the gravity of his tone and found myself staring at his eyes which were a rather attractive green. I also noticed that his hair needed cutting again to be fashionable, but that there was something rather raffish about the style which I liked.

'Not at all, Mr Bennett. Or may I call you Peter? It's how Kate always refers to you and I can't help thinking of you that way.'

He turned away. 'I don't think so, Miss Wyndham-Brown,' he said. 'Not unless you want to alienate your entire family.'

I looked over to where his gaze was directed and saw Aunt Augusta among the bouquets of lilies and gardenias. She had out her pince-nez now and was glaring at us.

'Has Aunt Augusta said something to you?'

'She and I spoke just before lunch,' he admitted.

'Really?' I could feel myself getting heated again. 'And of what did you speak, Mr Bennett? The weather? The flowers? The bride's dress?'

He gave a faint smile. 'I don't remember discussing any of those subjects.'

I took a deep breath and making sure Aunt Augusta could see me properly, I slipped my arm through Mr Bennett's.

'Perhaps I should make it clear to you, Mr Bennett, because my family don't seem to understand this yet: I'm twenty-one years of age. My behaviour, scandalous or otherwise, is no longer the concern of my aunts and uncles.'

He looked down briefly at my arm through his, but made no move to take it away. 'Is that so, Miss Wyndham-Brown? Because Lady Faversham seemed to think differently.'

'Oh yes? And what did she say?' I asked. A mischievous grin appeared on his face.

'Do you really want to know?'

'I really do.'

The grin grew wider. 'It's going to annoy you.'

I raised an eyebrow. 'Even so.'

'She said that, taking into account the tenderness of your years, certain conditions in your parents' will meant that she and your uncle were still able to bear the greater burden of responsibility for your fortune until such time as you were capable of doing it for yourself.'

I glared at him.

'The *what* of my years?' I asked angrily, and he chuckled.

'I told you it would annoy you,' he said, as I tapped my parasol impatiently against the stone lions guarding the pond.

'I can't believe her! The old — ' I bit back my words. 'And to think I always considered Aunt Augusta my favourite aunt.'

'Really?' Mr Bennett looked back to Aunt Augusta, who was still glaring at us. He sounded incredulous and at any other time I might have felt constrained to defend her; but not today. Today I was fighting the urge not to agree with him.

'Basically I can't run my own estate yet,' I explained. 'And I can't marry without their permission until I'm twenty-five. If I do, I lose my fortune.'

He thought about this. 'It sounds reasonable,' he said eventually, to my great chagrin. I scowled at him.

'Oh really? And how would you like it if

153

someone told you you couldn't marry whomever you chose until you were twenty-five?' I asked indignantly, but he just grinned.

'I'm thirty-one, Miss Wyndham-Brown, so it wouldn't bother me at all. And besides, I don't have a fortune to lose. Under the circumstances, I . . . ' he continued, then looked at me and paused.

'Yes?' I asked sweetly. 'Do continue. Under the circumstances?'

'Under the circumstances, I think I'll change the subject, Miss Wyndham-Brown. Tell me, what is your opinion of the new American emporium in Knightsbridge?'

I tried to keep frowning, but he looked so serious that I found in the end I was biting my lip to stop laughing.

'Very good, Peter. You see, you can be tactful when you try.'

'Tact is my middle name, Miss Wyndham-Brown.'

'Really? You amaze me. Every time — '

'Bella, there you are! And Peter too. Thank heavens.'

We both turned round together to see Kate coming towards us, the long cream-coloured train on her dress trailing across the grass.

'Kate, you're going to ruin your beautiful dress,' I said running up to her.

'I don't care. The wretched thing is a

154

monster. I swear it's got a life of its own. I nearly tripped following Alice down the aisle. Did you see?'

'Of course you didn't,' I soothed. 'I thought you were marvellous. Like a swan.' She gave a sigh of relief.

'Thank goodness. Adam said no one was watching me, but I definitely saw those horrible little Hawes-Davidson girls giggling as I walked past. Peter, how are you?' she added, as he helped me lift the train over a patch of mud.

'Very well, thank you. Where's Adam?'

'He'll be coming in a minute. His mother and father have trapped him and his brothers and their families in the library, so I took the opportunity of escaping. 'They don't like me,' she added dramatically, as we walked back to the house, all three of us holding the yards of gossamer-like material free of the ground.

'Kate, don't exaggerate. They're delightful,' I said.

'In company they might be,' she retorted. 'But if you had to put up with them in private, you'd sing a different tune. Especially Mrs Ellis. Everytime she sees me, she can't believe I'm not *enceinte*.'

'Kate! That's not true!'

'It is, I promise you. Look, here's the conservatory. We can hide in here.' She lifted up the billowing skirts and Mr Bennett held open the door of the conservatory for her, while I helped her negotiate the steps. It was very warm under the glass and quite humid. The perfume from the late Sir Henry Faulkner's prize orchids was almost overpowering.

'There. We'll be safe here for a while,' said Kate. 'Anyway, as I was saying; last night after dinner, Mrs Ellis asked me very coyly when the family could expect to hear the patter of tiny feet.'

'Oh dear,' I said, stooping down to smell a large orange flower. 'What did you say?'

Kate grimaced. 'I said nothing, my dear, like a good, respectful daughter-in-law. Of course, Adam and his younger brother Thomas had great fun talking about Alice's new spaniel puppies and how much noise they made when they ran about the house. But I just have to sit and make polite conversation. Oh look, there's Adam,' she added, as Adam appeared from behind a large ficus. He was dressed in wedding finery too, his grey silk cravat showing signs of wear. Adam disliked ties of any kind. He smiled when he saw us.

'I thought I'd find you in here. It's the only place Kate feels really at home.' He turned to Mr Bennett. 'So? Have you told her?'

'Er . . . no. We didn't quite get round to it,' said Mr Bennett, looking awkward.

'Get round to what?' I asked.

'Oh it's very exciting, Bella,' Kate said, digging into her reticule and bringing out her spectacles. 'Peter found — but wait, you tell her, Peter. After all it's your surprise.'

'Surprise?' I echoed. Mr Bennett shrugged. 'It's what I came over to tell you this afternoon before we got distracted. I'd been thinking about the key you gave me in the envelope for quite a while and a few days ago I finally worked out where it had come from. I knew it was a key to a bank security box, so the letters F and H had to mean Fortescue and Hopkins. It's a small concern, but I know quite lot of people use it when they don't want to call attention to themselves or their affairs. Anyway, the fact that I no longer had possession of the key and couldn't even remember the exact number of the box, made things more complicated, but one of the clerks is a cousin of someone who owes me a favour, and he told me that one of the older security boxes had been opened recently after a considerable length of time. He couldn't remember much about the client except he was an old man with a foreign accent, although he didn't know from where. It's not much I know, but I can't help thinking it somewhat suspicious that this had happened only a day after I was attacked.'

I looked at him horrified. 'Good heavens, Mr Bennett, surely you're not saying you were attacked because of me?'

He smiled briefly. 'I certainly don't hold you responsible, Miss Wyndham-Brown. In my line of work, one expects the occasional thump. But yes, I have to say I'm beginning to think the burglars weren't just angry husbands out to destroy evidence.'

'Good Lord.' I sat down heavily on a grubby wooden bench. Kate perched next to me.

'Isn't it exciting?' she said. 'Just think, Peter was set upon by a gang of desperadoes and all because of the things you gave him.'

'They were hardly desperadoes, Kate,' said Mr Bennett, smiling. 'If I'm going to be honest it was a bit embarrassing really. There were only two of them and one of them was quite old really. If they hadn't taken me so much by surprise I would probably have been able to frighten them off.'

Kate looked at me and rolled her eyes. 'Of course you would, Peter,' she said soothingly.

'I would have done,' he insisted, before turning back to me. 'Anyway, the other thing is, I finally remembered one of the pawnshop addresses, so tomorrow I'm going to go down there and see what I can get out of them.'

'That's very kind of you, Mr Bennett. But what exactly are you going to say? After all, without the tickets, one can hardly expect people to remember trinkets bought and sold over twenty years ago.'

Mr Bennett smiled. 'These are pawnbrokers, Miss Wyndham-Brown: they have long memories, especially for expensive items.' He shrugged. 'It may be a wild-goose chase. But there's no harm in trying.'

I smiled. 'Thank you, Peter.'

I noticed Kate and Adam glance at each other as I said his name, but I ignored them. As we walked through the conservatory towards the ballroom, an orchestra was just beginning to strike up and Mr Bennett held out his hand to me. Thus it was that by the end of the day I found that I had not lied to my aunt after all: I found him very agreeable company indeed.

7

Three mornings later Kate, Adam and I were all sitting in Mr Bennett's office. It was still somewhat dilapidated, but Laurent's threats had had an effect on Mr Jenkins. The door and furniture had been replaced, and there was a battered old armchair in the corner. Mr Bennett looked a bit battered too. He had another black eye. Not as bad as the one last time, but it still looked painful.

'What happened?' said Adam, pulling the armchair up to the desk.

'Nothing. Just a scrape. Now, I've been to several pawnbrokers in the last couple of days and — '

'For heaven's sake,' Kate frowned, 'Where did you get that black eye?'

'It's nothing,' he said, but under Kate's gaze he sighed. 'Very well, if you must know, I visited a few old friends the other day and after one or two set-backs managed to find out who was responsible for my visit to Guy's.'

'Was that wise?' asked Adam.

Peter shrugged. 'I can't afford to have it known that I'm such an easy target. In my line of business, that's tantamount to retirement.'

'So what did you do?' asked Kate.

'I took a couple of my own friends along and we had a little chat.'

'Oh Peter! You didn't do anything — '

'No, of course not. I do believe in the law, even if I might . . . slide around the edges sometimes,' he said testily. 'I got this black eye because they thought they might be able to leave without answering all my questions satisfactorily and we had to convince them otherwise. Anyway we didn't get much out of them. Whoever hired them was probably an intermediary for the real client and just gave them instructions to rough me up and grab all your stuff, Miss Wyndham-Brown. They got their money after they delivered the tickets and the key, meeting in an alleyway, dark night etc. They said they could barely make out who it was who was paying them and I believed them. It was a good rate of pay for a few minutes' work and no questions asked.'

'So it *was* my business they were interested in.' I felt a little dazed by this.

'Perhaps we should go to the police,' said Adam, but Mr Bennett shook his head.

'There's no point.'

'Why not, Peter?' asked Kate. 'After all,

you've been badly beaten; Bella's belongings have been stolen, and it appears that a — '

Mr Bennett smiled at her. 'As much as I appreciate your concern, Kate, believe me the police won't see it in the same light. As far as they're concerned, getting beaten is just one of the drawbacks of my profession and it's probably my own fault. So long as no one gets murdered, I'm on my own. And although they might be slightly more interested in the fact that it's Miss Wyndham-Brown who's had personal property stolen, even if I gave them the names of my two assailants there's nothing they could do about it. Those two idiots really didn't know who'd hired them so the police won't get any more out of them. And as for my suspicions about the bank security box in Fortescue and Hopkins — and that's really all they are, suspicions. The bank won't tell them any more than they've told me. That key was over twenty years old and anyone could have got hold of it. And since the person who opened it had a foreign accent, it's most likely he's fled the country now. Anyway, let me tell you about the pawnshop. It's run by a family who've owned it for fifty years and the old man who started it still goes in some days. His son's helped me out on a few occasions before and when I explained the situation to him he showed me something that I think you might be interested to see, Miss Wyndham-Brown.'

'What would that be?'

'A gentleman's pocket watch with an inscription on it. I wrote it down,' he said, searching in his waistcoat pocket and pulling out a slip of paper. 'It says 'To my husband, on our wedding day, 16th July 1887. Amelia'.' He looked at me and I nodded.

'That sounds right. I don't know the exact day they got married but I know it was in the summer of 1887, because Aunt Hermione told me an elderly aunt fainted during the ceremony because it was such a hot day. It certainly sounds like it could be Papa's watch. Why has the shopkeeper still got it?'

'He liked it. It's a good-looking piece and according to him keeps time extraordinarily well. The business is thriving and they can indulge their fancies occasionally. But he says he'll sell it back to you if you want it.'

'I do,' I said firmly. Mr Bennett smiled briefly.

'Miss Wyndham-Brown, I beg you not to sound so sure in the shop. Frank Redmond is a decent enough chap for a pawnbroker, but he dearly loves a profit. Go in with an attitude like that and he'll have the coat from your back before you even know what's happened. So are you ready for a visit to Cheapside?'

We found a cab easily and set off. Having spent some time in Laurent's motor car, I noticed the difference between the jolting of the carriage and the slightly smoother motion of the car and I mentioned this to Kate. She nodded.

'I know. Adam is keen to buy one, although I must say they're terribly smelly. But tell me, when am I going to meet this new cousin of yours?'

'I've no idea. I haven't seen him myself for some time. According to Aunt Hortensia, he had to go back to France because one of his nephews became quite seriously ill. She wrote to them two weeks ago and hasn't received a reply yet. It's all rather difficult, because really one doesn't know them that well and yet we don't want them to feel we don't care after all this time, especially when Laurent made the effort to come over here. I suppose we'll just have to wait and see what happens.'

By this time the carriage was slowing down. Mr Bennett opened the door and one by one we all climbed out. Directly in front of us was a shop with the traditional three golden balls hanging from a bracket above the window. Mr Bennett opened the door and we all walked in.

The shop itself seemed clean and well kept, although there was clutter everywhere, clothes hanging up above us and the most diverse items for sale from china tea-sets to violins and copper bath-tubs.

'Mr Bennett — back again, I see,' said a voice, startling me. 'An' with company this time. My watch *must* be an interesting piece. Perhaps I should charge admission.'

We all turned to see a middle-aged man addressing us from a counter against one corner of the large room. He had a thick greying beard and was dressed in a neat blue serge suit.

Mr Bennett grinned as he walked up to the counter. 'Frank, I've told these ladies that you're a decent sort despite the popshop. Don't go making me out to be a liar.'

The man picked up a cup and took a sip of whatever was within. 'I am a decent sort, Mr Bennett. That's why I'm not a rich man. So, do you want to see this watch then?' At Mr Bennett's nod, he pulled out a small box from beneath the counter. We all crowded round to look.

Nestling in the bottom of the box was a silver fob-watch with swirling intricate patterns around the edges. Mr Bennett pushed a clasp and the back fell away to reveal an inner shell on which was engraved the inscription he had told us about.

I knew it was my father's. I don't know

how, because I had never seen it before and there were no photographs of him wearing it. But somehow I just knew it was his. It seemed to be the sort of thing he would wear, expensive and elaborate and possibly just the tiniest bit too much and yet somehow endearing. I got the impression my mother had understood her future husband very well.

'Well, Miss Wyndham-Brown, what do you think?' asked Mr Bennett, as I passed it to Kate to examine.

'I'm sure it was my father's,' I said. 'And I would very much like to buy it back from you, Mr Richmond. If the price is right,' I added, remembering what Mr Bennett had said.

The pawnbroker gave me a wolfish smile. 'You don't want to go listening to 'im, a nice young lady like you,' he said, giving a contemptuous flick of his head towards Mr Bennett. 'I'll do you an honest price, miss. What are you prepared to offer?'

I could see Adam and Kate and even Mr Bennett preparing to intervene, but I held up a hand. 'Mr Richmond, I won't pretend I know how to haggle, because I don't. But I do remember the amounts on some of the tickets and the largest, if I recall, suggested someone had loaned my father seventy pounds. Does that sound reasonable?'

Mr Richmond gave me a shrewd look. 'Twenty years ago that would have been about right, miss. But it ain't twenty years ago now, is it? And there's me profit margin to be made on top. Now I've 'ad that watch for all that time and I've grown fond of it meself, so I couldn't let it go for anything less than a hundred and thirty.'

'Frank — ' Mr Bennett began, but Mr Richmond just shook his head.

'It ain't no good you coming in 'ere and thinkin' you can throw yer weight around, Mr Bennett. A man's gotta make a livin'. That's a nice watch and I've 'eld on to it for a good few years. Seein' as 'ow it was the young lady's dad's, I'm prepared to sell it back to 'er. But after you left the other day I 'ad it valued and a hundred and thirty's a reasonable price fer it.'

Mr Bennett scowled at him. 'Wait here,' he said, taking my arm and drawing me and the others away from the counter towards the front of the shop.

'What do you think?' He looked at me, then at Kate and Adam. Adam shook his head.

'He's right, Peter. That's a very nice watch. He's overpricing it a little, but not by much.'

'And, of course, he knows there's senti-mental value attached to it as well,' added

167

Kate. 'I suspect we won't be able to go much below his price.'

'Then let's not bother,' I said. 'Except — ' I looked at Kate and Adam. 'I hate to have to ask you this, but I need to borrow the money from you. I only get fifty pounds a month and I absolutely cannot go to Uncle Charles on this to get the trustees to advance me any more.'

'Of course, darling,' said Kate. 'Don't worry about that.'

As we walked back to him, Mr Bennett nodding his head rather grimly, Mr Richmond grinned at us.

'I knew you'd see sense, Mr Bennett. An' anuvver fing — the old man came in today. 'E was int'rested when I told 'im the story — says 'e remembers yer dad. Sarah!' he yelled, and a girl of about fifteen came out from the back of the shop. 'Go and get Grandad. Tell 'im the daughter of that bloke with the watch's 'ere.'

Without a word the girl nodded and disappeared.

'Walter came in?' asked Mr Bennett. 'I thought you said he'd vowed never to come back after he handed over the business to you, Frank.'

''E said 'e'd never do any more work. That don't mean the old fool don't turn up

168

occasionally pokin' 'is nose in and tellin' me 'ow to run things.'

Before Mr Bennett could reply, Sarah returned and held the door open. A very old man walked out. He was bald and his face was a mass of wrinkles, but he held himself upright and there was a bright spark to his eyes.

'Is this 'er?' he asked, poking a finger at me. Mr Richmond nodded.

The old man came up close and stared at me for a few seconds, his rheumy old eyes squinting as a ray of sunshine flooded the shop. Then he shrugged.

'Nah, 's too long ago. I can't really remember what 'e looked like. All I remember was 'e was posh. An' there was a woman in the carriage waitin' for 'im.' He sniggered. 'Always is with 'is type — '

'Now hold on a minute, Walter,' Mr Bennett said, his face flushing.

The old man didn't even bother turning round. He waved a hand behind him as he wandered back to the door. 'Desperate to get 'er on that ship, 'e was. I remember thinking when I first saw that watch I was gonna offer 'im eighty, but then I could see he was so desperate, I knew I'd make a tidy sum. 'E even fanked me. One thing about the nobs, they 'ave lovely manners.' He sniggered again.

169

'I remember 'earing 'im say to 'er as 'e lef' the shop, 'Don't worry, darlin', I've got enough now. We'll get you that ticket and then Amelia won't be able to do a thing about it'.'

I put a hand to my mouth, trying to stifle the gasp. 'Are you sure?' I asked, following him to the back of the shop. 'Are you sure he said 'Amelia'?'

He turned round and nodded. 'There was this girl I used to — ' He stopped and gave a short laugh. 'Anyway, I remember the name.' He looked at me shrewdly as I felt my cheeks grow hot with shame. 'That yer ma's name was it?' he asked surprisingly gently. I nodded.

He sighed. 'Well, can't be 'elped, darlin'. 'Appens all the time. Way o' the world.' He opened the door and disappeared, the girl following him and closing the door behind her.

I stood for a few moments, stupidly unable to think what to do next. I have vague recollections of Kate helping me out of the shop and the next thing I remember is the two of us back in the cab, the jolting making me feel slightly queasy.

'Where's Adam?' I asked after a while. 'And Mr Bennett?'

'They stayed behind to talk some more to

170

Mr Richmond,' said Kate gently. 'Oh my dear. I am so sorry.'

I was grateful she didn't try to pretend there might be a perfectly acceptable and honourable reason for Papa's business there. I just sat in the jolting, bumping cab, while she held me like a child, tears falling down my face.

★　★　★

I returned to Woodruffe Manor the next day. I had been staying with Adam and Kate at Mrs Whitaker's house, but although they tried to persuade me to remain, I took the first train back. It had been hard enough pretending I felt fine last night at dinner; I knew I couldn't stand another day doing it and I needed to go home and be alone with my thoughts.

I spent the next few days wandering the gardens or sitting in the study, refusing to see or speak to anyone until even Marnie became concerned.

'What's the matter, darlin'?' she asked me one morning, but I just shook my head and muttered something about feeling under the weather and after several tries she threw her hands up in the air and left me. I did not want to talk about this to anyone. I needed to be alone.

The truth was horribly clear now. Everything I had ever heard about Papa had turned out to be correct. He was charming, handsome, feckless and unreliable and had allowed my mother to rescue him from financial ruin only to betray her at what should have been the happiest time of her life. He had pawned her wedding gift to him, along with other sundry items, including a priceless family heirloom, in order to have his mistress accompany him on their travels. My heart ached for her as it had never done before. Until now, Papa with his charming smile and excitingly reckless ways had always captured my imagination and Mama had been the dull killjoy who had spurned pretty dresses and insisted instead on bills being paid on time and money being spent carefully. It was depressing to think that I took more after him than her.

On the sixth morning of my self-imposed isolation, I was just about to take my morning walk around the grounds when the telephone rang. Nicholls appeared.

'Mrs Ellis would like to speak to you, Miss Bella.'

'Tell her I'm unavailable, Nicholls,' I said, feeling guilty, but also a little irritated. Kate had rung every day since I'd been here and I was beginning to wish she would give up.

'Very well, Miss Bella.' He went out again and I could hear him speaking briefly before putting the telephone down.

I walked out into the grounds, pulling my coat tightly around me. It had rained almost non-stop for the past few days, not hard but with that irritating fine drizzle which seems to seep in everywhere and the gardens had turned to sloshing mud. Even the flowers had had enough, their heads bowed down with the weight of the water. The sky was a uniform grey and since it seemed to mirror exactly how I felt, I decided to trudge on down to the lake at the bottom of the field. Mama had apparently at one time had ideas for a pavilion here, but she had died before it could take proper shape and all that was left of her designs was a short jetty sticking out towards the middle of the lake.

I sat down on the edge, letting my muddy boots dip in the water, wondering for the hundredth time why Mama had married Papa when he was clearly a cad, when I heard the sound of footsteps crunching on the footpath leading up to the jetty. Assuming it was one of the servants, I didn't bother to turn my head.

'Whatever it is, it can wait until lunchtime,' I said disagreeably. 'I'm busy now.'

'You don't look it.'

I jumped up in surprise. Mr Bennett was standing on the jetty, wearing his usual, rather scruffy clothes. Even in my misery, I couldn't help wondering why he had been allowed into the grounds.

'What on earth are you doing here?'

'Well, I tried to speak to you this morning but apparently you weren't available.' He raised an eyebrow. 'You haven't been available all week, Miss Wyndham-Brown.'

'That's right.' I frowned. 'I've been busy.'

'Really? Doing what?'

'That's none of your business, Mr Bennett.'

He shrugged. 'As you wish. Here.' He reached into his pocket and drew out Papa's watch. 'Adam and I went back the next day and retrieved it.'

'Thank you.' I took the watch from his hands and flicked the catch. The inscription, in its elegant engraving, seemed a mockery of the union between my parents and Papa was to blame. I lifted up my hand, intending to fling it in the lake, but Mr Bennett caught my arm.

'Don't,' he said.

I glared at him. 'Why not? It means nothing to me.'

'Well, it might do, some day. Besides,' he said, pulling my arm down, 'It's expensive. If you don't want it, sell it back to Frank and put the money in the church poorbox. Then at least someone will get some good out of it.'

I looked at it for a moment. 'Here,' I said, throwing it at him. 'You take it then if it concerns you that much.'

He caught it deftly. 'Thanks.' I ignored him and began walking up the path towards the house. A couple of ducks had appeared and waddled towards us, quacking hopefully. My walks around the lake had become a ritual over the past few days and they were used to me throwing scraps their way. I fumbled in my coat pocket and pulled out a slice of bread, scattering the pieces on the muddy ground before walking on. After a few moments Mr Bennett caught up with me.

'So, how much longer do you think this attack of the vapours will last then, Miss Wyndham-Brown?' he asked, as we walked towards the house. I looked up at him in surprise.

'I'm sorry?' I said, unsure I'd heard him right. He stopped walking and looked at me, the expression on his face not entirely friendly.

'When are you going to stop wallowing in self-pity? I only ask because I came down here especially to see if you would like me to continue with the investigation I started, and to be frank I can't waste my time coddling you if all you're going to do is hide away in a corner, feeling sorry for yourself.'

I stopped walking and turned to face him and then suddenly, barely aware of what I was doing, I slapped him. The crack resonated around the lake and made the ducks look up momentarily from their feeding. Then they resumed.

He frowned and put a hand up to his cheek, rubbing the reddened flesh tenderly.

'Feel better?' he asked.

I began walking again. 'Much better,' I replied angrily. 'And in reply to your extremely rude question I have no idea how long I intend to remain here and it's none of your business anyway. I certainly don't require your services any longer and I'm amazed you have the impertinence to think I might.' I turned back and looked at him. 'Don't you think you've done enough, Mr Bennett?'

To my surprise he hooted with laughter. 'Do you mean you actually blame me for what happened? That's rich. Your father has a mistress and I'm the one who — '

'Don't be absurd,' I snapped. 'Of course I don't blame you for what — what happened. But I certainly don't want to know — '

' — what happened after that? No, of

course not, a nice young lady like you. You certainly shouldn't have to be bothered with any of the unpleasant aspects of life.'

'I didn't mean that at all!'

'Then what *did* you mean?'

We had both stopped walking now and we looked at each other, our faces flushed with anger.

'I meant that I don't want to know any more about my parents' failed marriage. I don't want to know what my father did to my mother. I don't — ' I turned away, suddenly unable to stop the tears falling.

He stood beside me for a moment, obviously unsure what to do. Finally he sighed and put his hands on my arms, holding me gently at arm's length.

'Listen, Bella, you really have to grow up. So your father wasn't a paragon of virtue. Well, neither was mine. He drank all his inheritance and then abandoned my mother to bring up four children by taking in lodgers and living in genteel poverty.'

'Well at least he didn't have mistresses,' I sobbed, fumbling in my pocket for a handkerchief and failing to find one.

'Oh he did. Two from what I found out later. And he left them in the lurch as well, as soon as he'd worked his way through their money. I have two other brothers that I know of and probably more elsewhere. At least my mother was lucky enough to have been legitimately married to him. The other poor women he conned didn't. Here.' He handed me a handkerchief.

'Thank you.' I sniffled and wiped for a few moments, trying to regain composure. 'I'm sorry. He sounds awful. Just like — '

Mr Bennett shrugged. 'It's an unfair world, and men generally have the upper hand.'

I had to laugh. 'Harriet would fall in love with you for saying that. Is that why you usually work for women with unfaithful husbands?'

'What?' He looked surprised for a moment. 'Oh, you're thinking of what I said to that idiot at Mrs Whitaker's wedding. No, I'll take any case so long as it pays, Miss Wyndham-Brown. It just so happens that those are the most lucrative cases.' He paused. 'And women are much better at paying me promptly as well. I suspect they generally have a better understanding of what it means to be on time with payments. Or maybe you're just nicer than men.'

I took a deep breath. 'Mr Bennett, I think you're trying to make me feel better.'

'Is it working?'

'Yes. But then I'm clearly very gullible.'

He smiled. 'No, you're not. Well, maybe a

little. But it won't last. Time will soon change that.'

At the same moment we both realized we were still standing very close to one another and with embarrassed looks we moved back a little and began walking slowly towards the house again.

'Forgive me, Mr Bennett, not that I'm not pleased to see you — '

'Really?' With an ironic glance at me he rubbed his hand across his cheek again.

'What exactly are you doing here? It seems a long way to come just to ask me if I still require your services.'

'How true. But as I pointed out you weren't answering any telephone calls and even Kate couldn't get through to you.'

'Mr Bennett, I find it hard to believe you came all this way out here out just out of courtesy.'

He smiled. 'I still owe you money, Miss Wyndham-Brown. And I thought I'd explained I admire people who pay their debts.'

'You owe me? I'm not sure I — '

'You paid my hospital bills and my rent — on the office as well as my room.'

'You don't owe me anything, Mr Bennett. As far as I'm concerned, the matter is over and all debts paid.'

'Really?' He seemed surprised, disappointed even. 'You don't want to know anything about that diamond — what was it called? The Dragonshead?'

I had told him about the Dragonsheart on the day of the wedding.

'Dragonsheart. No, I don't think so, Mr Bennett. I've had quite enough of my father's secrets.' I took a deep breath. We were close to the house now. 'But since you're here, won't you please stay to lunch?'

He looked rather doubtfully at the house. From the back it probably isn't as imposing as the front, but I found myself, in a rare moment of empathy, staring at it through eyes not my own and it is a huge house.

'I don't think so, Miss Wyndham-Brown. I should be getting back to the station. There's a train at three.'

'Splendid. Then you have plenty of time.'

'I'm not really dressed for polite society, Miss Wyndham-Brown.' He looked down at his clothes as he said this, but I was determined not to take no for an answer.

'Then we match, Mr Bennett, as I'm not dressed to receive company. Come along.' I took his arm and started to walk up the path towards the kitchen, then noticed his reluctance. I smiled. 'Mr Bennett, you're not frightened, are you?'

'No, of course not,' he said frowning, but still he didn't move. I raised an eyebrow.

'How did you get in, Mr Bennett?' I asked, curious now. 'I gave strict instructions I was not to be disturbed.'

He grinned. 'I went round to the tradesmen's entrance. I know my place, Miss Wyndham-Brown. And that old woman you brought with you to my office was sitting in the kitchen. Nice old bird. She gave me a cup of tea and told me where you'd gone. Easy really.'

Now it was my turn to mutter under my breath. Sometimes Marnie goes too far. 'Come on, Mr Bennett. Let's outrage the servants. I'm sure you'll enjoy it.'

He looked at me for a few long moments. 'If you say so, Miss Wyndham-Brown.'

'I do. Ah there you are, Nicholls,' I added, as I opened the door and found my entire staff sitting around the long wooden table drinking tea. 'This is Mr Bennett. He'll be joining me for lunch. Come, Mr Bennett.'

I beckoned him to follow me and turned towards the door to the hall, but not before I caught Marnie winking at him broadly. I decided to ignore her and we swept through to the drawing-room to await the luncheon gong. In fact, it wasn't until much later when we were actually sitting down that it occurred to me that she might not have been winking at him at all. One might even imagine she was winking at me.

There were times when Marnie really did go too far.

8

'Please come in, Miss Wyndham-Brown,' the clerk said, showing me into Uncle Charles's office. 'Mr Woodruffe won't keep you a moment. Would you like some coffee?'

'Thank you.'

As he closed the door behind him, I unpinned my hat and laid it on the huge rosewood desk. I had been to Uncle Charles's office a few times before, but had never really paid it much attention. Uncle Charles was always vague about what he did; 'Investments, dear girl, nothing to bother your head about'. I had the feeling he'd never said that to my mother.

The room was decorated in dark mahogany panels and with a carpet of deep brown. Above the fireplace was a portrait of King Edward, with black ribbons adorning the sides. His sudden death last week had shocked my family along with the entire country and there was a feeling that no one knew quite what to do. Next to him hung a slightly smaller painting of Joseph Woodruffe, my grandfather. He was dressed in the usual uniform of dark frock coat and black tie with a starched white collar and his face looked grim, much as I remembered him as a little girl. He had died when I was ten and I cannot say I was terribly upset by his demise. I always had the impression he didn't think me much of an exchange for my mother. As I stood contemplating his stern features, the door opened.

'Bella, my dear, how are you? What a surprise, seeing you here.'

Uncle Charles walked in followed by three minions holding documents for him to sign. All four of them wore black armbands. Uncle Charles sat down at his desk and wrote his name with a flourish then looked up at me.

'Would you like me to take you to lunch? It seems somewhat disrespectful, but I suppose one has to — '

'No thank you, Uncle Charles.'

'So, what can I do for you, my dear?'

I sat down opposite him in a large leather chair, waiting until the minions had scurried out.

'I notice you didn't say 'What a *pleasant* surprise', when you saw me.'

Uncle Charles put down his pen. 'Well, your aunts have not had very pleasant visits from you these past few days and I see no reason to assume I should fare any better.'

I drew off my gloves and smiled back at

him. Since Mr Bennett's visit I had done a lot of thinking and had come to several conclusions, not the least of which was my mother would not have thought much of a daughter who just sat around feeling sorry for herself. I had therefore returned to London and haunted the offices of Mr Saunders, the solicitor. At the end of two weeks I think he truly hated the sight of me, but I found I no longer cared what others thought. I had badgered and harassed him until he finally gave in and allowed me access to all of Mama and Papa's dealings with his firm. Mama, it transpired, had no illusions about her future spouse and had managed to negotiate a wedding contract that meant she retained control over the investments that she had brought to the marriage, in effect giving her financial control over the marriage and affording Papa little more than an allowance, much as I now had. This was probably just as well, because, as I had learned to my horror, Papa was on the verge of being declared a bankrupt when he had proposed to Mama. I had had to work hard to get Aunt Augusta and Aunt Phyllis to admit this when I ambushed them one afternoon over tea and they both seemed shocked that I should insist, but finally they had reluctantly admitted that Amelia Woodruffe's agreement to a union with the *ancient* and *honourable* name of Wyndham-Brown was as beneficial to us as it must have been to her to ally herself to our noble heritage etc etc. As I looked at Uncle Charles in front of me now, I found myself more in sympathy with him.

'I see you've been chatting to Aunt Augusta,' I said, as a clerk brought in a tray of coffee. 'And I always thought you two didn't get on.'

'Your aunt and I naturally have your best interests at heart, my dear, and we talk often to those ends. She tells me you have had many questions regarding your mother and father.' He leaned forward and poured out a cup of coffee for me, offering the milk jug and sugar bowl. 'I hear Mr Saunders has also had the pleasure of your company this week. Many times this week.'

I *tsked* as I picked up the cup and saucer. 'Whatever happened to attorney-client confidentiality?'

'As you are still regarded as a minor in the matter of your inheritance, I remain Mr Saunder's client and therefore privy to any matters arising from it.'

'My business with Mr Saunders had nothing to do with my inheritance and, as an adult, I am outraged by this behaviour.'

The battle-lines thus drawn, Uncle Charles

put down his cup. 'What can I do for you, Isabella?' he asked in a neutral tone.

'Why did you never tell me what a rogue and a scoundrel my father was?'

'A rogue and a scoundrel?' Uncle Charles picked up his pen again. 'Wherever did you hear that, my dear?'

'I didn't hear it anywhere, Uncle Charles. I concluded it when I found out he had a mistress he took abroad with him.'

The nib of the pen snapped as Uncle Charles pressed down too hard on it. 'And where did you hear *that*?' His voice was no longer neutral.

'From a pawnbroker in Cheapside. Where I also found the watch my mother gave to him on their wedding day which he pawned in order to buy a ship's ticket for this woman.'

'A pawnbroker? What on earth were you doing at a pawnbroker's?'

'I was taken there, Uncle Charles, by Mr Bennett, the private investigator I employed to find out these things.'

Uncle Charles put down his pen, not even pretending to be interested in his work any more. 'Mr Bennett? I see you did not take my advice and discontinue this unfortunate liaison with him.'

'I seem to remember it was more in the nature of an order, Uncle Charles, which was

187

quite galling really. Besides,' I smiled at him. 'Fifty pounds actually goes rather a long way when one is not spending it on clothes.'

Uncle Charles gave me a dry look. 'I knew fifty pounds was too much,' he muttered. 'Well, since you've found out so much on your own, I don't see what else I can tell you.'

I felt suddenly cold and put my fingers around the cup to warm them. 'Why did no one tell me about Papa?'

'Tell you what, Isabella? That your father was a feckless, unreliable wastrel who betrayed my sister?' Uncle Charles's face was hard. 'Your aunts certainly would not have thanked me for that description, even if it was the truth.'

'I would have done,' I said, but even to me it sounded hollow. Uncle Charles smiled grimly.

'I don't think so, Isabella. Your mother certainly didn't.'

'My mother? You mean you told her?'

'Of course.' Uncle Charles got up from his chair and walked over to the window, his hands gripping the sash. 'I did not like your father, Isabella. I cannot believe this comes as a shock to you and it comes as no surprise to me that your father had a mistress. I always suspected as much. I did everything I could to dissuade your mother from marrying him. But she refused to listen to reason and my father — your grandfather — could refuse her nothing. From the first moment she set eyes on Robert, your mother seemed to be bewitched by him and nothing would please her but to become betrothed. The only good I could see out of the whole affair was that even she realized how incompetent he was with regard to finances and she made sure he never had control over her fortune.' He turned back from the window.

'Despite my objections, the wedding went ahead and it seemed moderately successful at first, even if they did have no children. I knew Robert was unhappy to be tied to his wife's purse strings, but after a while even he could see how much better suited she was to that side of the marriage.'

Uncle Charles spoke softly, but I could tell he despised my father for this failing. After all, what kind of a husband would put up with a woman controlling his finances? I knew this would have been the prevailing opinion from every section of society and for a moment, I felt sorry for Papa. Then I remembered the watch and my heart hardened towards him again. If Uncle Charles was to be believed the marriage was a love match, at least on my mother's part, and

Papa had betrayed her — used her and betrayed her and for that he deserved no sympathy.

'You should have told me. Someone should have told me,' I insisted, but Uncle Charles merely raised an eyebrow.

'I think not, my dear. Anyway, you found out yourself. Perhaps that was the better solution. I must say you've shown more initiative than I would have given you credit for. Most unusual.' He walked back to his desk and sat down again.

'Thank you, Uncle Charles. But this wasn't the only reason I came to see you this morning.'

'Really?' Uncle Charles looked suspicious again.

'Yes. I'd like you and the trustees to approve an advance of money for a trip abroad.'

'Abroad? Where?'

'I intend to travel to Europe,' I said. 'Then eventually to Algeria.'

'Algeria?'

'Yes. I want to go and see my parents' graves. I want to see where they died.'

Uncle Charles sighed. 'Isabella, I really don't think — '

'I don't expect you to understand, Uncle Charles. I just need you to advance the

190

money. Unfortunately fifty pounds doesn't go *that* far.'

He smiled briefly and picked up his pen again. 'On the contrary, I do understand, my dear. I just don't think it's practical at the moment. I believe your aunt and uncle Faversham intend to remain in England for several months yet and I don't see that anyone else will be — '

'Oh that's all right. Doctor and Mrs Ellis have already agreed to accompany me. They're planning to go out there anyway.'

'I see.' Uncle Charles put down the pen again. 'Isabella, I don't think this is a good idea,' he said gently, but I shook my head.

'I need to go, Uncle Charles. Not just to see their graves; I need to get away.'

'From us?'

'From *everything*.'

Uncle Charles looked at me for a moment before finally nodding his head.

'Very well. You *are* twenty-one now, I suppose. One must trust you sometime. And heaven knows Amelia wasn't always right,' he ended drily.

I got up and kissed him. 'Thank you, Uncle Charles,' I said, as he stood up and walked me to the door. 'I'll make arrangements immediately and be out of your way in no time.'

191

'You're not in my way, Isabella,' he said rather sadly, as I walked out, which didn't mean much to me at the time. But later on I reflected that this was the most affectionate thing he had ever said to me and I wished I had acknowledged it.

★ ★ ★

The cab pulled up outside the dingy building in Bermondsey and I alighted. Telling the driver to wait, I walked up the rickety stairs once more to the first floor and knocked on the door; then, without waiting to be invited, I walked straight in. Mr Bennett looked up, a surprised expression on his face.

'Good morning, Peter,' I said. 'I must say it amazes me that every time I visit you're always here. Shouldn't a busy private investigator be out pounding the beat, or something?'

'Miss Wyndham-Brown. What can I do for you?' Peter asked warily, as I sat down on the chair. I smiled as I removed my gloves.

'Well, let me see. It's been nearly three weeks since we last met and I haven't had anyone shout at me, or call me a spoilt brat, or tell me how to run my life. I'm feeling bereft, Peter. Have you lost interest in me?'

'Not at all, Miss Wyndham-Brown. But you

192

said you no longer required my services, so I assumed — '

'I thought we'd decided to use first names,' I said.

'Did we? I mean — '

'Yes. I distinctly remember you calling me Bella when you came to visit me. Only once it's true, but I rather liked it. And it seems more appropriate if you're going to tell me off all the time. Now, do you want to know why I'm here, or should we bicker a little more first?'

He rubbed his forehead in confusion and pushed his shirt sleeves back. Since it was now the middle of May, he no longer wore his coat indoors and although the cuffs of his shirt were somewhat frayed, the material was of good quality and his black waistcoat matched the jacket hanging over the back of his chair. I particularly liked his tie. It was a very bright blue.

'Very well, Miss — Bella. Why are you here?'

I opened my bag, pulled out another brown envelope and placed it in front of him. He looked at it suspiciously.

'Why do I get the feeling this is more money?' he asked, one eyebrow raised.

'Because you're very clever, and this also seems to be compulsory whenever we meet. I try to give you money and you behave as though I'm the Devil tempting you into sin, although really, darling, I was under the impression you're running a business here. Now before you tell me all the reasons you can't accept this,' I said, forestalling him as he opened his mouth, 'let me explain. I managed to get Uncle Charles to advance me a rather nice sum and instead of using it on fripperies and clothes I don't need, I paid Kate and Adam back what I owed them straight away and I've kept the rest for emergencies. It's a bit underhand really, but if this whole episode has taught me anything, it's that one can never be sure when one might need cash in a hurry. Open the envelope, Peter, and then I can explain to you what I want.'

He looked at me even more suspiciously, but picked up the envelope. After scrabbling around in a drawer for a few seconds he found a rather grubby-looking paper-knife and slit the top. Then he pulled out the contents. There were five crisp ten pound notes inside.

'What's this?' he asked.

'It's fifty pounds, darling.'

'I can see that,' he said testily. 'What's it for?'

'I'm going abroad for a while — '

'Abroad?' he interrupted. 'Where?'

'To Algeria. I've decided I want to see where my parents were killed. Marnie tells me they were buried in a very nice cemetery and I think it would be' — I paused searching for the right word — 'cathartic if I went out there myself and made peace with them. Don't you agree?'

'I've no idea,' he said rather crossly, adding, 'What's this for?' as he flicked a finger at the fifty pounds.

'That's a retainer.'

'A what?'

'A retainer. You know, I retain your services and — '

'Yes, I know what a retainer is. But what's it for? You said the other day you weren't interested in the Dragonshead.'

'Dragonsheart: I changed my mind. As I told you, it's a lady's privilege. What I'd like you to do while I'm gone is see if you can find out any more information. Of course, I wouldn't expect you to spend all your time on it. I realize it's probably never going to be solved. But if you did have a few spare moments, I would be grateful. After all, you do seem to know so many interesting people. I'm sure you could find something out.'

He picked up the money again and flicked through it. 'There's far too much here.'

'You don't know that. You might find out

195

lots and be very busy for me.'

'I doubt it. 1 can't see me ever getting any further on this case.'

'Darling, don't be so pessimistic. I have every faith in you.'

'Flattered though I am, I really can't see me being able to do any more than I already have done.'

'Well, it's my money,' I said. 'Will you do this for me?'

He leaned forward, smiling wolfishly. 'For fifty pounds, Miss . . . Bella, I'll scrub your front doorstep for you.'

'You don't have to do that, just find the Bowood diamond.' I began to pull on my gloves. 'You know, that reminds me. There's something I've been meaning to ask you.'

'Ask away,' he said, opening a little tin box and depositing the money inside.

'Well, despite your insistence on being seen as a man of the people and your evident pleasure in taunting me over my wealth and position in society, you don't exactly behave like a savage you know. In fact, on occasions, in a very flattering light, one might almost mistake you for a gentleman.'

'Thank you so much.'

'Not at all. So my question is this: where did you learn — '

'To be well-bred? The same place as you,

Miss Wyndham-Brown. My family.' He frowned at this and I knew I'd annoyed him, but since I did this regularly without even trying, it hardly seemed a problem. I waited for him to elaborate but he said nothing more.

'Your family?' I prompted. His frown deepened.

'Yes, my family. And the small, but exclusive, school where my brother and I had manners and education beaten into us whether we wanted it or not.' There was a great deal of acrimony in this statement.

'I see.'

He looked up at me. 'I doubt you do,' he said, before placing the money tin into a drawer and closing it with more briskness than was absolutely necessary.

'All right,' I agreed. 'I probably don't. Tell me.'

'Tell you what?'

'Tell me how two boys who came from what I believe you described the other day as genteel poverty could afford the fees of a small exclusive school.'

He looked at me, the frown being replaced by an expression of amused resignation. 'I didn't realize you were paying so much attention the other day.'

'I always pay attention, at least when things

interest me. So how did your poor mother manage to send you to school?'

He sighed and stretched his hands upwards, before resting them on his head.

'Well, if you really want to know, she didn't. It was my aunt — my father's sister — who decided out of the goodness of her cold, unfeeling heart to educate us.'

'Good heavens, Peter, correct me if I'm wrong, but it really doesn't sound as if you liked your aunt.'

His smile grew cynical. 'I hated the old bat. Almost as much as I hated my father for leaving us to ruin.' He said this with so much venom, I almost backed away a little.

'Why? If she paid for your education, she must have — '

'She paid for our education because we were boys who had legitimate claim to the almighty Bennett surname and that apparently meant we were worthy enough to have money spent on us, whereas my mother and my two sisters and my illegitimate brothers didn't get a penny ha'penny to rub between them. God knows why the old — why she thought so much of the Bennett name: my grandfather was apparently a tyrant who wouldn't let her marry until she was nearly thirty and even then it was to force her into a union with an ageing industrialist nearly twice her age. Nevertheless, she still thought Bennett men could do no wrong and if my father had left us it was somehow my mother's fault.'

'Poor Peter. And I thought I had evil aunts and uncles.'

'Lady Faversham is a fairy godmother compared to my aunt Beatrice.'

'Of course. But even so, you still got an education out of her,' I pointed out.

He looked at me for a moment or two and I thought he might ignore the comment; then he nodded.

'We certainly did. Only the best was good enough for the Bennett boys. So she sent word to my mother that she had had us enrolled at the Slane School in Wiltshire and we were to present ourselves on the first Monday in October. Since she didn't bother to send my mother any money for the train fare or anything else, my mother had to come up with that herself. So we arrived three days late with none of the equipment the other boys had and worn, second-hand clothing.' His smile was not infectious. 'You've no idea how much fun that was.'

I looked down at my gloved hands, no longer amused. Some of my cousins had attended Slane; it *was* exclusive and very snobbish.

'I'm sorry, Peter. I'm sure they were little brutes.'

He shrugged. 'Will and I learned to look after ourselves very quickly. And we made a few friends after a couple of years. That was how I got a commission in the army.'

'You were an officer in the army?' I must have sounded amazed because he laughed.

'I even made captain, Miss Wyndham-Brown.'

'Then what on earth are you doing here?'

His face hardened. 'Because I happen to like being here.'

I sighed. 'I apologize, Peter, I shouldn't have said that. You're not going to start shouting at me again, are you?'

He stood up and came round the desk. Suddenly he was very close to me and I could see that his eyes seemed to have changed colour again. Now they were a pale green.

'You've just paid me fifty pounds,' he pointed out. 'One thing we peasants never do is bite the hand that feeds us.'

'I'm so glad to hear it,' I said, as I stood up and walked towards the door. 'Oh, by the way, if you do discover anything, please forward any correspondence to this *poste restante* and I'll get in touch with you as soon as possible.'

I handed him a card with the address I

always used whilst abroad and he took it and studied it for a moment.

'How long will you be gone?'

'Oh, I don't know. A few months. Why? Will you miss me?'

'Of course not. I mean — how could I? We barely know each other.'

'On the contrary, Peter, I think we're beginning to know one another very well,' I said. 'Goodbye.'

As I walked down the stairs I heard the door slam loudly and then the sound of someone swearing. I smiled. I do enjoy these little moments of triumph.

9

I glanced idly at the English newspaper by my side as I finished my breakfast. I was alone in the Hotel le Lutèce in Paris because Kate and Adam had left early to visit the Louvre before we caught the night train to Nice. Since this was going to be our last day in Paris I needed go shopping in the Champ-Elysées. Uncle Charles had been extraordinarily generous over this trip and although I had learnt the value of keeping money available, that still didn't mean I had to look like a pauper. Just as I was about to leave Monsieur Martin, the hotel manager, appeared at the table.

'Good morning, Mademoiselle Wyndham-Brown. There is a gentleman who wishes to see you in the lobby.' He handed me a card and I smiled.

'I'll come directly, *monsieur.*'

'Of course, *mademoiselle.*' Monsieur Martin gestured me towards the magnificent, marbled lobby of the hotel.

'Bella, *ma chère,* how are you?' Laurent stood in front of me, looking even more handsome than the last time I had seen him.

'Very well, Laurent. And you?'

'I am enchanted to see you again, *ma petite cousine*. You are as beautiful as ever.' He drew me towards the huge windows of the hotel that allowed us to look out on to the Seine and we sat down on a plump white-draped sofa.

'You know, Laurent, I'm beginning to lose confidence in your exquisite French manners,' I said. 'They're all very well, but you left London without even saying goodbye. Why on earth should I speak to you?'

'Always you accuse me of abandoning you, *chèrie*. It is most unfair. Did Charles not explain about my nephew?'

I pouted. 'So some horrid little boy sprains his ankle. I still don't see why you had to rush away as eagerly as you did.'

'Beautiful and cruel; I always knew it, *ma chère* Bella. Next time I promise you, even if Thierry is at death's door, I will ignore him to please you.'

I smiled. 'Good; that's settled then. So, to what do I owe the pleasure of your company this morning?'

'*Eh bien*, I received a letter from Hortensia yesterday and when I heard you were in France, in Paris no less, I thanked *le Bon Dieu* for giving me this opportunity to see you again. I had business here and what could be more pleasant than combining business with pleasure. But come, do I distract you? Do you have commissions to make?'

I shook my head. 'They can wait, since I have to grab my chance to speak with you, Laurent.'

'You see, cruel still. But tell me, *ma chère*, what became of your private detective, your Mr Bennett. Is he recovered now from his injuries?'

'Oh yes. He's quite well. And his office is in better condition too, thanks to you.'

'That's good, *ma belle*. I know you like him. Now' — he leaned forward — 'I will tell you why I am here. When I got Hortensia's letter I was very happy because I too have business in Algeria and hope we will be able to meet there.'

'Really?' I felt my whole face stretch into a ridiculous grin. 'That's wonderful. What takes you there?'

He shrugged. 'Again, business. I spent some time there in my youth. And you? I assume you mean to make a pilgrimage in memory of your parents?'

'Yes. I decided that it was time I saw exactly where Mama and Papa died. I found out some information about Mama and Papa that was not very flattering.'

'Ah.' Laurent took my hand in his.

'Particularly your father, I assume.'

I nodded. 'One hears stories when one is young and it means very little really. But to discover that one's father had a mistress and, what was even worse flaunted her in the presence of one's mother — that is somewhat hard to bear.'

He patted my hand. 'So. Monsieur Bennett is as excellent a detective as you said. I must admit I am surprised. I did not think he would be able to find out anything at all from those little pieces of paper.'

I smiled. 'Yes, Peter was rather wonderful.'

Laurent raised an eyebrow. 'And did the excellent Peter also manage to discover the name of this lady?'

'No, I didn't ask him to. To be honest, Laurent, I don't really care who the woman was. I suspect she wasn't the first and if Papa and Mama hadn't died in Algeria, she wouldn't have been the last either, and really that is as much as I wish to know about my father's less than noble character.'

'Of course. Well, *ma chère*, let us not dwell on unpleasant subjects when we can discuss instead when our itineraries will combine.'

So we ordered coffee and spent the next hour comparing our travel plans and by the time he left we had agreed to meet in the capital of Algiers in September. It was a very pleasant end to my time in Paris and I found I was looking forward to the coming months immensely.

* * *

I had had the romantic notion of going exactly the same way as my parents, taking their rather convoluted route through France, Italy and then across to the Island of Sardinia and over to Tunisa. This was not as eccentric as it sounded, since we had left England at the end of June and if we arrived too early in North Africa we would probably die of heat exhaustion. This way our leisurely tour down through Europe gave us plenty of time to become accustomed to the heat and our planned arrival in Algiers in early October would make the climate more bearable.

We spent most of July and August in Rome, Kate and Adam passing days wandering dusty ruins, whilst I contented myself in the absolutely mouth-watering shops in the capital. In September, we travelled down through the rest of Italy, stopping for a week in Naples before taking the train to Reggio di Calabria. The weather became hotter and hotter the further south we progressed and the landscape changed dramatically as we journeyed further down the country, the lush greens giving way to dry arid countryside and parched earth. The longer we spent lazing in the swaying train carriage, with its monotonous rhythmic noises the longer we seemed to sleep, rising only to eat or gaze out of the window at the olive groves, a cool drink in one hand and book in the other as we read or played desultory games of cards or dozed. Looking back, I can't help thinking there was something almost unreal about that part of my journey to Algeria.

The short trip across to Sicily and through Tunis to Algeria passed without incident and we arrived in Algiers shortly after the first week in October. It was still incredibly hot and although the long journey down Italy had acclimatized me somewhat for the change in cultures, I found myself staring mesmerized at the women clad from head to foot in layers of colourful clothing, the men in their flowing robes and the camels laden down with burdens as they began their journeys into the desert. The city itself was a curious mixture of European colonial architecture and the more stunning, exotic Arabic structures. The overwhelming impression was of brilliant whitewashed buildings which reflected the light and made one keep scrupulously to the shade even in the early morning or late afternoon. The ornate stucco-work and tiling on the walls was truly magnificent. Our hotel, a beautiful building fronted by arches and stone columns and decorated in mosaics, was situated in the city centre and reflected the best of both worlds, having the cool shaded courtyards of the wealthy Moorish houses and the modern plumbing of the West.

On the third morning of our stay, Kate and I left Adam after breakfast and walked the short distance to the post office. Even at ten o'clock in the morning, the sunlight already was blinding as we made our way across the noisy market square, ignoring the urchins who ran up to us, demanding we buy dates, peaches, apricots and figs. It was only a five-minute walk, but I was relieved when we saw the white pillars of the post office and we retreated inside eagerly to its vast, cool, dungeon-like chambers. After retrieving our mail we found a quiet spot near an open window.

'Ah here's a letter from Laurent,' I said, as Kate perched her spectacles on her nose and sorted through her own correspondence. 'Oh he's already here. He's given me his address and says he looks forward to meeting us all.'

'Wonderful. I'm looking forward to meet-ing him too, after all this time. You must contact him immediately.'

'I shall,' I said, running an eye quickly over

the rest of the letter, before sorting through the rest of my post. There were several documents from Uncle Charles for me to sign (how like him to wait until I was thousands of miles away before deciding he needed my authority to expedite changes to various investments), two from Aunt Augusta and a scrawl from Marnie, reminding me, among other things, not to drink the water. I was surprised, however, to find that there was nothing from Peter.

'That's odd,' I muttered.

'What is?' asked Kate.

'There's nothing from Peter.'

Kate looked up. 'Still? You were expecting a letter at that hotel in Palermo, weren't you?'

'Yes. And there was nothing at the hotel in Tunis, either.' I put the stack of letters down beside me on the bench and went through them more slowly this time, but still there was nothing.

'When was the last time you heard from him?'

'When we were staying in that little *pensione* in San Giovanni.'

'Oh yes. I remember. That little boy brought our post up from the town and one morning his donkey nearly ate the lot.'

'That's right' I said. 'I suppose Peter must be very busy and there's nothing for him to say. But I did think he'd have written something to me by now.'

'Well, no news is good news I suppose,' said Kate. 'I'm sure there'll be something from him soon.'

'I expect so,' I said. 'Let me just post these letters and then we can go.'

And we walked back outside into the hot morning sun.

⋆ ⋆ ⋆

'Your cousin certainly has good taste, Bella. I'll say that for him.'

As Adam spoke he looked around the restaurant in which we were seated. It was quiet and cosy, yet somehow sumptuous in its simplicity, with tables arranged around a courtyard of black and white tiles with a large fountain at its centre and pots of sweet-smelling thyme, flaming orange orchids and geraniums and scarlet dianthus. Waiters in snow-white robes padded around silently offering exotic delicacies such as couscous, spiced meats and salads of tomatoes and cucumbers as well as the more recognizable European staples. In one corner of the room a small group of Algerians sat, playing mournful, haunting tunes on lute-like instruments and colourful drums.

'Have you noticed we're the only non-French Europeans here,' Kate whispered, leaning across the table with its dazzling white cloth and gleaming silver cutlery. It was true; the clientele, apart from us, was exclusively French. Adam's eyes narrowed slightly.

'The French always seem to know where the best of everything is,' he remarked grimly.

I smiled. 'You make it sound as though you think they're deliberately keeping the Anglo-Saxon element out, Adam.'

'Ignore him, Bella. It's an Englishman's prerogative to be annoyed with the French. Haven't you ever noticed that?' Kate asked, as she sipped some red wine. The waiter had brought it for us as soon as we arrived, explaining that it was ordered with the compliments of Monsieur Marivaux. It was excellent. Adam scowled at us both.

'Well really — trust a frog to — '

'Laurent darling, here you are at last,' I said loudly, as Laurent appeared. He was resplendant in his formal evening dress of black coat and white bowtie and I could tell that he had heard Adam's unfortunate reference to amphibians.

'*Ma belle*,' he said, taking my hand and putting it to his lips as I stood up. 'It is wonderful to see you again. And this must be

Madame Ellis.' He turned to Kate, taking her hand and kissing it as well, ignoring Adam's glare. 'I have heard so much about you, Madame Ellis. It is a pleasure to meet you.'

'I'm very pleased to meet you too, Monsieur Marivaux,' said Kate. 'May I introduce my husband, Dr Adam Ellis?'

Laurent turned to Adam. '*Monsieur*, how do you do? I trust you enjoyed the wine I ordered for you.'

'Very nice,' said Adam somewhat stonily.

'Excellent.' A waiter appeared and poured wine into Laurent's glass as we all sat down. 'The waiters are inclined to use up the more mediocre bottles on English customers who come here. Not that many do.' He beamed at Adam, then turned to Kate and I. 'This restaurant is one of the best-kept secrets at the French Consulate.'

'How long have you been in Algeria?' I asked.

'Since late August.'

'Really? Good Lord,' said Kate in surprise. 'It must have been roasting out here then. However did you endure it, *monsieur*?'

'I am used to it, *madame*. I spent several years out here in my youth. As I believe you did in Egypt.'

'Yes, I did actually.'

'Then you know that it is simply a matter

of acclimatizing oneself to the heat and taking all the precautions the natives take. But come, let us consider the menu. The food the chef prepares here is particularly suited to European palates that have not yet had the chance to . . . '

He began to explain the menu to us and since, as Adam rather sourly pointed out later, the French were so obsessed with food, his suggestions were all excellent and soon our table was groaning under the weight of glistening salads and vegetable dishes of peppers and chick peas and plates that had fish still in its whole form and kebabs and small dark rolls of bread. We were hungrier than we realized and the aromatic smells of the many different spices only served to spike our hunger. As we ate the tension round the table eased slightly until at last Adam and Laurent managed to find common ground on the subject of the different ethnic groups in Algeria, the Berbers, the Maghrebs and the Tuareg.

'So, *ma chère* Bella,' said Laurent eventually as the waiters served us thick, dark coffee and placed a dish of sweet sticky honey cakes and stuffed dates in the middle of the table. 'What is your itinerary now you are here in Algeria? How do you intend to honour the memory of your parents?'

'Well,' I said, stirring a spoonful of treacly sugar in to my coffee, 'I've been giving this a lot of thought since I left England and I've decided that the best thing I can do is go to visit the last place they stayed in before they died. I know there won't be any graves or anything, but at least I'll be able to walk round the village and get some idea of what their last days were like. I've always felt that just seeing where they were might bring me closer to them somehow. Even now, knowing what I know about Papa, I'd still like to go.'

Kate took my hand in hers but said nothing and for a moment there was silence round the table.

'Of course,' said Laurent eventually. 'But I understand their last stop was in a little town called In Salah. Is that correct? This is what my father told me before he died.'

I nodded. 'So I believe.'

Laurent rubbed a finger thoughtfully round the gold rim of his coffee cup. 'I do not believe it would be a good idea to go to this place, ma chère,' he said finally.

'Why ever not?'

'Algeria is not the most stable of countries, chèrie, even with the French presence here. North-west Africa in general is somewhat volatile.'

214

'I know there are problems in Morocco,' I said. 'But our governments — '

'Our respective governments have more pressing problems in Europe than merely maintaining their interests here. But it is not that so much of which I speak. Here on the coast and in the towns, western influence is strong and you and your companions are safe. The further into the desert you go the more dangerous the situation becomes. And In Salah is a long way from Algiers. I think perhaps you should — '

'Laurent.' I put a hand on his arm. 'I did not come all this way from England just to spend a few day visiting some mosques before returning to Europe. I don't intend to be as foolhardy as my parents, but certainly I will visit this town even if only to lay a few ghosts.'

He said nothing for a few moments, before turning and looking at Kate and Adam.

'And you, Monsieur and Madame Ellis? What are your thoughts on this?'

'Well Monsieur Marivaux,' said Kate. 'We do understand your concerns. We've both lived long enough in foreign countries to know that one should always be sensitive to the political structures of the region. But we did agree to accompany Bella here and I would like to see something of the

215

interior before we leave.'

Adam nodded. 'There are a few archaeological sites we thought we might visit.'

Laurent looked at us all intently for a moment before nodding. 'Very well then, if I cannot persuade you to remain in Algiers at least let me organize some protection for you. I have contacts here. Give me a few days and I will be able to arrange a party to take you to In Salah.'

'You're very kind, Laurent,' I said. 'But really, I'm sure — '

'Please, Bella, indulge me. I can arrange this easily. Besides,' he smiled, 'how could I face Charles or any of your other relatives if you came to any harm?'

I smiled. 'Since we looked after your sister so badly, I don't think we'd have a right to make a fuss.'

He nodded gravely. 'Even more reason to attend to you, *chèrie*. I want the pleasure of knowing that we frogs are better at something than you English.'

He looked slyly at Adam as he said this and after a pause Adam had the grace to laugh and our meal ended in much better spirits than it began.

★　★　★

216

Two days later I was standing in the high, vaulted hallway of the hotel, drawing on my gloves as I prepared to launch myself on the streets for a short walk to the post office again. True to his word Laurent had departed Algiers the very next morning after our dinner to go to a place called Sidi bel Abbes in order to marshal his forces for our travels. He was very serious about it and made us promise not to move out of Algiers until his return.

I was grateful for the chance to sit and reflect on the next step of my journey. I still wasn't really sure what I expected to find in the tiny little town where my parents had died. I still couldn't think with any clarity on my father's betrayal of my mother, but as the weeks had given way to months on my journey down through Europe I had found myself wondering more and more what had made Mama so determined to drag her new-born daughter and errant husband out to such a strange and alien place. It helped somehow; she became, if more eccentric, at least less pitiful.

So there I was standing in the beautifully decorated hallway with its cool marbled floors and the brightly coloured, intricately pat-terned Berber rugs on the wall, glancing idly at the fountain in the courtyard when I

217

became aware of a commotion going on in the large doorway. I couldn't understand what they were saying, but it quickly became clear the servants were attempting to stop someone from entering the premises and this person was equally as determined to come in. The manager of the hotel, a middle-aged Frenchman with a high, starched collar and a magnificent moustache of which Uncle Charles would have been extremely envious, appeared from his office and walked over to them briskly and I heard him speak first in Arabic, then in French and finally, to my astonishment, in English.

'No, no, *monsieur*, you cannot come in. Please leave immediately — there is no one here who wishes to speak to you. If you do not leave I will call the — '

I caught a glimpse of a very scruffy, dirty-looking individual on the steps and turned back to the fountain, losing interest. There were a number of down-at-heel foreigners in Algiers who spent most of their time trying to persuade ex-patriots to lend them money and we had been warned not to approach them or allow them to approach us. So, I was just about to leave by the side exit when I heard my own name mentioned. I looked up.

'*Absolument pas.* I will not allow my

clients to be deranged in this way. I do not care what letters you have, Miss Wyndham-Brown will not — '

Intrigued, as one always is when one hears one's own name, I moved back to the front of the hotel and stared across at the three Algerian servants who were pushing someone back down the steps. For a moment he seemed just another dirty, bearded ex-sailor trying to beg for a few francs, then suddenly I realized with horror that I recognized him.

'Peter!'

The scruffy creature looked up at me with wild eyes.

'Bella! Thank God! I thought I'd come too late. I thought I'd missed you again. I — '

As he spoke he stumbled on the steps, slipped and fell.

'Peter!' I screamed.

'*Mademoiselle*, do you know this man?' Monsieur Besson stared at me in amazement and I couldn't blame him. Peter looked awful; his clothes were torn and stained, a wild growth of beard covered his face and he *smelt*, to be perfectly honest.

'Of *course* I know him,' I said in exasperation. 'Please, get a doctor straight away. And prepare a room for him,' I added, kneeling down on the steps beside him. Monsieur Besson came over.

'And a bath too, *mademoiselle?*' he enquired coldly. I glared at him, then caught another whiff of my employee and sighed. One could only take pride so far.

'By all means,' I said, as the servants, finally realizing the new status of this hitherto undesirable person, now grouped around us and took Peter from my arms. Slowly they helped him up the stairs, leaving me to shake my head and wonder what this strange new turn of events meant.

★ ★ ★

'You may go in now, *monsieur, mesdames.* Your friend is awake,' said the dapper little French doctor as he walked out of the hotel bedchamber.

'Is he all right?' Kate asked. He gave a little bow of assent.

'He is tired, somewhat dehydrated, mal-nourished, but he is young. He will mend very quickly. He is however, most anxious to speak to you. Especially you, *mademoiselle,*' the doctor continued with a smile. 'From what I can understand he has come a long way to deliver his message.'

Peter had lost consciousness almost as soon as we got him into the bedchamber and the few words he had said had made no sense to me at all. Whilst Monsieur Besson arranged for a doctor I had sent a servant to find Kate and Adam. They had arrived back at the hotel within the hour and we had waited impatiently for the doctor to attend to Peter.

I pushed open the door and saw him sitting up in the bed, a clean white nightshirt on, his face freshly shaved and a hand-painted glass of tea in his hands. He smiled wanly as we all came in.

'This is getting to be a habit, Peter,' I said briskly, as I walked over to the bed and sat down. 'Really, I can't leave you alone for five minutes.'

He shook his head. 'I didn't have any choice. You weren't answering any of my telegrams and — '

'What telegrams?'

'The ones I sent you. I knew you weren't getting them,' he said, with a certain amount of satisfaction as I frowned. 'I've been sending you all telegrams since the beginning of August, telling you to get in touch urgently and not had one reply. I did hope after the first two that if I sent it in Kate's maiden name it might get through, but it obviously didn't. I sent two to that unpronounceble place in Italy, three to Palermo, and I even sent one to Tunis, although I was pretty convinced by that time that it was a waste of time. *And* money I'd — '

'Wait a minute, old chap, you're going to have to slow down.' Adam and Kate had pulled up chairs by this time and were sitting opposite me. 'What exactly has been going on? What on earth are you doing here?'

'I had to come,' he insisted. 'I had to warn you about that French chap. Is he here yet?'

'What French chap?' asked Kate, her eyes widening, but I felt a stab of fear in my stomach, even before Peter spoke.

'That damned Frenchman who's been following Bella around. Marivaux.'

'Do you mean my cousin, Laurent Marivaux?' I asked.

Peter nodded firmly. 'That's him. I knew there was something funny about him the moment I set eyes on him, but you telling me he was your cousin threw me off the scent. He's the one who set those thugs on me back in March. And he was the one who went to the bank and took out whatever was being kept in there. I'll bet you a pound to a penny he's also been responsible for — '

'Wait a minute; stop,' I said. 'What on earth are you talking about? Laurent was the one who helped me get you to a hospital when you were hurt — he even helped stop those awful men from taking all your belongings. What are you talking about?'

Peter looked at me, his face suddenly calmer, even compassionate as he took my hand.

'How much do you know about him, Bella? Really?'

'I know he's my cousin,' I said indignantly.

'Why?'

'Why? Why should he lie about it?'

'Any number of reasons. You're rich is my personal favourite and he knows there's that familial guilt about the dead sister. Although I'm not ruling out the possibility he's working on behalf of somebody else, probably to get that diamond. Or he could even have heard about that and combined the two — he's got quite a reputation in Paris and — '

'A reputation? What for?'

Peter shrugged, obviously realizing again that he was still somewhat ahead of me.

'For sharp practices. The *commissariat* in Paris weren't very keen to talk to me until I mentioned his name and then they opened up quite considerably. He's not at all popular with them and I can understand why — '

'The police?' I shrieked, but Kate put a hand on my arm.

'Peter, what *are* you talking about? What exactly has Monsieur Marivaux done to attract the attentions of the French police?'

'He's a private detective. Like me,' Peter

added. 'Although from what I could gather from them, he sails very close to the wind. They're quite certain he killed a chap last year for a client although they can't prove it. He's very popular with the monied classes in France though. Apparently he only takes on a couple of cases a year if they interest him and he charges through the nose.' For a moment Peter sounded almost wistfully envious, then he seemed to remember what we were talking about. 'Anyway, I doubt very much he really is your cousin, Bella.'

I stood up. 'Don't be ridiculous. Of course he's my cousin. And he's not a private detective, he's a dairy farmer and he lives with his family in a little town in Normandy called — '

'How do you know?' asked Peter. 'Have you spoken to anyone else in the family? Have you seen any documents that prove this?'

'Well, no, of course I haven't,' I said. I glared at him. 'This might come as a shock to you, Peter Bennett, but among normal people, when one is introduced to new members of the family, one does not usually demand written proof of their identity.'

He smiled faintly. 'Then perhaps you should start doing that. And by the way, may I say you sound exactly like your uncle Charles. The family resemblance is uncanny.'

224

'You've spoken to Uncle Charles?' I said.

'Of course I did, as soon as I realized what we were dealing with. And he was as stuffy as you are about it. I got a long lecture about family loyalties and people who didn't know their place and bad manners about poking noses in where they weren't wanted. Still, I think he was bit more suspicious when I left, although it's hard to tell when you're being slung out through the tradesmen's entrance.'

'All right, wait a minute here.' Adam put up a hand. 'When did you start to get suspicious about this fellow, Peter?'

Peter motioned to me to fill his glass up with more tea and I did so. 'After you left I decided I wasn't happy with the situation as it was and I thought I'd give Arnold and Henry one last chance to confess their sins. They're the two who roughed me up, by the way. It took a bit of persuasion, but in the end they saw the error of their ways and Arnold admitted that they'd been given an address in Peckham if they encountered any problems. I won't go into detail but suffice it to say I got a good enough description of their employer to start making me thinking that he bore a strong resemblance to the chap you'd brought with you to my office that day. Then I went back to Fortescue and Hopkins and although the assistant there couldn't give me much more information, he admitted there was a strong possibility the foreigner could be French. So then I started asking around about your so-called cousin and found that no one had actually seen or spoken to any other members of this banished branch of the family and when I got your letter from Naples mentioning you'd met up with him so fortuitously in Paris and had arranged to meet again in Algiers, warning bells started to go off in my head. I sent a telegram straight away but heard nothing, which was when I decided to take a little trip to Paris.' He spread out his hands. 'After I'd spoken to the police I became even more worried and I wasted about a week there not wanting to leave in the hope you'd reply. But you didn't so I had no choice but to follow you here as quickly as I could.' He took a sip of the tea. 'I had forty pounds of your advance left and I travelled as cheaply as I could. I got thrown into jail briefly for vagrancy in Sicily. At least I *think* it was vagrancy. Their English was as poor as my Italian.'

While he was speaking I felt my head spinning round. All the things he was saying sounded incredible, ludicrous. Laurent, some kind of hardened private detective, a thug who arranged to have Peter beaten half to death, following me across Europe for his own nefarious means! It was absolutely ridiculous.

And yet — and yet — what did I really know of Laurent? Or any of the family for that matter? None of us had actually spoken to any of the others; we had simply taken his word that he was who he said he was. And now that I thought about it, some of Laurent's absences had been rather strange. He had disappeared at odd times with very little explanation and none of us had felt able to question him.

'Bella! Bella!' I looked up to see Kate staring at me in concern.

'I'm sorry,' I said. 'I was just — '

'I know, my dear,' she said kindly. 'I realize this must be terribly distressing for you. He seemed so pleasant — '

'Not to me he didn't,' Adam muttered. 'I knew there was something a bit off about him.'

'Did you?' asked Peter eagerly. 'Because I thought — '

'You thought no such thing,' said Kate briskly. 'And no more did you, Peter, until you got a more detailed description of your foreign person. But this is not helping at all. Bella dear, do you think it's likely that Laurent might not be all he pretends to be?'

I nodded dismally. 'I'm afraid so, now that

Peter raises all these questions which I can't answer. But why? What could he possibly want from me?'

'Money,' said Peter. 'That's what it usually boils down to. I think he heard about that diamond from somewhere and whatever he took from the bank only gave him some of the information he needed. He knows you know something about the diamond and probably thinks you've got more information and you've come out here to retrieve it.'

'But that's ridiculous. I told him what I was doing out here. Why would I lie to him?'

'People who routinely lie and steal themselves tend to find it easy to believe others are capable of the same kind of behaviour, Bella,' said Adam. 'Why should he think you're telling him everything?'

'Besides, you brought Adam and Kate with you,' Peter said. 'That's probably made him more suspicious.'

'Why on earth would the fact that Kate and Adam are here as well make me more likely to be searching for lost treasure?'

Peter smiled cynically. 'You may not have done any homework on him, my dear Bella, but you can bet he's done all his on you. Adam and Kate are well-known archaeologists and they very recently found the Scarlet Queen. Who else would you ask to

228

accompany you on just such a trip?'

We all looked at each other in amazement. Put like that it sounded very plausible. Suddenly Adam gave a gasp.

'I've just thought of something.'

'What?' we all chorused together.

'He made us promise to remain here.'

'What?' asked Peter frowning.

'He got us to promise to remain here. The other night when we met for dinner, he tried to dissuade Bella from going to In Salah, but she insisted. He was probably sounding out her resolve and when she insisted, he got us to promise instead to remain here whilst he organized a safe party to take us there. He's been gone for two days now.'

We all looked at one another in horror. It was true. Whilst we had been sitting here in Algiers, Laurent was gone. He could be anywhere, doing anything and we had no way of knowing what he was up to. It might already be too late.

'Don't worry, Bella,' said Kate, trying to sound reassuring. 'We'll work something out. We'll find out what he wants.'

But I shook my head, knowing her words were empty. Whatever Laurent wanted from me, the chances were he already had it.

10

'Peter, are you sure you're all right?'

'I'm fine. Will you stop asking me that. It's been nearly two weeks now and I haven't had any problems.'

I bit my tongue to stop myself from saying anything I might regret. We were all tired and hot. At least Peter was well enough to feel irritable. I caught Kate glancing at me and we exchanged a smile. Then I set my sights on the interminable dull, almost silent road ahead and steeled myself for hours more of the same thing.

We had left Algiers four days after Peter's arrival, Adam and Kate arranging a guide and enough equipment and provisions to last us for a month, the amount of time the guide insisted it would take to get to In Salah. I had been torn between almost febrile desperation to get going before Laurent returned from wherever he was, and a desire to give Peter enough time to rest. I did not want him to come with us at all at first, but he would not hear of us leaving without him. Also both he and Adam seemed to think the problem was not that Laurent might return to Algiers any day, but that he had already left for In Salah and we would not be in time to confront him. They had both decided by then that Laurent was after the Dragonsheart and that somehow he had discovered it was to be found at my parents' last resting place.

The first day of travel seemed almost too much for Peter; he was pale and wan and twice he had almost fallen from his horse and we had stopped early and started late the next day to give him extra time. But gradually over the past few days he seemed to improve, growing stronger every day and by the time we entered the desert on the fifth day he did seem much better. As I watched him now surreptitiously, I noticed that the colour had returned to his face and althought he was snappy, it was no more than any of us were after hours in the saddle and nothing to look at but endless dull yellow sand-dunes, punctuated by the soft clicking of the mules' hoofs and the smell of over-heated bodies.

'*Monsieur*,' shouted the guide, a thin young man called Hassan. 'We should think about stopping now. It will be dark soon and the animals need to be rested.'

'So do we all, Hassan,' said Adam wearily. He nudged his horse around to the front of the line and began to consult with Hassan about the best place to camp.

I pulled back slightly and fell into line with Kate. She was all but unrecognizable in the long white desert robes we had all taken to wearing, with our heads bandaged up in turbans and folded loosely over our faces to keep out the sand and the flies. Adam and Kate had adopted the Algerians' mode of dress as soon as we encountered the dunes and Peter had followed suit soon after, but foolishly I had tried to remain a respectable young English lady in my riding habit. However, after two and a half days fighting the heat and constant buzzing of the mosquitoes and other vile-looking insects that seemed to thrive in such appalling conditions, I had given up, removed the thick serge jacket and wrapped myself up in the mummy-like shroud Kate had wordlessly provided me with. I felt much better.

'Are you sure you want to carry on?' I asked her, as Adam, Peter and Hassan began unpacking the equipment with the help of the four Algerians Hassan had brought with him. 'This is getting more unpleasant by the day and we don't even know what we're going to find when we get to this place. You don't have to come, you know.'

Kate gave me a dry look from beneath her veil. 'I certainly do. How would it look if I left you alone with only male company? Although

232

I do wonder if perhaps this is the most sensible thing we could be doing.' She pulled the gauzy fabric from her face and looked out at the dunes cautiously.

'What do you mean?' I found myself following her gaze and seeing nothing there but miles and miles of empty desert. Hours of silent riding must have made me nervous, because although I could hear and see nothing, still I felt uncomfortable.

'I'm not sure,' Kate said, as she turned back to me with a grim smile. 'It's just that — I've been out in conditions like these so many times, Bella, with Papa and now with Adam and never once have I felt so . . . vulnerable as I have these last few nights.' She shivered before shaking her head and leaning over to pat my hand. 'Oh just ignore me, Bella. I'm being fanciful. Tomorrow we should reach Ghardaia. Hassan says it's quite a large town which I think is just what we need. There's nothing like a noisy, crowded market-place to drive the whimsies from one's mind.'

I smiled, but I couldn't help glancing out at the desert. It was still, peaceful even as the sun began to sink into the horizon, turning the yellow dunes rose and gold and with the gentle noises of the night animals, the fennec foxes and the jerboas as they began to forage and hunt it was not without its own special beauty. But now her words haunted me and even through dinner that night I felt a sense of foreboding that simply wouldn't go away.

After dinner I wandered towards the small, makeshift corral where the horses and mules were kept. They eyed me in a bored fashion for a few minutes, becoming mildly curious when I held out some honey cake for them, but soon losing interest when the tasty piece of sticky sweet was gone. I couldn't blame them; after all when morning came we would round them up and weigh them down with heavy loads again.

'I thought you'd gone to bed.'

I turned round. Peter was behind me.

'Not yet. I'm not tired enough. How about you? Are you — '

He held up a hand. 'For the hundredth time I'm fine. Really. Would you like a note from my doctor to prove it?'

I walked over and sat down next to him. 'Yes.'

'Well when we get back to London, I'll have one forged and posted to you.'

I smiled. 'Seriously, Peter — '

'Seriously, Miss Wyndham-Brown. I've survived much worse than missing a few meals. I promise you. Although it's nice to have a client who takes such an interest in my welfare. I could get used to it.'

I nodded. 'I want to know my money's being well spent. One wouldn't want an employee who couldn't do his job.'

'Really? And how am I doing so far?'

'So far I'm satisfied.'

'Satisfied?' he echoed. 'Is that all? I had to travel down Europe in the worst train carriages, twice with the livestock, cut down to one meal of dry bread a day by the time I reached Rome, nearly got locked up in Sicily and all you can say is — '

'I thought you said you'd survived much worse than missing a few meals?' I asked.

He shrugged. 'I was lying,' he admitted, his grin spreading to his eyes. 'I was hoping you'd be impressed by my manly indifference to hardship.'

I grinned back. 'Oh, I see.'

'Well? Did it work?'

We turned and looked at one another, and I was very aware that we were alone under a black sky with the warm breeze of the desert night blowing gently behind our backs, the cicadas making their soft clicking sounds. This was far worse than the time Henry had encountered me alone in that stupid maze in Hertfordshire. I hadn't even liked him particularly, let alone wanted to kiss him, but I found as I looked at Peter, his eyes no longer sparkling but deadly serious that not only did I want to kiss him, I wanted —

Suddenly there was a shout from the tents and the sound of a gunshot exploding nearby. Peter and I jumped, just as the horses and mules began neighing and jostling into each other, their fear at the unexpected violence of the noise feeding our own disquiet. For a few seconds we were thrown together, as a horse pushed against us, then we both realized simultaneously that figures were running around our tiny camp, shouting in Arabic and French.

'What — ?' Peter began, but before he could say anything else, I felt hands reach out and grab me from behind and drag me away from the corral. I screamed and lashed out, but before Peter could do anything, another figure ran up suddenly behind him and dealt him a blow to the head. The last thing I saw was him crashing to the ground, but as I flailed my arms about, another hand clamped a soft rag around my mouth and nose and within seconds the world became an endless black hole that I was falling into.

★ ★ ★

When I finally came to, the sun was up and slowly shedding pale light on the desert. I felt

236

groggy and queasy and for the first few seconds I had difficulty remembering where I was. I seemed to be jogging up and down although since I wasn't running there seemed to be no rational explanation for this state and for some reason someone had apparently tied me to a pile of rough, smelly carpets.

Slowly I remembered what had occurred the night before and, as I struggled to sit up, I realized simultaneously why I was being jostled up and down and why there were carpets under my nose. I had been tied to the hump of a camel and its rolling gait carried me along to the rhythm of regular padding. As I struggled to free myself the bonds seemed to tighten and I panicked and began shouting.

I felt rather than saw several camels and their riders come closer to me and the swaying motion of the camel slowed down and finally stopped. Arms, swathed in blue fabric, reached out and began untying me.

'Let me down!' I shouted at the nearest figure. 'Who are you? Where are my friends?'

As the rope finally fell away I was able to sit up and I turned around stiffly to see a sea of blue figures atop camels. They were all dressed in the same pale-blue material, their heads and faces concealed so only the eyes were visible. One of them, the person who had untied me, began to talk in a soft gentle voice, presumably to soothe me, but since I didn't understand a word he was saying and I was still bound by the ankles to the camel, it didn't help much.

'Who are you?' I said again, frowning to try to conceal how frightened I was. 'What do you want with me?'

The man began again, speaking more slowly this time and eventually I realied he was speaking French. For some reason this enraged me.

'Hah! Too bad!' I said, scowling at him, as I tried to keep steady on the stupid camel. 'I don't speak French and even if I did I doubt I'd understand your appalling accent. So if you expect me to give you any information' — I don't know why I said that, I was babbling really — 'you're going to be sadly disappointed.'

The blue-clothed man turned round and shouted something to his companions. Obviously I didn't know what it was but it amused them all and they began laughing. Being tied up and dragged away from one's friends is bad enough but being laughed at by one's captors really is too much.

'Oh very droll,' I said acidly to my new friend. 'I'm sure you think — '

'*Drôle, oui, oui,*' he said excitedly, nodding

at me. '*Drôle*, hah, hah.'

Vague memories of long ago French lessons suggested '*drôle*' might be the French for 'funny', but I was in no mood for a vocabulary lesson.

'Well you might think this is *drôle, monsieur*,' I said, 'but I can assure you I don't. So, unless you're prepared to speak to me in English, or even better turn this wretched animal around and take me back to my friends, then I have nothing else to say to you.' And to demonstrate the point I turned my head away from him.

I heard him speak again to his companions and more muted laughter, but he didn't try to engage me in conversation again and as the sun rose higher in the sky and the brutal heat of the day began I found I had no energy left to care.

★   ★   ★

We stopped some time, I don't know when, rested, ate and continued travelling when the worst heat of the day had passed. I can't be sure, but I think my captors did this out of deference to me as they seemed capable of riding all day without stopping, sitting atop their smelly, docile camels and plodding along in a semi-daze. As I was feeling more than a little nauseous due to the rolling motion of the camel, I found the best way to cope with my general misery was to do as the blue men did and doze in the curious chair-like saddle on top of the camel.

As the sun set on this appalling day, we stopped again, this time by a small oasis, with a few spindly palm trees dotted around it and I was only mildly surprised when the beast I was riding knelt down and I was helped off and allowed to totter along to a pile of rugs where I sank down gratefully to watch them set up their brightly coloured tents. I counted twenty of the brutes altogether, with at least ten more camels which were being used as pack animals in the same way we used the mules. All of these people — I couldn't tell if they were men or women — were clothed the same in blue robes with their faces hidden by the thin fabric and, as they worked together, I began to get the impression I was by no means the most important part of their cargo. Some packs they unloaded flashed silver and gold in the harsh sunlight. They laughed and joked a lot between themselves as they worked and I have to say I felt quite bitter that they were having so much fun when I wasn't.

Just then, one of them came up to me and held a water bottle to my mouth, trickling in small amounts gently and stopping every few seconds. I was desperately thirsty, but knew enough not to bolt the water down. I had done this during our midday break and vomited copiously, much to everyone else's amusement.

My benefactor nodded encouragingly as I took small sips, his eyes through the gap in his turban crinkled up. He was the same man who had spoken to me at dawn and I got the impression he had been elected as the lucky person given the job of minding the truculent, stupid white woman. He had by now given up any hope of having me understand him, and he contented himself instead with small smiles and reassuring pats on my shoulder which frankly weren't reassuring at all.

'Who are you?' I asked, as I lay back on the rough carpet, panting with heat and effort. 'What do you want with me?'

But the dark brown eyes just crinkled up again and with one final pat he left me, unable to move from heat and exhaustion and with nowhere to go even if I could.

★ ★ ★

I awoke with a start. There were noises outside the tent, shouts of concern and I could hear scuffling.

I stood up, pulling my now extremely dirty robe around me. Beneath it my thin cotton blouse was stained and ripped in places. Picking up the lamp that was still burning weakly, I moved as quietly as I could to the tent flap. I had done this earlier on and found a man in blue squatting outside. He had stood up and motioned me back in, and since he clearly had the upper hand, and I was in no mood to fight, I had just retreated and picked listlessly at the dishes of food they had left for me, plates of couscous, spiced lamb and a jug of mint tea. If I had had any idea of what they wanted with me, I might have been hungrier, but since no one could understand me, nor I them, communication was non-existent and there is nothing like not knowing one's fate to ruin the appetite.

However, this time my guard was nowhere to be seen and I was just about to move cautiously out of the tent when suddenly a group of about five of the men appeared, dragging someone or something between them, none too gently. On seeing me, one of them shouted something in Arabic and I was pushed back into the tent without ceremony.

There was a certain amount of grim laughter as the figure being hauled in was cast to the ground in front of me and the lead man said something. His accent was still terrible, but a few long forgotten words of French must have come back because I caught what sounded like the words 'anglais' and 'ami'. I looked at him in confusion for a moment and he pointed to the bundle in front of me. With a sudden shock I realized it was Peter. But before I could say anything, they walked out again.

'Peter!' I gasped, sinking down to my knees. I put the lamp down beside him to examine his wounds. He looked awful; his face was bruised and dusted with sand and there was a trickle of blood coming from his mouth. 'Peter, are you all right?'

He groaned and his eyelids flutttered sickeningly for a few moments before opening. Slowly he levered himself up on to his elbows and rolled over to one side, before rubbing at his eyes.

'Are you all right?' I asked again. His response was to groan, so remembering the jug of mint tea, I got up and brought it over to him, pouring out a little in a thin china cup.

'Here, have some of this. Slowly now.'

He drank a few sips before sinking down on to his back again. There were rips in his robes and one boot was hanging off at the ankle. Finally he pushed himself upright again.

'We've got to stop doing this, Bella. I don't think I can survive much more of your way of life. Have you ever thought of taking up embroidery?'

'I'm an excellent needlewoman,' I said, pouring more tea into the cup. 'When we get home, I'll show you the set of chair-backs I decorated for Aunt Augusta's fiftieth birthday.'

'I'm looking forward to it already.' He took the cup rather shakily and drank some more.

'What happened?' I asked. Peter gave me a dry look.

'Well, let's see; since life with you is never normal we got waylaid on a main road to an Algerian market-town, you were abducted and the rest of us left beaten and gagged.'

'Beaten!' I said horrified.

Peter shrugged. 'Well, Adam, Hassan and I were. Kate was left with enough rope on her wrists to make it over an hour before she was able to untie herself and then us.'

'They're all right then?' I asked eagerly.

'Kate is, but Hassan had a cracked rib and Adam was concussed and was having a bit of trouble seeing when I left. He wanted to come after you as well but Kate and I managed to persuade him he'd only slow me

244

down and besides they'd taken all the horses. We managed to rig up a travois behind the donkeys and got to Ghardaia before sunlight and I left them there to follow you.'

'You came alone?'

He nodded again. 'No choice really. I couldn't leave Kate alone and Hassan at least seemed to have some sense of loyalty. He managed to get the — '

'What about the others? The men he brought with him?'

'Ah.' Peter spotted the dish of spiced lamb kebabs and, picking one up, began gnawing at it hungrily. 'It seems Hassan is not the best judge of character and our employees were actually better paid by your abductors than by us. At least as far as we can work out. They'd disappeared even before those thugs turned up according to Adam, and since all the horses are gone and most of our equipment, it seems reasonable to assume they were in cahoots with those people outside even before we left.'

'Oh.' I looked at him a moment. 'You don't suppose Laurent — '

He shrugged and picked up another kebab. 'We don't know. Hassan assured us he hadn't heard of any Frenchman who was interested in our trip, but to be frank that doesn't mean much. I don't think Hassan has had much experience at this kind of thing. Anyway, he found Adam a doctor, or some sort of medicine man, in Ghardaia who seemed to have some idea what he was about, so I left as soon as I could and managed to pick up your trail with the help of a group of villagers. They'd seen the Tuareg moving before daylight and — '

'The what?'

'The Tuareg,' Peter repeated. He found another cup and poured out some of the mint tea, passing it to me as he sat down cross-legged opposite me. 'That's what these people are called. They're quite distinctive due to the blue robes they wear; actually that's their other name: 'the blue people' or 'the blue men'. Anyway the villagers weren't too keen to get involved at first since they have quite a fearsome reputation, but Kate managed to bribe them into showing me where they were headed and I caught up with you around midday and just kept plodding on behind you until they slowed down for the night. It was funny really,' he added, taking a sip of the cold tea, 'camels can go really fast you know, much faster than horses but they didn't seem to be in any hurry. Which was a good job because I would never have kept up otherwise. Anyway, I saw them set up camp and I waited until it was dark, meaning to try

246

to slip down to your tent and get you, but they must have been aware I was here because they seemed to be waiting for me. Why do they want you anyway?'

He asked this quite casually as thought I should know the answer and I stared at him in surprise.

'Good heavens, Peter, why on earth should I know? Because they're ignorant, uncivilized thugs I suppose.'

'Surely you asked them?' He sounded a tiny bit cross.

'How can I ask them? I don't speak their language and they don't speak mine.'

'They speak French,' he said, taking a piece of the flat bread I'd been left and dipping it into some humous. 'It might be a bit rough, but I know Kate and Adam have no problems.'

'I can't speak French,' I said, getting cross myself now. He stopped what he was doing and looked at me in amazement.

'You can't speak French,' he echoed. 'I thought you heiresses were raised on stuff like that.'

'Stuff like what?' I asked irritably. 'And will you stop eating my supper?'

'You aren't eating it.'

'I wasn't hungry before; I might be now.'

'Well, nobody's stopping you. And I

haven't eaten all day.'

'Oh for heaven's sake, eat it if you must. And why don't *you* ask them if you're so clever?'

'Because I can't speak French either,' he admitted.

'Oh really? And how did you manage to get through five years at Slane without learning French?'

'Because it's a stupid language. And everyone can speak English anyway. Everyone who counts,' he added.

We looked at one another. 'Except, of course, in situation like these,' I said. He thought about this and shrugged.

'The French master at Slane told me one day I'd regret not paying attention in lessons,' he said at last. 'I'm sure if he could see me now he'd be laughing his head off.'

'So would Mademoiselle Berthier,' I agreed. 'But this doesn't help us a great deal at the moment.'

'I know. I suppose that means you don't know what the rider earlier on this evening wanted, then?'

'What rider?'

Peter sighed as he stretched out. 'They had a visitor just as the sun set. He seemed to cause a bit of agitation at first, then they all sat down together and after a lot of talking he rode away again.'

'I didn't even know they had a visitor. I heard some shouting, but as soon as I went to the tent flap, my guard waved me back in.'

'Ah. Talking of which.' Peter stood up and picked up the lamp, throwing long shadows across the heavy folds of the tent. He walked across to the opening again to be confronted by another blue-veiled Tuareg. Through the eye slit we could see a grin crinkling up his face, but he waved Peter back vigorously, barking a firm order in Arabic.

'Yes, yes, I get the point,' muttered Peter, as he moved back. The Tuareg nodded and we saw his shoulders shaking with laughter. 'Well it's nice to know someone's happy.'

'Oh they're very jolly fellows,' I said. 'Especially when they strap you to a great huge smelly camel and force you to ride for hours.'

'Hmm.' Peter began to rub his forehead again.

'Are you sure you're all right, Peter?' I asked. 'I forgot you've had an even worse day than me.'

'Actually I do feel a bit tired.' This time he didn't even bother to argue with me. 'Let me just lie down for a bit and then when it's quietened down out there, we'll see if there's any way we can escape.'

Having spent a lot longer in the company of the Tuareg than Peter had, I didn't feel at all confident about this plan, but I didn't say anything to him. I just nodded and watched him lie down on the pile of carpets that had served as my bed. Within a very short while he was asleep and I pulled a light blanket over him before settling down near to the doorway myself.

★　★　★

I awoke with a start. I had only meant to doze for a bit, but I felt as though I had been asleep for hours. For a moment I sat without moving, accustoming myself to the silence.

After a few moments of waiting to see if anybody was moving outside, I got up slowly and crept towards the tent-flap, cautiously pulling it open. It seemed absolutely still; even the guard outside was fast asleep, his eyes closed behind the blue face-cloth.

I stared at him for a second, not fully comprehending at first why this was a good thing. Then, as I realized that Peter and I now had a small chance of escaping, it occurred to me that everywhere else in the encampment was eerily still. No one moved, no one sighed, not even the night breeze disturbed the absolute peace. The long dark blue shadows where the full moon shone were completely still.

I crept back to where Peter lay and began shaking him.

'Peter!' I hissed as loudly as I dared. 'Wake up. They're all asleep. I think we might have a chance of — Peter! Peter!'

As I shook him, he rolled over on to one side, but made no sign that he was waking up. Indeed, I could hardly see him breathing.

'Peter! Wake up!'

I shook harder and harder but he barely stirred, just rolled over a little more to one side. Panicking, I ran outside, glad even to have woken up our captors if only in the hope they might succeed where I had failed, and then I heard the unmistakable jingle of horses' reins, a lot of them. It must be Kate and Adam, I thought. They must have found a way to catch up with us.

About thirty feet or so ahead of me, covering the vast empty sandy space of the desert, was a crowd of people on horseback, at least twenty, if not more. Even at this distance and despite the coverings over their faces, I could tell from the way they sat on their horses that they were Europeans and I felt a sudden lifting of my heart.

'Thank heaven you've found us,' I shouted, not caring if the Tuareg heard me. I ran towards them, pointing to the tent I'd come from. 'My friend and I have been abducted by these people and I think he's ill. I can't get him to wake up. Are you the leader here?' I added, as I reached them and stared up at the rider on the largest horse, who pulled at the material covering his face. 'I think he needs to — '

But as I looked up at him the words died in my throat and I felt a sudden stab of fear in my stomach. For looking down at me, with the familiar expression of urbane, mild amusement on his face, was Laurent.

11

'Bella, at last I have found you. You make life very difficult for me, *ma chère.*'

He looked down at me from the horse, a chiding, almost playful note in his voice, whilst I just stared up at him, dumbfounded. I don't remember falling to my knees, but I must have done, because suddenly I was crawling backwards in fear.

'Keep away from me!' I yelled. 'I know what you want and you're not going to get it. Help!' Even then, I couldn't help thinking how ridiculous it was to be shouting for my captors to come and rescue me.

Laurent watched me with an expression of interest as he nudged the horse so it followed my painfully slow progress. I wanted to get up and run, but my legs refused to obey and stand up. He made no move to get off his horse and neither did any of the others, which somehow frightened me even more.

'Bella, this is not a very polite way to behave. Especially after all the extra work you've created for me. Did I not tell you to remain in Algiers?'

'Don't come near me! You — you

253

murderer!' I was screaming at the top of my lungs now, but still none of the Tuareg stirred and at the back of my mind, I knew this was a bad situation.

'Murderer?' Laurent frowned, as he swung one leg over the back of the horse and jumped down nimbly. 'Who have I murdered?'

'I — I — someone in France, although I don't know who,' I said, still backing away. 'I've heard about you. You're a notorious brigand who kills for money, but you won't get anything from me.'

Laurent smiled. 'Ah. I see Monsieur Bennett has been talking.'

'Yes, he has. And he told us all about you. And we know you tried to kill us.'

He had come closer to me now, but, as he held out the reins of his horse to one of his men, he stopped and looked at me in surprise.

'I tried to kill you? Why would I do that?'

'Because you want the Dragonsheart.'

'The Dragonsheart?' He shrugged his shoulders carelessly. 'I already have that.'

'What!' I stared at him. He had said this in such a casual manner that, for a moment, I forgot to be frightened. 'What do you mean, you've got the Dragonsheart?'

He shrugged again. 'I got it in London.

Many months ago. Don't worry; it is quite safe,' he added, holding out a hand to help me up.

'Safe? With you? What an absurd thing to say.' I looked at his outstretched hand in disgust and finally got myself up on to my feet. 'Why should a precious diamond be safe with a thief and a murderer like you?'

The mildly amused expression faded from his face and he frowned again. 'You keep saying that. Why do you think I wish to hurt you?'

'Because you've stolen my property; you sent people to murder Peter in London and, no doubt, sent these dreadful savages to do the same here. That's why.'

Laurent considered this. 'Very well,' he said eventually. 'Perhaps I can see why you might think I wanted to hurt Monsieur Bennett. Actually I did order the attack on him.' He smiled at me wickedly. 'And it did not cause me any anguish at all, although I had no intention of having him murdered. But I did not steal your diamond and I did not send these people to abduct you. On the contrary, I have had to spend a great deal more effort and money finding you.'

'Do you really expect me to believe that?'

'Of course.'

'Well, I don't. For a start poor Peter is lying

255

in there, probably dead because of all the — '

'I doubt that very much, *chèrie*, unless poor Peter has the appetite of a horse.'

'What?'

'Unless he ate so much this evening that his stomach is about to burst he will suffer no worse than a bad headache. Come, let me show you. Alain,' he added to one of the men on the horses and then he spoke in rapid French, before moving towards my little tent. He pushed the sleeping Tuareg guard to one side as he entered.

'Wait a moment,' I shouted, following him in. 'You can't come in here.'

Laurent crouched down beside Peter. 'Why not?' he asked with interest.

'Because I say so.'

He laughed. 'I thought you wanted me to help him,' he said, taking Peter's chin in his hand and turning it briefly before pulling up his eyelids to inspect his eyes. I knelt down beside him and pushed his hand away.

'I don't want you to do anything,' I snapped.

'Really? You don't want me to wake him up?' He shrugged his shoulders and stood up. 'Very well.'

As I knelt there, with Peter unconscious beside me, I very desperately wanted to kick Laurent. But practicality has a nasty habit of

256

rearing its ugly head at the most unwelcome moments and I was worried about Peter.

'Can you really wake him up?' I asked, as I stroked Peter's darkred hair.

'Of course, *chèrie*. All you have to do is ask.'

'You promise you won't hurt him.'

'I will be as gentle as a lamb,' he replied innocently.

The innocence should have warned me, but I was desperate so I nodded.

'Very well.'

He beamed at me and pulled an animal-skin water bottle out from under his white robes. Grabbing my arm, he briskly pulled me back before upending the bottle over Peter's face. The water splashed out in a torrent, soaking his hair and most of his shirt, but it appeared to be working because Peter began coming to, waving his arms about ineffectually and trying feebly to roll away from the cascade.

'Stop it!' I yelled, as Peter's eyes fluttered open. Laurent sighed and lifted the bottle the right way up again.

'If you think this impresses me, Laurent, you're very much mistaken,' I said angrily, as I knelt down beside Peter. 'You're behaving like a brute.'

'I don't understand, *ma chère*. I woke him

up for you, did I not? And I used almost a whole bottle of precious water on him. What more can I do to prove my good faith?' But there was a wicked gleam in his eyes as he regarded poor sodden Peter.

I ignored him. 'Peter, are you all right? Please wake up!'

Peter continued to cough for a few more minutes. Eventually he pushed himself up and stared at me blearily.

'What the hell are you trying to do, drown me?'

Laurent crouched down again a little way away from us both.

'No, it was I, Monsieur Bennett.'

Peter turned, frowning, blinking several times as though he couldn't believe his eyes. I knew the feeling.

'You!' he said, realizing who he was seeing. 'How did you get here?'

He tried to get up, but he was still too groggy, so he contented himself with sitting upright and pushing me behind him. Laurent seemed to find this amusing.

'Very chivalrous, Monsieur Bennett. You know I might grow to like you, yet.'

Peter, meanwhile, rubbed at his head. 'Oh God, I feel like I've got the most appalling hangover. We didn't drink anything last night, did we?'

I shook my head.

'Only the mint tea. And you ate quite a lot of that — ' Suddenly I remembered what Laurent had said about Peter's appetite. I turned round to see him watching us both, an innocent look on his face.

'What did you put in the food? It *was* you, wasn't it? Oh it's just the sort of devious, unpleasant thing I can see you doing. *He* drugged the food,' I added, pointing to Laurent. 'Don't try to deny it.'

'Certainly I will not deny it, *ma belle*.' Laurent held out his hands, palms up. 'It was the easiest and simplest way of getting you back from the Tuareg.'

'How did you — wait a minute.' Peter frowned. '*You* were the rider who visited them last night, weren't you? It was you.'

'Yes. I posed as a trader and distracted their attention whilst one of my *confrères* drugged their food and water. It was not hard.' He said this modestly as though one of us had just congratulated him.

Peter's frown deepened. 'But I only saw you. There was no one else.'

'You did not see any one else, Monsieur Bennett, because we did not wish you or the Tuareg to see anyone else.' He shrugged. 'Although they were distracted anyway, once I'd told them about you hiding in the dunes.'

'You did what!' Both Peter and I glared at Laurent who merely smiled at our outrage.

'I needed them to accept me as an ally, not an enemy. Telling them about Monsieur Bennett, casually, so it seemed innocent, was the best way of achieving that. It also meant I knew where you both were, so I didn't have to waste men keeping an eye on both of you.' He beamed at Peter. 'I also enjoyed knowing you were in some discomfort.'

'Oh did you?' Peter's eyes narrowed as he tried to push himself up, but he was still too weak from the drugs and the general abuse his body had taken over the past few weeks and he collapsed again.

'Gently, Monsieur Bennett,' said Laurent. 'You must rest. You know, you really should have stayed in Sicily.'

'In Sicily?' Peter's eyes narrowed. 'I suppose I've got you to thank for that too, haven't I?'

Laurent nodded.

'What are you talking about?' I said.

Peter turned to me. 'You remember me telling you I got thrown into jail in Sicily?'

'Vaguely. Why?'

'Well, that was the work of your dear cousin too, by the look of things. Let me guess — you've got friends there.'

'Many, Monsieur Bennett. I am a very

260

amiable person. For example, even though you were intending to tell Bella some, let us say, less than flattering tales about me, I still arranged for you to have a comfortable cell in the local prison, until I could speak to her myself.'

'Comfortable!' Peter's glare got darker. 'It stank. And it was crawling with rats.'

'Well, I couldn't arrange it straightaway,' said Laurent, with a semblance of regret, but the wicked gleam in his eyes had returned. 'Anyway, you escaped. Which, by the way, impressed me, Monsieur Bennett. Well done. I had not expected you to be so resourceful.'

'Oh really. Thank you so much. And I hadn't expected you to be so devious and underhanded and morally bankrupt and — '

'Yes, I get the point, *monsieur*.'

'I'm sure you do. Is there anything to drink in here? Anything that isn't drugged, that is.'

Laurent stood up. 'I used up all my own water awakening you. No matter. I will fetch some more. Unless you would like something a little stronger?' As he said this he pulled a silver whisky flask out from beneath his robes. Peter glared at him.

'I'd rather die than drink with you,' he said with dignity. Laurent just shrugged.

'Very well. Wait here.' And he disappeared out through the tentflap.

'Do you feel a little sick?' I asked gently, crawling closer to him. He nodded.

'If I drink anything stronger than water I may be sick,' he confessed, hanging his head and taking deep breaths. He looked deathly white again.

'Never mind. It'll pass. And you sounded very brave,' I said. He smiled weakly.

'Thanks. If only I had some strength in my legs. I don't know how long — ' Suddenly he stopped and looked at me. 'You feel all right, don't you?'

I nodded. 'I hardly ate anything last night and only drank a little of that tea. I felt a bit groggy before, but it's passing now.'

'Good. If you get any chance, any chance at all, Bella, you must try to escape. I can — '

'Don't be ridiculous, I'm not leaving you here on your own. Either we go together or we don't go at all.'

'Bella, you must! You're in much better shape than I am and it's obviously you he wants. He won't — '

'Exactly. It's me he's interested in. I can't possibly leave you alone. Besides, I don't think he wants to hurt either of us.'

'Oh really? Did you not hear any of that explanation earlier? He had me thrown into a prison in Sicily and then he told the Tuareg about me, and there was no guarantee they wouldn't have killed me, you know — '

'Yes, but they didn't, Peter,' I said, urgently now as I could hear sounds from outside, rapid, incomprehensible French which meant Laurent was nearby again. 'And he's admitted he's got the Dragonsheart — '

'He's got the diamond?' Peter's voice also dropped to an excited whisper.

'Yes! And he didn't even seem that bothered. It was as though it wasn't what he was really here for. And he did seem genuinely surprised at the idea that I thought he wanted to kill us. Well, kill *me* anyway. I suppose he didn't seem that worried about you.'

'Oh wonderful!' said Peter sarcastically. 'Suddenly I feel so much safer.'

'He did say he was going to get you a comfortable cell,' I muttered feebly.

Peter gave me a withering glare. 'And you believe him?' he hissed, as soft footfalls came nearer the tent.

'No, of course not,' I hissed back. 'But — ' Before I could continue, however, Laurent returned, bending through the tentflap once more.

'Here, *monsieur*,' he said, handing a water-bottle to Peter. Peter just stared at it. Laurent sighed and shook it before putting it to his own lips and taking a long swallow.

'*Voilà, monsieur*. Now if it is drugged, so am I and very soon you will be able to overpower me and escape.'

'I'm sure. No doubt your men outside are ready for any such attempts on our part.'

Laurent merely shrugged as he sat down crosslegged on the carpet near to us, then offered the water bottle to Peter again. This time Peter took it. After several deep mouthfuls, he handed it back to Laurent and, as he reached across, I saw a gun tucked into his belt. I shivered.

'*Eh bien, mes enfants*, it pains me that you think yourselves prisoners,' said Laurent. 'After I have gone to such lengths to help you. Now we should talk seriously, should we not?'

Peter laughed curtly. 'Yes, let's. Shall we start with how interested the *gendarmerie* in Paris are in you? Especially Commissaire Fréret.'

'Ah, Monsieur le Commissaire Fréret,' said Laurent happily. 'How is he? Has he recovered from the leg wound yet?'

Peter ignored the question. 'He said that under no circumstances should you be trusted or even approached. In fact, according to the records in the thirteenth *arrondissement*, you are considered a dangerous criminal.'

Laurent shrugged again, unconcerned. 'We French like to overdramatize. I wouldn't worry about Monsieur Fréret. He's still angry with me for getting — but I am becoming distracted; forgive me. So, Bella, now we must discuss our family.'

I glared at him. 'You're not my cousin, are you?'

'No, I am not.'

'Who are you then? What's your real name?'

He laughed softly. 'My name really is Laurent Marivaux, *chèrie* and I am the grandson of Evelyn Woodruffe. All that was true.' He paused for a moment. 'Do you remember asking me once if I had a picture of my sister?' he asked, as he reached inside his robes. Peter flinched and started to draw me back, making Laurent glance up. I was surprised to see real sadness in his eyes as he realized why.

'Do not fear, Monsieur Bennett. It is merely a photograph.'

I frowned. 'A photograph of your sister?'

'Yes. Look.'

He turned the photograph round so we could see it properly. It was faded, the sepia bleeding yellow and brown into the surrounding cardboard and for a moment, it was hard to take in the entire image. Peter gave a gasp of surprise and for a few seconds I wondered why. Then I saw it too.

'This is your sister?' Peter glared at Laurent, who nodded.

'*Oui, monsieur.*'

'It's old enough, it can't be — ' He looked over at me. 'She's the very image of you, Bella.'

And she was. It was so obvious that if she hadn't been wearing a hopelessly old-fashioned bustle dress I would have thought it was a picture of me.

'Actually, it would be fairer to say Bella is the image of her, don't you think, Monsieur Bennett?' said Laurent gently, but he was looking at me as he said this.

'Well she's very — I mean, the family resemblance is very strong — I didn't realize — ' I was babbling, trying to ignore what logic insisted was the case, but just *couldn't* be true.

Laurent meanwhile was shaking his head. 'I am sorry that this upsets you *chèrie*, but it is the truth. I am not your cousin: I am your uncle. And my sister Agnès was your mother.'

'No! My mother was Amelia Wyndham-Brown. That woman is just some French girl my parents brought with them when they came here.' But even as I said the words, I remembered my father's odd behaviour just before he left, selling off his watch and other jewellery, the pawnbroker's insistence that he was bringing his mistress with him on the trip to humiliate my mother, the entry in his diary: 'A grows sicker every day'. 'A' didn't stand for Amelia, it was for Agnès! I felt the blood rush to my face and then leave again almost as quickly and I was utterly sick to my stomach.

'This isn't true. It can't be,' I wailed, but looking at Peter's face as well as Laurent's I knew it was. 'So this . . . this *strumpet* who made my mother's life unbearable, who humiliated her beyond decency, who behaved like a — a — '

'*Sois sage, chèrie,*' warned Laurent. 'I know this is a shock to you, but she was my beloved sister.'

'So I see. The family resemblance is uncanny,' I said unpleasantly. 'And so my poor mother had to bring this little — but wait a moment, she's not my mother, is she? Poor Amelia, who had to watch her pretty little French cousin seduce her husband and then bring her along on this godforsaken trip isn't my mother at all. She is.' I pointed to Agnès's picture; then in a rage I picked it up and ripped it to shreds before running out of the tent and into the heat of the early morning sun. I heard shouts behind me, loud

267

declamations in French, but I ignored them all and ran as fast as I could away from the camp, away from Laurent, away from everything.

I didn't get very far. It was too hot, even so early in the morning and there was absolutely no shade at all, just miles and miles of dry, dirty yellow sand and the fearsome heat baking everything it touched. For a while I just sat where I had dropped far enough away from the camp so that I could no longer hear any voices. I didn't think; I did my very best not to think because then I would have to start considering things that were abhorrent to me. I just sat and breathed deeply, concentrating on not crying. For some reason I had decided it was very important I did not cry.

After a while I heard noises and turned around. Walking slowly towards me, his feet sinking deeply into the dunes, was Peter.

'Go away,' I said, but he ignored me and carried on walking. Finally he reached me and sat down beside me in the sand.

'Go away. I don't want to talk to anyone.'

'Don't be foolish, Bella, you'll cook out here.'

'I don't care.'

'Well, I do. We do,' he added, and I looked at him, my eyes narrowing.

'We? Would that be you and my newly discovered, notorious uncle, brother to that little French whore whose bas — '

'Bella, don't,' he said quietly, and I stopped, putting my hand up to my mouth. He waited a while before taking my other hand in his.

'You don't have to talk to anyone if you don't want to, not even Laurent. He's promised to take us back to Ghardaia immediately.'

'Has he? How nice of him. What a wonderful uncle I now have in place of Uncle Charles and Uncle Geoffrey and — ' Suddenly I couldn't bear it any longer. The thought that Uncle Charles and Uncle Geoffrey weren't my uncles any more and Mama wasn't even my mother suddenly seemed to rear up out of nowhere and hit me squarely in the pit of my stomach and I turned to Peter and bawled my eyes out like a little girl.

He held me in his arms and patted my shoulders gently, whispering nonsense at me, waiting for the storm to pass. Finally I had no more tears left.

'I can't believe it, Peter. I just can't,' I croaked, my voice hoarse from all the crying. 'It can't be true. How can I be the daughter of — of — perhaps there's been a mistake.' I

269

looked up at Peter as I said this, but he shook his head gently.

'You — er — Laurent showed me a picture of — er — Lady Bowood. You really don't look at all like her, do you? He said he had other evidence which had convinced him of who you are. And anyway, Agnès was very pretty. Like you. And Amelia' — he paused and cleared his throat — 'she wasn't really, was she?'

I thought back to the photograph of my parents — or at least the people I thought were my parents — in my bedroom at home in Woodruffe Hall. Poor Amelia, as I must now start thinking of her, was a clever woman with much better business sense than amusing, charming Papa, but no, she was not pretty at all. And Agnès was.

'She may not have been pretty,' I said tartly, 'but handsome is as handsome does, as one of my old governesses used to say. And it appears neither of my parents — my real parents — behaved very handsomely at all.'

Peter sighed and pulled me close again. 'They did what they did, Bella. It wasn't your fault. And I think we can all agree they paid for it.'

I sighed as well before dabbing the last of the tears away. My mouth felt dry now as it always does when one has cried and the heat and dusty desert wasn't helping at all. I stood up.

'Shall we go back?'

'Oh — er — of course. If you're up to it,' said Peter, getting up as well. 'You're sure you want to?'

I nodded. 'I'm thirsty. And sitting out here, as you pointed out, isn't going to solve anything. And I'm feeling calmer now, thanks to you.' I put a hand through his arm and smiled at him.

'Not at all. You really don't have anything to feel bad about, you know. None of this was your fault.'

'No,' I sighed. 'But it's going to make a lot of difference to my life from now on. In which case, I suppose I had better go and get better acquainted with my new uncle. How was he when you left him?'

'Upset . . . for you,' Peter admitted grudgingly. 'He's probably not as bad as that *commissaire* chap in Paris made out. Although I wouldn't go calling his sister a strumpet again. I got the impression he was very fond of her. He's certainly very protective of her memory.'

As we walked back to the camp a voice called out, '*Mademoiselle*?' and I turned round and saw the fellow Laurent had called Alain. He was of middling height, in his late thirties with deeply tanned skin and black hair that was going grey around the temples. Like all the other men Laurent had brought with him he wore the swirling white robes which reflected heat and kept the sand at bay.

'*Monsieur?*' I said coolly.

'*Le capitaine est là-bas.* Over there,' he added in heavily accented English, pointing to a large tent near the edge of the camp. '*Venez vite, mademoiselle. Il vous attend.*'

Peter raised his eyebrows at me. 'Apparently your uncle is waiting for us. Do you get the impression we shouldn't dawdle?'

Ignoring his ironic stare, I picked up the skirts of my robes and walked towards the tent. As we reached it, I heard the sound of someone being beaten and howls of pain. Glancing quickly at Peter I tried to push my way inside, but found it was barred by several guards.

'Let me pass, please,' I said, but the two nearest the opening just grinned at me and held me at bay as though I was a child. There was something very unpleasant about their manner as though they were used to making people do things against their will and they enjoyed the sensation. But before the exchange could get any nastier, a voice snapped something and they let me go and came smartly to attention.

'Bella, *ma chère*. You are back.' Laurent appeared at the opening and taking my arm, gently but firmly propelled me through to the outside again. 'Are we friends? Have you forgiven me?'

He smiled at me in a relaxed way, oblivious to the reddened flesh on his knuckles. I tried to ignore them, too.

'There's nothing to forgive, Laurent, although I have to say I really wish that you were just a distant cousin and that — Agnès and Papa hadn't done what they did.'

He nodded. '*Eh bien*. Let us just say that no one behaved as they should have done and leave it at that. Now' — he continued to walk me away from the tent and we caught up with Peter who was hovering nearby, gazing idly at the packs on Laurent's horses — 'we still have much to talk about you and I, but it must wait. There is some business I must take care of here. I have instructed Alain to take you and Monsieur Bennett back to Algiers and I would be obliged if you would wait for me there — without leaving this time,' he added, grinning. 'Alain speaks some English, and he will look after you well in my absence. *N'est-ce pas, mon vieux*,' he added to the man who had walked up to us again.

'*Oui, mon capitaine*,' the man said. They began speaking in French to one another and then Alain walked away, beckoning us to follow him.

'Go, *ma petite*; you have a long journey and it is best to travel whilst the sun is still low in the sky. I will be back as soon as I can.' He took me by both arms and moved as if to kiss me, but I backed away.

'Yes; just a moment, Laurent. Why aren't you coming too?'

'I told you, *chèrie*. I have business to attend to.'

'Really? And would that business be something to do with those people in that tent there?' I looked down at the bruises on his knuckles.

A slight frown passed over his face. 'It is not for you to concern yourself with, Bella. You must do as I ask now, please.'

I pushed his hands away from my arms. 'Actually I think it is something for me to concern myself with, Laurent. After all I'm the one they abducted.'

'Nevertheless you must — '

'And since I'm the one they abducted and now they're the ones in captivity, I think I'm entitled to know why they did it, don't you?' As I said this, I began walking back to the tent again, only to find my way suddenly blocked by a group of burly Frenchmen. I turned round to see Laurent looking at me, no longer amused or indulgent. The cruel spark had returned to his eyes and it occurred to me that I did not really know this man very well at all.

'Go. Now, Bella.'

'Why? Because you don't want me to see you beat and torture those men?'

'No.' He moved closer to me, his eyes dark. 'Because I say so.'

'Do you? And is that how — ?'

'You know I've just realized something,' said Peter suddenly, positioning himself between us.

'What is it you have realized, Monsieur Bennett?' asked Laurent calmly, never taking his eyes off me.

'These men you brought with you — they're all legionnaires, aren't they? The French Foreign Legion?'

'Yes.'

'Hmm. The French Foreign Legion, eh,' said Peter, in the same chatty way. 'You wouldn't want to argue with them, Bella. They've a fearsome reputation.'

'It is a reputation well deserved, *monsieur*.' Laurent's lips barely moved.

'Right. Right. And if they're legionnaires and they keep calling you 'sir' and '*capitaine*', is it? That must make you — '

Laurent's eyes left mine for the first time

and moved to regard Peter, which I suddenly didn't want at all. I was Laurent's niece after all — Peter had no such protection.

'Ex-legionnaire, Monsieur Bennett. I am retired now.'

'Ah.' Peter nodded slowly, then turned to me. 'You know, Bella, if your uncle really wants us to go, then I think we should do just that. Any man who makes commissioned officer in the French Foreign Legion probably knows what he's talking about and who are we to question him?'

For the first time, the blank look left Laurent's eyes and he seemed to come to life again. He looked back at me in confusion. But before he could say anything, there was a shout from the tent and a legionnaire appeared, waving for Laurent. He glanced back at us briefly.

'I have to speak to my sergeant. Stay here. Please,' he added to me and slowly I nodded. We watched him run back to the tent and disappear inside it.

'His sergeant, eh? I thought he said he was retired. Pity we can't ask any of these others here.'

I looked around at the men Laurent had brought with him, seeing them properly for the first time. They still wore the white desert robes, but with the face coverings down it was obvious they were all soldiers, with the strong sinewy bodies of fighters, their faces all burnt by the pitiless African sun, youngish faces like Alain's but with hair going prematurely grey. Most of them had scars either on their faces or arms and I remembered the long white mark on Laurent's arm now and wondered where he had really got it. A childhood riding accident no longer seemed plausible.

'How did you know they were legionnaires?' I asked, stepping closer to Peter. He shrugged.

'I thought I recognized a remnant of uniform one of them was wearing earlier on, but I wasn't sure.' He looked at me intently. 'They really do have the most filthy reputation, Bella. Not the sort of people you argue with.'

I raised an eyebrow. 'Even Laurent?'

'Especially him.' He turned and looked back at the tent; it was eerily quiet now. 'That veneer of sophistication he's got is rubbing off fairly fast I'd say.'

I frowned. 'What do you mean?'

'I mean any civilized manners he's relearnt since being retired are losing ground.' He squinted as a tent flap blew lazily in the minutest wind. 'I think Uncle Laurent is starting to remember all the fun he had in the Legion. That's why I thought it might be better for all of us if he was reminded that non-civilians don't always appreciate being ordered around — especially when they're also new nieces.'

I moved closer to him and put my arm through his. 'I'm so glad you're on my side, Peter.'

'I'm always on your side, Bella,' he said seriously, taking my hand in his. 'Although to be honest, I'd quite like to keep Uncle Laurent on our side too. Just because he's got the morals of a tiger on the prowl doesn't mean he isn't a good ally to have. The Tuareg don't exactly lead the world in good works either. Apparently one of their commercial successes is in slave-trading.'

Just then the tent-flap opened up and Laurent came out again. He barked a few orders to the men lounging nearby and they got up and walked down to the oasis where they began filling water-skins.

'Bella, you said you wanted to speak to the Tuareg. Now is your chance. Come with me. You too, *monsieur*.' He beckoned Peter to follow.

'Why? Aren't your methods working then?' I asked rather unpleasantly, as we trotted behind him. I still couldn't forget the blank look in his eyes when I had refused to obey him. He stopped and turned around.

278

'You think I am a thug?'

'Yes,' I said. 'I do actually.' From the corner of my eye I could see Peter flinching, but I didn't care. Laurent, however, just grinned at this.

'*Bravo, mon ange*. There should be honesty between relatives. I believe Monsieur Bennett here, he thinks I am a thug, too. He thinks I am intending to slaughter these natives like animals because they took something of mine. So do my *confrères*. And I have to admit, *chèrie*,' he nodded, as we reached the opening to the tent — 'the idea had occurred to me. But I have not acted on it yet. I am curious as to why they took you alone and not your friends as well.'

'Yes, I was wondering that, too,' admitted Peter. Laurent favoured him with a dry look.

'No doubt, Monsieur Bennett. It is an interesting situation, is it not? Why would the Tuareg, who are well-known for their practice of abducting and selling people into slavery waste so much time and expense transporting just one woman across the desert, when they could have taken two and made themselves twice as much. The problem is they won't tell me. Or any of my colleagues, despite our best persuasions. They insist they will only speak to you. So, *mon ange*, are you ready to talk to your captors?'

He pulled up the tent-flap and I smelt the sharp metallic odour of blood. I stepped back.

'You don't have to, if you don't want to, *ma chère*,' he said softly. 'They will tell me eventually.'

I stared at him. 'Laurent, what exactly did you mean when you said 'they took something of mine?''

He burst out laughing and walked in. After a few seconds, Peter and I followed him.

12

Inside the smell was awful. All the Tuareg were sitting huddled in a corner, their uncovered faces caked with dirt and vomit and dried blood. Their blue robes were ripped and torn from their bodies and several of them were unconscious. I had a feeling they were the lucky ones. Surrounding them were several of the legionnaires, all holding rifles.

'My God,' I whispered to Peter, as we walked into this little hell.

Peter gripped my hand. 'Keep steady, my love. None of them is dead. Yet.'

Sitting some way away from the others, tied with his hands behind his back to a central post, was an older man. He seemed familiar and I realized he was the one who had tried to communicate with me yesterday. Without his face-covering, I could see he was about forty or fifty with greying black hair. He was not as dark-skinned as most Algerians — in fact all the Tuareg were lighter-skinned than I had expected. He looked at me briefly then noticed Laurent standing nearby. With great effort he managed to spit at him.

I must have jumped; I was not expecting such a poisonous display of dislike, but Laurent merely grinned.

'It might have taken Monsieur Bennett several hours to recognize who we are, but the blue men spotted us in seconds.'

I turned from my former captor to my uncle. 'They don't seem to like you very much.'

'They have good reason not to,' he answered grimly, but said no more and I did not press him. I didn't really want to know.

The man looked across at me and began speaking, slowly and in obvious pain. He was still using the same heavily accented French as before and I shook my head, as I stepped closer to him. The smell of sweat and blood was stronger and despite the fact he had been responsible for kidnapping me and causing me a great deal of fear, I couldn't help wishing he was not tied up and in such discomfort. After all, they had treated me a lot more gently.

'I'm sorry, I don't understand you.' I looked over at Laurent. 'Haven't you explained that I don't speak French.'

'I have, *mon ange*, but for some reason he doesn't believe me.' He shrugged sardonically, then looked at both me and Peter. 'I know neither of you speak French and I realize Arabic is out of the question, but is there any chance either of you speak German? Even a little bit?'

We both shook our heads and he gave a grunt of disgust. Peter frowned.

'You mean they know French and German but not English?' he asked in amazement.

'For some reason they don't think it is an important language to learn,' Laurent said drily. 'What can they be thinking of?'

I turned to the Tuareg. 'I'm sorry, *monsieur*,' I shouted. 'I really don't understand French.'

'Bella, *ma chère*, I appreciate the effort, but if he does not understand English, how is shouting at him in it going to help?'

I scowled at him and tried again. '*Monsieur, je ne parle pas français*. Only *anglais*. Really.'

At this the Tuareg turned to Laurent and said something. Obviously I couldn't understand the words but there was no mistaking the incredulity in his voice. Laurent just shrugged and the man looked back at me with disbelief.

'Oh for heaven's sake. Laurent, you'll have to make him understand he's got to talk to you and you'll translate. What's his name?'

'His name?' Laurent looked surprised, but he spat a few words at the Tuareg, who replied equally brusquely.

'He says his name is Ishmail.'

'Monsieur Ishmail, why did you bring me here? What do you want?'

The silence in the tent seemed to grow and swell. Then finally Ishmail nodded stiffly and began to speak, Laurent responding angrily to his words. He scowled as he turned back to us.

'He says he cannot give you an answer. It is not for him to reveal the purpose of his mission. That is for someone else to do — someone he calls the Foreigner. But he asks you to go with them. Apparently they regret the necessity of abducting you,' he added with heavy irony.

'What else did he say?'

'Nothing,' he snapped, throwing his hands in the air impatiently. 'Come. You will get no more intelligence from this savage.'

'Wait. Wait. All right.' I rubbed my hands together nervously. 'Tell him I'll come.'

'*Quoi*?' Laurent looked at me in horror. 'Absolutely not. You will not go with him anywhere.'

'Yes I will,' I began angrily, when Peter interrupted.

'Ah listen, Bella,' he said, taking my arms in his hands. 'That really isn't a good idea.'

'No, it is not,' Laurent barked. 'And you

284

will not even entertain it. These people are savages — if they even think — '

'Oh really?' I said, pulling away from Peter. 'And you're the image of civilized society are you? So why is it I was treated with respect, fed with the best they had and given my own place to sleep while these men now lie here, half dead? Tell me again exactly who is the savage here, Laurent, because I'm a little confused.' I stared at him with contempt, but he shook his head.

'So you think they treated you well because they respect you? Because you are too *sympathique* to be sold into slavery?' He gave a snort of laughter. 'Don't be so naive, *ma chère*. They kept you well because a woman in good condition sells better. And I have come a long way to find you. I have no intention of letting you go now.'

'He's right, Bella,' Peter insisted more gently. 'It would be madness to go with these people. I'm glad they didn't hurt you, but they *did* attack us. Remember what happened to Adam. You can't possibly trust them.'

'Listen to him, *chèrie*,' said Laurent, in a more honeyed voice. 'These people have no interest in you except as merchandise. Anything they say is just trickery — lies to steal you away.'

I looked at Peter and Laurent, their faces

creased with concern for me and I knew they were both right. Going with the Tuareg, voluntarily, was madness. And yet . . . there was something inside of me, some tiny voice, barely audible, telling me I should trust Ishmail, that I might just learn something important.

'I want to go anyway. Listen,' I insisted, as they both started to speak at once 'I know what you're saying, both of you, is right. They probably are all you say and I'm not completely stupid, Laurent, despite what you might think. I do realize that if they'd known who you were last night you'd be the one slumped against that post all bloodied and bruised now, not Monsieur Ishmail. But think for a moment: why is it they took only me? You said it yourself, Laurent, if it was for slavery alone they could have taken Kate as well and made twice the profit. There must be another reason for them taking only me.'

Laurent frowned and opened his mouth to speak, but I didn't give him the chance. Crouching down to Ishmail again, I dredged up the only French I'd ever learnt at school.

'*Monsieur, mon nom? Vous savez?* What's my name?'

The man looked at me through bloodshot eyes, but smiled faintly as he nodded. 'Windabrow,' he said, faintly.

'There! He knows my name,' I said triumphantly. 'Why would he know my name if he was just stealing me to become a slave? There must be another reason why he was sent here for me.'

Laurent stared at Ishamil. 'Very well. He knows your name. I grant you that it is unusual but what difference does it make? You still have no guarantee that you will be safe with them.'

'It's a good point, Bella,' Peter agreed. I frowned.

'I don't care,' I said. 'I'm going with them whether you like it or not. Untie him, Laurent. I'll take my chances.'

'Don't be ridiculous.' Laurent snapped something at one of his legionnaires and walked out of the tent without another word to Peter or me. I ran after him.

'Wait a moment, you can't just give me orders; I'm not one of your horrible soldiers,' I said. 'I don't care whether you agree or not, I'm not asking your permission. I'm going on with Ishmail and his men.'

Laurent turned to me. 'How?'

'What?' This wasn't the response I'd been expecting.

'How?' he asked again, in a tone of sweet reason. 'I am not inclined to let the Tuareg go after their offence to me and it is I who command these men, not you. In fact, *ma chère*, I can order Alain to put you on a horse right now, tie you to it if necessary, and Monsieur Bennett as well and there is nothing you can do about it. And by the way, Monsieur Bennett, your gun has no bullets, so there is no point aiming at me or my men.'

I turned to see Peter staring at a small pistol in his right hand. He frowned and checked the barrel, swearing in disgust as he shook it and realized it was indeed empty, before turning back to Laurent who just shrugged.

'You had a gun!' I shrieked at Peter. 'How long have you had that?'

'Well, of course I've got a gun,' he snapped irritably. 'This is a dangerous place. Although having one that actually works is always a bonus,' he added, glaring at Laurent.

'You are safe with me, Monsieur Bennett.'

'That's such a relief.'

'Never mind that,' I interrupted. 'Don't you dare tell me what I can and can't do. Release those men in there immediately and let us be on our way.'

Laurent looked down at me in disdain for a moment, then said something briskly to Alain, who was standing nearby. I was prepared however, which is more than can be said for Alain. As he walked up to me, with a most unpleasant grin on his face, I kicked him smartly on the shin. The look of agony on his face was very gratifying.

'Bella, you have just kicked Alain,' said Laurent in surprise as Alain hopped about the sand, screaming in pain and the rest of the legionnaires laughed at him.

'I know. It must be the savage in me coming out,' I snarled. 'I wonder which side of the family I get it from.'

Laurent smiled at this as he walked back towards me. Suddenly he swooped down and picking me up, threw me across his shoulder.

'Let me go!' I yelled, as he walked over to the nearest horse and slung me across the saddle. 'I want to go with the Tuareg. You have no right to — '

'Forgive me, *ma chère*. But you are going back to Algiers. When I have attended to these people then I will follow you and we will — '

'I am not going back to Algiers,' I shouted, trying desperately to free myself from his grip. 'And certainly not with that oaf Alain. Let me down immediately.'

'You are very spoiled, do you know that,' said Laurent calmly, as he tied me to the saddle. 'You cannot have everything you want just because you demand it. Monsieur Bennett, are you going to get on your horse sensibly, or should I instruct my men to have you restrained as well?'

'Well, if you'd just stop and listen for a minute — ' Peter began.

'Leave him alone,' I yelled, from the undignified position of my head hanging down on a level with the horse's belly. 'You are a brute and a savage and — '

'I may well be all those things, *ma petite*, but you are still going back to — '

'Could you both stop and — '

'I refuse to believe I'm related to you, Laurent Marivaux,' I spat as he continued inexorably to tie me even more tightly to the saddle. 'You have no manners; you think you can order everyone around; you have — '

'Actually I can order you around. At the moment anyway. Later on perhaps when we return to Europe, I will have to ask your forgiveness for this behaviour, but for the moment, there is nothing you can do about this so you will just have to — '

'Shut up!'

Peter's roar was so loud, it not only stopped Laurent and me from arguing, it attracted the attention of all the other legionnaires and made one of the camels bellow in surprise.

'I'm sure this dispute is very entertaining for all your men and I have to say the family ressemblance is very strong at the moment, but have neither of you ever heard of the notion of compromise?'

'Compromise?' we both chorused.

'Compromise. Let her down, for God's sake Marivaux. She looks like she's going to be sick.'

Laurent frowned and looked at me briefly before pulling at the knots he had just tied.

'Thank you,' said Peter, as I slid back down on to my feet again. Laurent waved a hand irritably.

'What do you mean by compromise?'

Peter shielded his eyes as he looked back towards the tent where the Tuareg were still being held.

'Listen, Bella, he's right. You just can't go riding off with those men. It's suicide. You won't know how to get back even assuming they'll let you go and there is no guarantee you'll be allowed to leave. That Ishmail character might be sincere, but I doubt all the others will be prepared to be so reasonable, especially after what he and his men did to them — '

'What is your suggestion, Monsieur Bennett?' snapped Laurent.

'Let them go,' Peter said. 'Tell them we'll wait for them back at Ghardaia, or wherever you think is a reasonably safe place for us to meet. That way if they really do have some important information for Bella, they've got no excuse. They can make compromises too. If they're in earnest, they'll come. And admit it,' he added, turning to Laurent, 'aren't you the slightest bit curious about what they've got to say?'

Laurent stared at him for a long second, before turning to me. Slowly he nodded.

'Very well,' he said finally. 'Wait here.'

'Where are you going?' I shouted, as he walked back to the main tent again.

'To speak to my men, *chèrie*. To try to persuade them this time the Tuareg must leave unharmed.'

And without turning back he disappeared. I let out a deep sigh.

'Are you all right?' asked Peter. I nodded.

'Thank you,' I said, as I sank down rather shakily on to the sand.

He grinned. 'Someone's got to make sure you frogs listen to reason,' he said, as he sat down next to me.

'That's not funny.'

'Yes it is,' he said, putting an arm around me and pulling me close. I could feel his body shaking with laughter and soon I, too, was laughing.

Just before the Tuareg left — or rather were allowed to leave rather grudgingly by Laurent and his surly band of mercenaries or whatever they were — Ishmail came and found me. His face covering was back in place now, but I knew it was him; I don't think I would ever have trouble recognizing him again. He bowed from the waist, rather stiffly, his palms pressed together.

'Mademoiselle Windabrow.'

'Monsieur Ishmail.'

'Ghardaia. I will come. *Avec l'Étrangère,*' he said. I nodded.

'I will wait, *monsieur*. As long as it takes.'

He bowed again and turned back to his people. We watched until the line of camels ran off into the distance and disappeared over the horizon. Peter was right; they did go much faster than horses.

The journey back to Ghardaia did not take long. We waited until later in the afternoon when the sun was less ferocious and after filling the animal skins, set off.

Laurent and I did not speak much. I was still smarting from his cavalier behaviour towards me and I couldn't forget the brutal way he had treated the Tuareg. He, in his turn, seemed displeased by my contempt and he made no attempt to talk to me. Or perhaps he was too concerned with the disgust his legionnaires were clearly showing at having to let the Tuareg go without killing them.

We arrived at Ghardaia to discover we had missed Adam and Kate by only a few hours. Adam's injuries had improved a little and a passing caravan had agreed to take them back to Algiers where Kate felt he would get better medical attention. She had left me a heartbreaking note, apologizing for not waiting for me but pleading with me to understand that she was worried about Adam. Laurent, who had stopped at Ghardaia briefly, had been so helpful during the last few frightening hours before he went off in search of me that she couldn't help feeling we were in good hands. I felt horribly guilty at her words. How could I have led my two best friends into such dreadful danger? I prayed that Adam would be well soon.

We stayed in the same small hostel that they had recently vacated. The owner, a tiny, fat man bundled in dirty robes, could hardly contain his glee at having so many rich foreigners in his grasp and showed me into a bare, dingy room. I was exhausted by the long, uncomfortable journey in the heat and dust and just fell on to the hard, rather grubby mattress on the floor. I was asleep instantly.

When I woke up there were strange noises coming from somewhere and I sat in confusion for a few moments, trying to remember where I was. We had arrived at Ghardaia in the early evening and I remembered seeing the first few stars begin to twinkle in the gloom of the night. Now hot sunlight streamed in through the cracks in the dry wooden door. Donkeys brayed, dogs barked and people were shouting at each other very close by. I could also smell bread baking and there was the sizzle of frying meat coming from just beyond my doorway.

I stood up and opened the rather creaky wooden door gingerly; it seemed so ancient I feared it would fall from its hinges at any moment. Just beyond my room was a courtyard with the obligatory fountain, covered over with a fragile looking roof of branches from which it was possible to find some rather random shade. The fountain was cracked and neglected and the pots of shrivelled looking plants badly needed paint-ing again. A figure was slumped by the door on a dilapidated wicker chair, but jumped up at the noise.

'Bella?'

'Peter, is that you?'

He came over to me. 'How are you?'

I nodded. 'I'm fine. What time is it?'

'It's midday. You slept for nearly fifteen hours.'

I yawned. 'Are you all right?'

He smiled. 'I feel a lot better than I did. Are you hungry? I can get us some food. The legionnaires have made themselves at home in the bar and the owner of this place is very keen to keep them happy.' He frowned. 'I can't quite work out if it's because he likes the money they spend, or because he's frightened of them. A little of both probably. Anyway, the service is marvellous.'

I looked more closely at him. He was cleaner and his wounds had been dressed properly now.

'I'd love some food, but would it be possible to have some water brought to my room first? And some clean clothes?'

He grinned. 'No sooner said than done, *mademoiselle*,' And before I could say anything else he disappeared through the courtyard.

Soon a large bowl and a jug of warm water was delivered to my room by a pair of giggling, veiled girls. The jug was filled with jasmine petals which made the room smell divine and to my delight they brought some of my luggage as well. Apparently Hassan's assistants had not been able to make off with all our possessions.

After cleaning half the desert from myself and putting on a simple cotton blouse and riding skirt, I went outside to the covered courtyard. Peter was sitting at a rickety table filled with plates of food. There was flat bread, still warm from the oven, a colourful, spicy stew, couscous and even a few spikes of lamb kebab, as well as the inevitable tea. As I sat down opposite Peter, I noticed a small door opening out into the bar beyond our private courtyard where Laurent's little army had gathered to drink and smoke and play cards. I noticed they were all wearing red trousers and blue jackets.

'Thank you,' I said, as he passed me a plate filled with the vegetable stew. It smelled delicious, pungent with spices and herbs, oily pools swirling delicately around the rich red sauce.

'You look nice.'

'Thank you darling, so do you,' I said. He had taken off the desert robes and had on white trousers and shirt to reflect the sunlight. 'Tell me, is Laurent wearing the same as them?' I asked, as I pointed through the door.

Peter shook his head. 'No, he's retired, remember? But they're all dressed in uniform because they really are all legionnaires. They're all on leave as far as I can gather and joined him voluntarily on this jaunt for a bit of recreation. The uniform's to impress the locals. Strictly speaking they shouldn't be wearing it off-duty, although I doubt anyone will complain.'

I took a bite out of a piece of bread. 'Where is he?'

'Went off to feed the horses or something, I think. I had quite a long talk with him this morning actually.'

'Did you? How nice. What did you talk about?'

He must have noticed the rather brittle tone in my voice, because he glanced up at me briefly. 'Oh you know. The political situation out here, the heat, — er — '

'Me?'

'Not at all,' he said awkwardly. I frowned at him.

'Peter, for a private detective, you're a very poor liar at times.'

'No really — ' he began, but I threw my knife down and got up.

'Oh for heaven's sake, don't treat me like a fool,' I said, walking over to the little indoor pool with its broken fountain. He sighed.

'Very well, we talked about you. But I don't know what you're getting so upset about? What's so wrong with me talking to him?'

I stared at the faded patterns painted around the pool.

'Because you're beginning to like him and I don't want you to. And I know it's childish and ridiculous but that's how I feel. You're supposed to be on my side, remember?'

He got up and walked over to me. 'I *am* on your side, Bella. Always. But what would you have me do? Tell you what a rogue and a scoundrel he is? He's your uncle. Whether you like it or not. And she was your mother.'

'Thank you so much for reminding me. That's really helped.'

'No, that's not what I — damn it Bella, you always do this to me.'

'Do what?' I asked indignantly.

'Make me feel like a bumbling idiot.'

I smiled. 'Peter, you're terribly sweet. Have I ever told you that?'

'Yes,' he said rather snappily. 'It makes me sound like a puppy, which isn't very flattering.'

'I don't think of you as a puppy, Peter.'

'Really? How do you think of me then?'

We were very close now, probably too close in fact. I doubted Aunt Augusta would have approved, or Uncle Charles. Or Laurent either, come to that. The last thought made my mind up.

'Like this,' I said and pulling him closer still, we fell together against the faded stucco walls, our lips searching each other out, our hands working feverishly as we melted into each other. I had often wondered what this moment would be like and had discussed the time and place and manner of my first kiss with Harriet and Helen and all my other female cousins endlessly and innocently, but nothing could have prepared me for the aching sweetness that travelled up my belly like wildfire, leaving me breathless and aching for more.

'Ahem.'

For two pins I would happily have ignored the loud cough from the doorway, but Peter pulled back reluctantly and we both looked up to see Laurent standing there, an unfathomable expression on his face.

'Hello, Laurent,' I said, curtly.

He glanced briefly and none too amicably at Peter, but forbore to say anything. Instead he shrugged and moved into the dilapidated little courtyard.

'Good afternoon, Bella. Did you sleep well?'

'Very well, thank you.'

A painful silence ensured, which I felt no compunction to break. I still remembered the humiliating way he had thrown me across the horse.

'I am not interrupting anything, I trust?' he enquired, glaring at Peter.

'You know perfectly we — '

'Not at all,' said Peter. 'Do come in, old

chap. We were just finishing off a meal. Have you eaten?'

Laurent looked at us both, me glaring at Peter and Peter beaming effortlessly at him. Finally, with a shrug of the shoulders, he smiled.

'*Ah, les anglais*,' he said, walking across and sitting down rather gingerly on the cracked wall of the fountain. 'I came to see how you are, *ma chère* and to apologize for my behaviour yesterday.'

I went back to the table. 'Very well.'

'*Quoi?*' He looked confused.

'By all means apologize. You were horrible yesterday. I was very offended.'

'Bella — ' Peter began, but Laurent held up a hand.

'*Non*, do not, I beg of you, mediate between us again, Monsieur Bennett. If Bella and I are to become friends we cannot always rely on you to be on hand when we argue. As much as you would perhaps like to be,' he added somewhat drily. 'I apologize, *ma chère*. I am desolated that I behaved so badly towards you. It will not happen again.'

'Very handsomely done,' Peter said, joining me at the table. 'You have to admit, Bella, the French certainly know how to apologize. Cheers.' He held a cup of tea up in a brief salute. Laurent ignored him, instead searching through the pockets of his jacket and pulling out an envelope.

'Here. I have something for you. I have been carrying it around for the last five years, wondering when I would summon the courage to give it to you. I think it is now time.'

He passed it over to me and I took it, wondering what it might be. I pulled the fold back and a slip of yellowing, rather cracked parchment-like paper fell out. I turned it over and tried to read the writing, but it was written in an incredibly fancy, florid style and the ink had run in a few places. It was also in a foreign language.

'It is a record of your birth,' Laurent said, leaning closer to me. 'See, Agnès's name is here, and your papa, and see, there you are.'

I frowned as he pointed to various words. It was hard at first, but as I became used to the style, I made out some recognizable words, 'Agnès Veronique' and underneath her name, 'Robert Lindsay Oliver Wyndham-Brown' and then, next to the word *femmina*, 'Angélique Marie-Odile Augusta'.

'Angélique? That was what they called me?'

Laurent nodded. 'It was her favourite name. I knew as soon I saw it that I had found you.'

'Where did you get this?' I asked.

'From the Santa Cecilia convent in Viggiano. It's where you were born. You understand this is not a legal record. It is merely a copy taken from the register there.'

I stroked the rough textured paper. 'You mean there's no official record of my birth?'

'No.' He rubbed a hand across his eyes. 'Officially you don't exist. Except from this document.'

I fingered the date on the sheet, 'il 3 febbraio 1889'.

'This is my birthday?' I asked. Laurent nodded. 'How appropriate. Even the date I've been celebrating for the last twenty-one years is not really mine.'

'*Chèrie*, you should — '

'So why *was* I celebrating the 23rd February as my birthday, then?' I cut in harshly, interrupting him. He hesitated before answering.

'Because that was the date of birth of the real Isabella Wyndham-Brown,' he said eventually.

'What do you mean, the real Isabella Wyndham-Brown? *I'm* Isabella — I mean — ' I faltered, not really knowing what I did mean. After all, I wasn't Isabella Wyndham-Brown, not any more. I was somebody called

Angélique Marie-Odile Augusta. No surname.

Laurent sighed. 'There was a real Isabella Wyndham-Brown, born in the Ospedale San Giovanni at Castrovillari on 23rd February. Madame la Vicomtesse was really with child and she delivered a daughter some three weeks after you were born. Of course the documents to that birth are legal and binding. As far as I can surmise, the infant died with the three adults at In Salah later that year.'

Peter took my hand as I studied the paper, saying nothing. I had thought I was used to the news by now, but somehow seeing it written down in black and white made it real in a way merely being told had not. And, of course, I should have realized I had a half-sister even if only briefly. How else could Marnie have got away with her story? I thought briefly and bleakly about Marnie. Soon she and I would have a long, hard conversation.

But not now. Now I turned to this strange, unfamiliar man who was one of my closest living relatives. 'How do you know all this? You said you'd been holding this document for five years.' I stared hard at him. 'How long have you known about me?'

He shrugged. 'For about ten years,' he admitted. 'Although at first I refused to believe it. Perhaps I should explain from the beginning.'

'Yes, perhaps you should,' I said harshly. He glanced at me, then Peter, before nodding.

'Very well. But first, a drink, *non?*' Without waiting for our reply, he stood up and went across to the rickety little door that led through to the tiny canteen where his men were carousing. He snapped something to a legionnaire and returned to us, dragging another chair through from the bar.

'You may not believe this, *chèrie*,' he said, smiling at me mischievously, 'but when I was a child I was very spoiled.'

'Oh I can believe it,' I said bitterly. He grinned.

'*Eh bien*, my mother pampered me. After Agnès's death she felt bereft, you understand. Her only daughter dead, her husband numb with grief and unable to speak of it, her three older sons too old to spoil, but too young to comfort her; I was the only one left she could turn to. So, she doted on me. Which was very pleasant for me but not good, really. Later on, when my father had recovered from his sorrow, he saw what was happening, but did not know how to stop it. And so, I became a very unpleasant little boy, always used to my own way, careless of others.' He paused, then held out his hands. 'I was not a nice child.'

Just then, Abou, the canteen owner came in with a tray, bearing three glasses and a bottle with a dubious-looking brown substance in it.

'*Monsieur*,' he said, setting the tray down. Laurent gave him a handful of coins and he walked away, clearly pleased.

'Here, try this. It is very strong. Monsieur Bennett,' he said, pouring out two generous measures and passing one to Peter before pouring a tiny amount out for me. '*Et toi, ma belle*. It will make you forget your sorrows. *Salut.*'

Clinking our glasses, he drank the whole lot down in one gulp. Peter and I glanced at each other before taking more conservative sips, then gasping.

'Oh my goodness,' I said spluttering. 'What on earth is it?'

'*Boukha, ma chère*. A spirit made from figs. It is excellent, *n'est ce pas?*'

Peter wiped a few tears from his eyes. 'Very nice,' he gasped. Laurent grinned.

'The first time is the worst. Soon you will taste the sweetness of the figs, ripening in the sun.'

I looked at the tiny trickle of fluid left in my glass and decided I could live without the experience. 'So, you were telling us about your childhood, Laurent?'

'Hmm? Ah yes. Well, by the time I was seventeen, I was wild, out of control, what you would call a brat, I think. My father and my older brothers became tired of my wilfullness and my mother's refusal to see how bad I was, and in consultation with the entire family — the male element that is — they decided I should join the army. I think my father felt it would make a man of me. My brothers probably hoped I would be killed. They were not very fond of me at that time.' He thought about this for a moment, then shrugged. 'Anyway, being the spoilt little brat that I actually was, I decided that no one was going to tell me what to do, and if they all hated me that much I would take myself away. Accordingly, I sold my mother's most expensive necklace, bought a train ticket to Seville in Spain and made my way to Algier. It was there I joined the Foreign Legion.' He paused for a moment and poured more *boukha* into his glass and Peter's, before swallowing it down in one gulp again.

'It was horrible,' he continued. 'Before I had been in the service ten hours I knew what a terrible mistake I had made, but, *hélas*, by then it was too late. The Foreign Legion does not care why one signs the papers, only that one has. So there I was spoilt, rich, arrogant and about to be fed to the wolves, so to speak. I doubt I would have lasted a week under normal circumstances.'

'So what happened?' asked Peter. 'Did Papa manage to buy you out?'

'Unfortunately not, *monsieur*. It was six months before my father and my oldest brother Guillaume found me and by then I was in Madagascar. However I was lucky. There were three older Englishmen in the barracks I was thrown into who found out that not only could I speak passable English, but that I could read and write it as well. Fortunately they could not.' He shrugged. 'They decided I was more use to them alive than dead, so they taught me how to survive in the service and in return I wrote letters to their various wives and sweethearts. It was a fair exchange. They each had several women.'

'Oh,' I said. I couldn't think of anything else to say.

'Anyway it was not long before I heard the story of the Englishman with two wives, although I didn't take much notice at first, being concerned as I was with other little things, like not being murdered in my bed or dying of dehydration on the training exercises. Besides, it was a kind of joke, you see, among the French. But my three mentors, they were very proud of their compatriot. And then, one night, after a particularly successful raid against the natives in Morocco, we were celebrating in a little bar in Tangier and the talk turned again to the English aristocrat who had lived in In Salah and kept two wives like a real Muslim. Even then I was not very interested, until it was mentioned that one of them was French, a pretty young woman, who, it was said, was *cousine* to the older one. I will not tell you all they said — it is not for the ears of women — but the story ended with this man and his women dying of typhoid and only a little child and servant left alive and transported back to Algier by a detachment of my *confrères*. Now my memories of that time were naturally vague, but I knew Agnès had died in In Salah of typhoid along with our cousin and her husband, whilst a baby and servant were found by some soldiers. I also knew that everyone, even the family in London, whose name my father would not permit to be spoken, were mystified as to why they had remained so long abroad. It seemed reasonable to assume that they were talking about the same people. And so I understood, at last, what the others did not. Your father had disgraced my sister and they could not return.'

He stopped and took a deep breath, then let it out in a sigh, before emptying the dregs of the bottle into his glass and staring at the translucent brown fluid.

'One really should not drink too much of this. It is too pleasant. *Tiens*, where was I? Oh yes. Well, I heard the story and thought a lot about it. I was still very young, you understand, barely twenty, and two years in the service had hardened me, made me eager to fight, and jealous of my honour. I will not bore you with the many sleepless nights I spent vowing revenge on the Woodruffes for the shame they had brought on my family.' He laughed. 'The fact that your father was already dead barely bothered me at all. But I still had three years left of my service and there was little I could do whilst a legionnaire. And then, one night I heard another detail to the story, one that had not been mentioned before, that there were two children born to this Englishman. This was told to me by an Algerian in Sidi. They had a different view of the matter, you understand and he was most amused that the foreigner had been burdened not only with an older ugly shrew of a wife, who, it was said, was mad and who ruled him like an emperor, but he could also not get a son from either of them and was cursed with two daughters, one from each.' He leaned closer to us now, a finger raised in the air. 'Now I knew a child had been brought back alive and had been returned to the family in London. For many weeks I pondered on this new twist of events, one day cursing *le bon Dieu* for allowing the Woodruffe girl to survive whilst my own sister's child must perish, the next grateful that the evidence of her shame died with her. I was not a pleasant person to live with during those weeks and my *confréres* soon learned to avoid me. Finally, however, one grew bored of my petulance and persuaded me to confide in him.'

'That was nice,' I said, thankful that at least one of these thugs had a modicum of grace. Laurent looked at me, confused, for a moment before smiling.

'He beat me to a pulp behind the stables and demanded to know why I was being a — but, never mind. The point is, when I told him, he asked me why I assumed the child who survived was the daughter of the Englishwoman and not my own niece. At first I cursed him for a fool, but gradually the notion took hold of me and soon I could not get it out of my head. By this time I had only eight months to go before my time with the service was complete. They were the longest eight months of my life. As soon as they were up, I left Africa, returning to Europe, stopping only to see my family briefly, as by this time, we were reconciled and they had forgiven me my youthful impulses. Besides,' he shrugged, in that peculiarly pragmatic Gallic way, 'I needed the address of the Woodruffes. It was not easy to get. Papa was still filled with rage at the carelessness of the family who allowed his only daughter to die and I did not dare tell him my suspicions as he was unwell even then and I hesitated to tell him something so monumental that might not even be true. *Eh bien*, I managed eventually to discover the address of the Woodruffes in London and I travelled there in the spring of 1904.' He stopped and leaned back in his chair before looking up at me and smiling. 'I saw you outside your uncle's house one afternoon, *ma chère*. From the moment I saw you I knew you were Agnès's child. You were so like her even at that age. It was astonishing. I remember standing on the corner of the street after you disappeared into the house, not able to believe my own eyes.'

I frowned. 'So what did you do?'

'I returned to France.'

'What do you mean?' I cried. 'You can't possibly have come all that way and made such a discovery and just meekly go home again.'

He shrugged again. 'What choice did I have? I did not want to leave you but after

I had thought about it for a while, it occurred to me that all I would be doing was ruining your life. Think about it, *chèrie*,' he said and I could hear the note of pleading in his voice. 'You were loved, well cared for, much richer than our family, with a respected name and a comfortable life. If I went to Charles and told him the truth, you would become an outcast, shunned by society. The more I thought about it, the more I realized I could not do that to you. So I left.'

'You left?' I said. 'You made a choice you had no right to make and just left, without telling me or anyone about your suspicions? I don't suppose it occurred to you that perhaps the decision wasn't yours to make, or even that you might just be wrong?'

'You are angry with me, Bella. Always you seem to be angry with me?'

'Of course I'm angry!' I shouted, feeling so enraged I wanted to throw something at him. 'I can't believe even you could be so arrogant as to believe you had the right to do such a thing. Did it never occur to you that perhaps I might want to know who my real mother was? That perhaps I might want to become acquainted with my grandparents or my uncles or aunts? But no, you made a decision and of course once Laurent Marivaux makes his mind up, no one else is allowed to have

313

any say in the matter!'

I stood up violently, the chair clattering behind me.

'Ah, Bella — '

'Not now, Peter,' I snapped. 'I'm too angry to talk.'

'No, but — '

'Really!' I turned round to see him standing by the beaded curtain that looked out into the street beyond. 'The last thing I want is to hear you try to defend him, Peter. I'm far too angry.'

He shook his head. 'Oh I'm not trying to defend him, Bella. You can yell at him as much as you want as far as I'm concerned. I just thought you ought to know that Ishmail and his friends have arrived.'

'What!' I shouted. Laurent and I both rushed over to where he was standing.

He was right. Out in the late afternoon sun in the market-square, surrounded by a crowd of fascinated stall-holders and passers-by, were Ishmail and his men, all blue-robed and silent atop their camels.

13

Just then, there was a tap at the door.

'*Monsieur, les Tuaregs,*' said one of the legionnaires.

'I'll go.' Peter turned away from the window. 'I'll tell them you'll be there in a minute.' He moved closer to me and spoke softly in my ear. 'Let him finish what he has to say, Bella. You might be surprised.' Then he surprised me by kissing me gently on the cheek. He walked to the door and was gone.

With the feel of his lips still on my skin, I turned back to Laurent again. He watched me, his hands behind his back. I knew he had seen the kiss and it had not pleased him, but he was no longer in control and he knew it.

'So what happened after you left London?' I asked in a neutral tone.

'You must understand I was confused. For five years I had been used to obeying commands, having my life ordered in a very simple way, without the distractions of family or any other complications. Now I had knowledge of something my training had not equipped me to deal with. What was I do? You were my niece, blood of my blood and the

315

only link to my sister. How could I leave you? And yet, link though you were, it could not be denied that the truth would harm many people besides you. I did not know what to do, so I returned home and did the only thing left I could think of. I consulted my brother Guillaume.'

'Indeed? And what did Uncle Guillaume advise?'

Laurent sighed. 'You are angry still, *ma chère*. I understand. But please let me finish. By the time I got back, Papa was dying. He was in considerable pain and we agonized about whether to tell him he had a granddaughter, but in the end it seemed unnecessarily cruel. He could barely see, nor hear, or speak, and we didn't even know how much, if anything, he would understand of what we said. Then he died. My mother was beside herself with grief; again it seemed that nothing would be accomplished by throwing light on to this situation. So together Guillaume and I decided we would wait. After all, in the end it was you who stood to lose the most by the truth. So we decided to wait until you were twenty-one. Then we felt you would be old enough to make your choice, to live with what we had to say,' he finished, gesturing with his hands.

I frowned. Angry as I was with him and

also this new uncle who made decisions on my behalf, I could see they had a point. Telling an adult news of such momentous proportions is infinitely preferable to telling a fifteen year old. And even I could see that I was not the only one to be devastated by this. How would all my aunts and uncles in London react? How would they feel about me now? I rubbed my head; it felt as though it was being spun round like a dervish. I tried to remember everything that had happened since last spring.

'So, you waited until I was twenty-one. And then you came to see me. But I don't remember you telling me any of this, dear Uncle,' I said bitingly.

He shook his head and had the grace to look shame-faced. 'No. I was a coward. I couldn't help thinking of all the things you would lose by admitting who your real mother was. You had been Isabella Wyndham-Brown for so long, what difference would it make really? After all, you are the daughter of Viscount Bowood.'

'The *illegimate* daughter,' I said. 'It makes a difference. And there's the question of Mama's money — Amelia's money,' I corrected myself. 'It's not mine. It's not right I should have it.'

'Well, that is your decision now. Anyway,

317

while I was trying to decide what to do for the best, you found your father's pawn tickets which led to Monsieur Bennett. Knowing what I knew about your papa, I was interested to see what he was hiding.' He paused. 'Also I confess I was curious to see what you would do next. You and Monsieur Bennett — '

'I don't want to talk about that,' I said curtly. 'It's nothing to do with you.'

He did not agree with me, I could tell, but wisely he refrained from commenting. Instead he nodded.

'Very well. The rest you know or must be able to guess. I hired some people to steal the tickets from his office. I knew when you showed them to Monsieur Bennett what they were and I found the bank and the security box easily enough. The diamond was inside. Then I returned to France; I knew it was time to tell you what you needed to know, but first I had to tell my mother about you.'

'And how did she take the news?'

'My mother has forgiven me much over the years but I think not telling her about you was the worst. She refused to speak to me for a week.' He smiled. 'Actually none of the family except for Guillaume spoke to me — it was rather peaceful, really. Anyway, by the time my mother had forgiven me, you were well on the way to discovering what your father had been up to and I felt it might be easier for you if you came to discover the rest for yourself. That is why I left you to travel down to Algeria. I went to Sidi where I knew I could get some comrades to accompany us to In Salah — it is really not a safe place to travel alone, *ma chère*, as you and your friends infortunately found out. I was going to give you the diamond and tell you about your mother when we arrived; I thought it be easier to hear near to where she died.'

'You know where she died then?' I asked, eagerly. He nodded.

'I found her grave. And your father's,' he added more bitterly. 'I can take you there. I was going to, but I did not expect Monsieur Bennett to become so interested in me and by the time I found out he had escaped from Sicily, you had already left Algier. So.' He held out his hands. 'Here we are.'

I nodded as I picked up my straw hat. 'Here we are. Come on.'

'What?'

'I think we've kept the Tuareg waiting long enough. Let's go see what they have to say.'

'Very well.' He opened the door and gestured politely for me to go through. As Peter said, he did have excellent manners.

Outside, the camels were beginning to get a little restless. They weren't the only ones.

'I'm glad you're here, Bella,' said Peter, eyeing the legionnaires nervously. 'I'm not sure these fellows can be counted on to keep their tempers much longer.'

I nodded. Laurent's comrades were gripping their rifles with whitened knuckles and they looked like they would enjoy nothing more than an excuse to open fire. Behind their blue face-masks, the Tuareg seemed implacable.

'Laurent,' I said cautiously, and he nodded and snapped some orders. The legionnaires glanced at him resentfully, but there did seem to be a slight lessening of tension.

'They want you to go with them,' Peter said, waving towards the camel at the front. 'Ishmail says — I think — that they have a camel for you.'

I stared at the huge smelly beast standing next to him. I'd wondered why it was riderless. 'Absolutely not,' I replied and walked over to him. '*Monsieur*, no camels. No camels. *Chevals* only.'

Laurent winced. 'The word is *chevaux, ma petite*,' he said wearily and rattled something off to Ishmail who shrugged. 'How can you be half French and have no feel for the language at all?'

I ignored this as I walked towards a horse and put my foot in the stirrup.

'Wait a moment. Where are you going?' Laurent asked, putting a hand on the reins.

'With them, of course.' I tugged at the reins again and he pulled them back.

'You cannot go alone.'

'Of course I can. That's why they're here.'

'You cannot go alone. It is far too dangerous. I will come too and so will — '

'Don't be ridiculous.' I kicked the horse and it began to trot towards the camel train. 'They'd kill you the first chance they got, and frankly I can't say that I'd blame them. They want me, Laurent,' I said more gently. 'And I want to know what they've got to say. There have been many surprises today and I've a feeling they're not over yet.' I nodded to Ishmail, who nodded back to me and shouted something to his own men.

Laurent sighed impatiently. 'Monsieur Bennett, can you please explain to this — this troublesome child that she is putting herself in danger by her actions,' he asked turning round to Peter. But he was already on a horse himself.

'I'll go with her. She's right; you won't last an hour if those chaps have their way.'

Laurent threw up his hands in despair. 'Very well. As you wish. Go with *les sauvages*. I am helpless. Go.'

The Tuareg had already begun to point their camels towards the desert and Peter and I followed them.

'You realize he's given in far too easily, don't you?' said Peter, leaning in close to me as we reached the outskirts of the little town. I frowned. Wheeling the horse round again, I trotted back to where Laurent was standing.

'I know you won't be able to resist sending someone after us,' I said, 'but can you please be as discreet as possible? I would like to find out what they have to say without bloodshed.'

'You won't even know we're there, *chèrie*,' he replied cheerfully.

I sighed. 'That's what worries me, Laurent. Suddenly I find myself feeling much happier when I know exactly where you are.'

'Many women have said that to me, *ma belle*. But mystery is good for the soul.'

I gave him one last long stare and spurred the horse back to Peter.

★ ★ ★

We seemed to travel for miles out on the sands. The camels plodded along in front, their soft feet padding over the dunes tirelessly, the metal bits chinking in a kind of monotonous rhythm. It was late afternoon and our shadows lengthened as the hot sun sank lower in the sky.

'So. Did it go well?' asked Peter, as we struggled to keep up with the Tuareg.

'I suppose so,' I said wearily. Already I was hot and sticky, the coolness of the canteen shade with its tinkling fountain no more than a distant memory. 'He's very plausible, but — '

'But you don't trust him?'

'Do you?'

'No. But — and I hate to admit this, so don't start yelling at me — I am beginning to have a grudging respect for him. They know he's going to be following us,' he added, pointing to our escorts. 'And that's going to make us safer. Don't think it won't, Bella.'

'I know.' I frowned. 'It's so annoying.'

Peter grinned. 'Cheer up. When we get back you can refuse to tell him what they said; that'll frustrate him for a change.'

We plodded on for a bit. The landscape seemed unchanging to me; dull yellow sand piled up in endless dunes. But the Tuareg clearly knew where they were going, swerving the camels this way and that and leaving zig-zag marks in the sand. Or perhaps it was the camels who knew where they were going.

'Peter,' I said after a while, 'how did you know about the Foreign Legion?'

He squinted up ahead for a moment. 'My old sergeant in the police force had been a soldier out here about twenty years ago. I remember him telling me once about a ruffian they'd picked up in a bar-room brawl in Tangier. He said this fellow was the nastiest brute he'd ever come across in his life and believe me, for Sergeant Anderson to say that was quite an admission. The worst thugs in the East End used to beg us not to lock them up when he was on duty. Anyway, he said they turned him over to the French Embassy who gave him the option of being returned to France for sentencing, or he could join the Foreign Legion. Apparently they needed new recruits. This fellow chose the latter because he thought it would be the easy way out.'

'And it wasn't?' I pulled my hat down lower over my eyes to shield it from the late afternoon sun.

'Anderson says he saw the chap about fifteen months later, by pure chance, when they were leaving Morocco. He couldn't believe it was the same man. Tame as a kitten, apparently. Respectful to his superiors, jumped when he was given an order, completely changed. Of course, he did add the chap wouldn't look anyone in the eye and there were some odd looking scars on his face that hadn't been there before.' He looked at me and shrugged. 'If your uncle managed to survive that, he deserves a little respect.'

I thought again briefly of the long scar on Laurent's arm and shivered.

'I didn't know you were in the police force,' I said.

He looked at me, one eyebrow raised.

'There's a lot you don't know about me, Bella.'

'I thought you said you joined the army after leaving school.'

He nodded. 'I did. I was in for five years. I left when I was twenty-three.'

'Why?'

He smiled at me faintly. 'People kept telling me what to do. Besides, by that time my sisters had married and my younger brother Will was rather good at his chosen profession of importing cotton so my mother didn't need me to provide a regular income any more.'

'Oh. You sent her money?'

'Somebody had to. Aunt Beatrice certainly wouldn't.' He took a long swallow from his water-bottle, then passed it to me.

'Whatever happened to Aunt Beatrice?' I asked lightly.

'Still alive as far as I know. The last time I

saw her was in the spring of 1901. I'd just left Slane and she ordered me down to the country to discuss my future. She'd decided that I was to repay her generosity by joining her late husband's factory staff in the exalted role of junior clerk. Apparently we Bennetts don't like giving something for nothing.'

'And you went?' I looked at him curiously. 'Now that surprises me, Peter.'

'Does it? Why?'

'I thought you were much more rebellious and insolent than that. Somehow the idea of you meekly trotting up to see your aunt at her summons is quite disappointing.'

He shrugged. 'She sent a first-class rail ticket; it was a pleasant spring day and I'd just escaped school. I was in a compliant mood. Actually she'd also made arrangements for me to be accommodated at the town's best hotel for the night, but as it turned out I decided not to avail myself of that particular piece of largesse.'

'Why?'

He grinned. 'Well, Aunt Beatrice also thought I'd trotted up there to do her bidding, so she was quite surprised when I told her to go to hell.'

'Peter!'

'What?' he said, laughing at my shock. 'You just said you were disappointed that I'd gone so meekly. What's wrong now?'

'It just seems so rude. After all, she was your aunt. And she'd paid for your education.'

He snorted. 'She was a penny-pinching, sour, old bat and I'd had enough of her manipulations. And so had Will actually. He's two years younger than me and we'd talked it over. He was hoping she'd be so angry she'd refuse to continue paying for his education so he could leave Slane too. The only reason I'd stayed so long was because Mother had been so desperate to see us through there. She'd put up with a lot of humiliation from Aunt Beatrice too.'

'And did she refuse to pay?'

Peter laughed. 'No. I think she decided to write me off and concentrate on Will instead because the last two years she actually sent Mother some money to equip him properly for school. Poor Will was stuck there 'til the bitter end. Still, he got his own back when she summoned him to the ancestral home for his lecture on repaying family debts.'

'Oh. And what did he say to her?'

'He never told me,' Peter admitted. 'But I think you should know Will isn't as polite as me.'

I laughed. 'Peter, you're quite horrible. When I get home, I shall make it my business to meet Aunt Beatrice. I'm sure she isn't nearly as wicked as you suggest.'

'You must do as you please, but don't expect me to make the introductions. Although the old girl will probably be tickled pink at the thought of being sought out by a viscount's daughter.' He stopped suddenly and glanced at me.

'Even an illegitimate one?' I said softly, and he shrugged.

'No. I don't think she'd like that quite so much.'

'Then you were right and she can go to hell,' I said briskly, and now it was his turn to be shocked.

'Bella!'

I laughed. 'Excuse me, I think you mean Angélique. Or Marie-Odile. Or perhaps Augusta. I haven't quite decided yet.'

He shook his head. 'No, I like Bella. It suits you,' he said, looking at me seriously now.

'Well, it's the name I'm most familiar with,' I said. 'But come, you must finish your story now. What happened when you left the army?'

'I told you. I joined the police force and became a detective and found I was rather good at it although I became restless again fairly soon. Then my old superintendent came into a small inheritance and invested in a private detective agency that was doing rather well in Chepstow. He knew I was thinking about leaving and asked me to join him. He guaranteed me more autonomy and better pay so I jumped at the chance. Then when we were approached by the Cavendish Museum, I was offered the job because they needed someone with genteel manners.' He looked over at me and smiled. 'And so there you have it. My life story in ten minutes.'

'And now? Why did you leave the agency?' I frowned. 'Did you get restless again?'

He sighed. 'My fatal flaw, I'm afraid. I just don't like being told what to do. Sadly, however, I've learnt the hard way that such magnificent independence doesn't pay the bills. I'm going to have to go crawling back to Joe Connelly when we return.'

I leaned over and patted his hand. 'I wish I could do something for you, Peter. But I can't get any real money until I'm — ' I stopped. 'Well, actually, I don't suppose I'll ever get it now. It's not even mine.'

'I wouldn't have accepted any money from you anyway, Bella.'

I raised an eyebrow. 'Is that manly pride speaking, darling?' I asked lightly.

He grunted. 'Something like that. Hello, now what's this?'

I looked up to where he was pointing and saw that finally the dull endless sand dunes had given way to a slightly larger version of the oasis we had camped at the other night. In the distance I could see several camels grouped around two brightly coloured tents, the blues and greens and red starkly contrasting with the dirty faded yellow of the sand.

'I think we've arrived,' said Peter softly, as a camel with a tiny rider atop came running towards us.

Our little train didn't stop however, even when the man in blue reached us. He and Ishmail exchanged a few words and then he galloped, or whatever the camel equivalent was, back to the tents. Ishmail turned to us.

'Come.'

We followed him up to the tents and dismounted, giving our horses' reins to a Tuareg who led them down to the oasis where they drank gratefully. I took my hat off and began fanning my face with it, wishing I too was a horse and could just sink my hot, dirty face into the cool green waters of the pool. Then Ishmail came up behind us, his flowing blue robes swirling little eddies of sand around his sandalled feet.

'Come,' he said again, this time beckoning us into the larger of the two tents.

Inside it was cooler and dark after the blinding light of the desert and it took a few seconds before my eyes became accustomed to the dimness of my surroundings. Then I saw two figures sitting cross-legged in the middle of the floor, the smaller one swathed in blue, with a blue face-covering, and propped up by pillows which I came to see were richly embroidered in greens and golds with fantastic images of peacocks and swaying forests. Around them were seated about seven or eight men, all straight backed with their face-coverings pulled up tightly so only a thin sliver of flesh showed around their eyes. On their laps rested long curved swords. Involuntarily I backed away, almost falling into Peter's arms.

'Gently, Bella. I think they're more scared of us than vice versa.'

'Really? Could you tell my heart that? It doesn't seem to want to believe you.'

'I think — ' he began, but was interrupted by the other figure seated in the centre of the semi-circle.

'Please? Come in. Sit down. You are welcome.'

I squinted closer. A young woman about the same age as me was pointing to a spot near her on the carpet. Her face, unlike the men's, was bare and, as I sat down, I got the eery sensation that there was something familiar about her.

'Please. Take some tea,' she offered, in a rather deep voice. She said something in Arabic and then more figures behind her that I hadn't noticed in the gloom, women, again without face-veils, passed little cups of sugary tea to us and the other men. We all sat and drank, Peter and I rather nervously.

'It is good? You like it?' asked the girl amiably, her accent strong but understandable. Her fingers and arms were covered in rings and bracelets, her clothes brightly coloured versions of Ishmail's blue robes. A thin scarf of red and green covered some of her head, but left a lot of glossy black hair still on view.

'It's very nice,' I muttered awkwardly. I looked at Peter, but he was staring at the girl as though he'd seen a ghost and I knew he wasn't going to be any help. Honestly, men are just useless when they're presented with a pretty face. 'You speak very good English,' I added.

She nodded. 'Of course,' she said with a hint of arrogance. 'Please, let me introduce myself. I am Aja, daughter of the Foreigner, adopted by the Imouhar, those you call the Tuareg.' She paused, before smiling sweetly. 'I am also the Honourable Miss Isabella Lavinia Wyndham-Brown.'

14

'What!'

'I am Aja — '

'Yes, yes. I heard that. What I mean is — '

I stopped. What *did* I mean? I turned to Peter. Now I realized he wasn't bewitched by her pretty face so much as by the similarity between us. Because I could see it too. The eyes, the mouth, the line of the cheekbone. All the same features that stared out at me whenever I looked in the mirror. The only thing that was different was the nose: it was longer than mine. It was Amelia's nose.

'Miss Wyndham-Brown?' he spluttered.

'Yes.'

'Isabella Wyndham-Brown?'

'Yes. My father was Robert, eighth Viscount Bowood and my mother was Amelia Woodruffe. Would you like to see my birth certificate?' she asked politely. 'Mama kept it.'

'We thought you were dead,' I managed to blurt out. It lacked grace, but she didn't seem upset. She merely nodded.

'Yes,' she said. 'But I am not.'

'No. You're here. Why *are* you here?' I asked, frowning. 'What's the daughter of an

English viscount doing in the Saharan Desert?'

She smiled. 'This is not the desert. But I am here because this is where my mother came to escape the illness that afflicted In Salah when I was a baby. We have lived here ever since that time.'

'Amelia didn't die from typhoid?' I could feel my frown deepening.

'No she did not die from typhoid. Neither did I. She left the village and begged for refuge with these people.' She indicated the Tuareg sitting around us, before bending forward and pouring more tea in our cups. 'Tell me, why do you have my name?' Although she looked at me with no animosity, I got the impression she knew exactly why.

'Because everyone thought I was you. No one . . . ' I paused, scowling, 'at least no one except Marnie — knew about the other baby. Up until today I thought I was Isabella Wyndham-Brown.'

'Now you do not?'

'No.' I took a deep breath. 'I know who I am now.'

'You are Angélique.'

'Yes.'

'Your mother was — '

'Yes. I know who my real mother was.'

Aja smiled rather seriously, her kohl

smudged eyes studying me with interest.

'Be at peace, my sister. I meant no insult. What our mothers did, they did. You are no more to blame for the fault than I.' She frowned suddenly. 'Marnie is the serving woman, yes?'

'Yes.'

'She was supposed to be my nursemaid,' said Aja. 'I wonder why she thought you were me.'

'Believe me, it's a conversation I'll be having with her when I return,' I said with deep feeling.

'I too would like to speak to her. So I am Isabella and you are Angélique. It is complicated, my sister, is it not?'

'Yes, it is.' There was a silence for a few seconds. I looked at Peter, who reached out and took my hand.

'How did you know about Bella, Miss Wyndham-Brown?' he asked her.

'Who are you?' she asked, looking at him. She wasn't rude or abrasive or confrontational, she just wanted to know.

'This is my friend, Mr Peter Bennett,' I said. She turned her head to one side.

'A friend? And you travel with him alone? This is permitted? Curious. My mother always told me young ladies were much less free in England than we Tuareg.'

'Yes, well, she has a point. It's a long story. So perhaps — '

'And the other man you travel with, the *legionnaire*' — there was stirring of dislike among the Tuareg in the tent — 'he is a friend also? I do not think I like your choice of friends,' said Aja, disapprovingly.

'That's a long story too,' I muttered. 'But Aja — Miss Wyndham-Brown — ' I stopped. 'I'm sorry, I don't know what to call you.'

'Aja is simplest, I think. It's the name I have been called all my life. And you? What should I call you, my sister? I think Angélique is as strange to you as Isabella is to me.'

I cleared my throat. 'If you don't mind, everybody — my friends call me Bella.'

She shrugged. 'I don't mind.'

'Aja, please, may we speak with your mother?'

Aja looked at me thoughtfully for a few moments. 'Amelia, Viscountess Bowood is dead.'

'Oh. I'm sorry,' I said. There was a short silence, which, being English, I felt compelled to fill. 'Was it a long time ago?'

'Long enough.'

'Aja, believe me when I tell you I knew none of this. All my life I have been Isabella Wyndham-Brown. I only learnt yesterday about my real mother and then you. We thought you were dead — at least, we thought Mama, I mean, Amelia was dead. Nobody even knew another child existed. Well,' I added somewhat acidly, 'Marnie knew. But she didn't tell anyone.'

Aja nodded. 'I believe you. My mother suspected as much when weeks turned to months and months to years and no one from her family came out here seeking us. She heard about the child — you — being rescued with the servant woman. It suited her purpose.'

'Her purpose? You mean she remained here voluntarily?'

Aja raised two well-marked eyebrows. 'Of course. Did you think she was kept here against her will?'

I glanced at Peter. 'Well, actually, yes. After all, they abducted me,' I said, waving a hand at Ishmail and his men behind her.

Aja laughed and translated my words quickly. In a few seconds all the others in the tent were laughing too.

'Forgive me, my sister, but they took you because I told them to. You asked me before, Mr Bennett, how I knew about my sister being here; I will tell you. My mother gave up expecting someone to return for her many years ago. She realized it was assumed both she and I were dead, even that you had taken

337

my place. But she suspected that one day some member of her family might become curious as to our final resting place and so she instructed various members of our tribe, those who work in the city to the south, to keep alert for the name Wyndham-Brown or Woodruffe. For years nothing happened. But then thirty nights ago you arrived. And I arranged for you to come here.'

I frowned. 'I can't say I like your methods.'

'It was regrettable,' Aja agreed casually. 'But I could not be certain you would come.' She made a moue with her lips. 'I don't think I would have come if I were you.'

As she spoke she poured more tea in our cups and I had an absurd sense of dislocation as though I was in the vicarage at Woodruffe and we were all about to discuss the plans for the harvest festival. I shook my head briskly.

'Aja, what can you tell me about my — our parents? I still know so little. Why did they all come here? Obviously Marnie lied about some things, but I'm sure she was telling the truth when she said both your mother and mine died. And why on earth didn't Ma — your mother come back to England to claim what was rightfully hers — and yours?'

Aja picked up the delicate glass cup, her many rings clinking against its painted surface. She nodded slowly.

'I will tell you all that she told me. You know that your mother and my father — our father — they did not . . . ' She paused searching for the right words. 'They did not behave properly, but by the time my mother discovered this, it was too late. Agnès was already pregnant with you. My mother wanted to send her back to France in disgrace, but my father refused to let her go, insisting that he would provide for them both. My mother laughed at this — he had no access to her money, thanks to her lawyers and what little she allowed him he spent immediately. But still he refused to have your mother sent home in disgrace. In the end, my mother reluctantly agreed to help — Agnès was her cousin after all — but she insisted they all go abroad, so no one would know of the disgrace to the family or the humiliation to her. She made him pay for Agnès's travel expenses. At the time it gave her some bitter consolation but afterwards, she always regretted her pettiness. When she came to live with the Tuareg, and she grew to enjoy being valued for herself, she knew she was wrong to have blamed our father completely for his actions. Or your mother. She used to tell me she should never have married him; he was not meant for her and she would have wished she hadn't except that he gave me to her and

339

that was the greatest gift in the world.' She paused and smiled at us mischievously. 'And I, because I was an arrogant child, would think, yes, it was a fair exchange after all.'

I smiled at her. 'You were very lucky, Aja. You had a mother who loved you.'

Aja nodded. 'And you did too, my sister. Even my mother did not deny that.'

'And what about our father? Did he love us?'

Aja nodded. 'But he did not know what to do. Soon after they left England, my mother found out she was pregnant too, to her horror. At first she was appalled at the thought of carrying the child of a man she despised, but as the months wore on she found I was a solace to her. She ignored our father and your mother completely and spent all her time preparing for my birth. She told me she did not even know when you were born because our father and your mother left for the convent without telling her. Then I was born some weeks later. The birth was difficult for my mother and for a while it was feared neither of us would survive. But we did. However in the aftermath she experienced a terrible form of melancholy. She grew more distracted and concerned with circumstances that had not bothered her before. She kept seeing or imagined seeing people she knew and thought they were laughing at her and her faithless husband. And so she refused to go back home and insisted on travelling further and further abroad. She told me she forced our father and Agnès across to this country and into the desert. There at last, she said, she began to find some peace. She met these people' — she indicated the men and women around us — 'in the market at In Salah and, as she began to learn to talk to them, to listen to them buying and selling and understand their customs, she found she had more in common with them than with her own people. But she would probably not have stayed if it had not been for the coming of the sickness.'

Beside her, her companion stirred and tapped her on the shoulder. She leaned forward and listened to the whispered words. Finally she nodded and looked back at us again.

'This is Amina. She remembers my mother well. She asks if you know of the sickness?' I nodded and Aja continued, 'It was bad. The Tuareg were only in the town a few days when they saw the first signs. They left but many people stayed, including our parents. Then Papa fell ill. He sent the nursemaid for help, but she never returned and then your mother was sick too. My mother was still well and so was I but she began to fear for me and so she went to the Tuareg and offered them money if we would be permitted to stay near the camp until the illness had gone. They agreed.'

There was a little silence in the tent, followed by a hiss and a whoosh as candles were lit. They were perfumed and their aromatic scents wafted around us, sending jasmine and freesia in delicate smoky trails through the air.

I breathed them in deeply, feeling heavy with emotion. At last I knew the truth about my parents and about the woman I had believed was my mother for so long. I did not doubt Aja's testimony for one moment. It sounded starkly honest.

'Why did your mother not return to England when the disease died away?' I asked, picking up the tea and sipping it again.

Aja shrugged with her hands and all her jewellery tinkled. 'Why should she? She loved the life here. She went to my people with as much wealth as she could carry from In Salah as payment for sanctuary, so they would know she was a woman of substance in her own country and no slave. And while she waited for the town to be safe once more, she turned her time to helping them accumulate wealth. My mother was clever at figures and

342

among the Tuareg such skills are appreciated whether one is man or woman. They named her the money-maker and soon every man in the tribe was calling on her to help him with his merchandise and trains and commerces. Every year she vowed she would leave next year.' Aja smiled, as she turned and took Amina's hand. 'She was happy here.'

'I'm glad for her,' I said. 'And I think you've been happy here, too.'

'Yes,' said Aja. 'This is my home. But England is my home, too. I want to see it. So you will take me there, yes?'

'What?'

I stared at her, shocked. I had no idea that this was the reason she had brought me here. Going home with all I now knew was bad enough, having to tell Aunt Augusta and Uncle Charles and all the other relatives that actually I wasn't Isabella Wyndham-Brown, I was Angélique, the bastard daughter of the French companion, was worse. It never occurred to me that there was a real Isabella and that she'd want to go back with me. As I stared at her, appalled, her appearance began to register properly too. Here in the desert, with the heat and dust outside and the incense burning inside, the candlelight flickering on the richly textured carpets, Aja blended in. Her shimmering head scarf, her rings and bangles and necklaces and her brightly coloured robes were not out of place. But what on earth would they make of her in London? But then, what would they make of me? I wondered if, under the circumstances, I could suggest we both remain here.

Outside the camels made the funny bellowing noise that signalled they were being fed and I heard little whinnies of pleasure which suggested our horses were being fed too. Our hosts were nothing if not generous.

'Yes,' I said eventually. 'Are you sure you want to do that? England is very different to this place.'

Aja shrugged and her heavy gold necklace swayed portentously. 'Of course. That is why I wish to go. Will you take me, my sister? Or would I be an embarrassment to you?'

I felt my face flush. Had my thoughts really been that obvious?

'Of course not,' I lied, as only the English can. 'It's just that' — I hesitated — 'you realize nobody knows you exist? Well, actually, nobody knows *I* exist. At least as Angélique. That is to say — '

I stopped. It was too complicated and anyway, why not take her? Uncle Charles and all the Woodruffes deserved a real Isabella after putting up with a fake one for all these years. As I thought this, I couldn't stop a little smile stealing over my face. The idea of introducing Aja to Uncle Charles was suddenly irresistible.

'Very well,' I said. 'When can you be ready to leave?'

Aja turned to her companions, the old woman sitting next to her swaddled in her blue robes and Ishmail and his men behind them. They talked rapidly and vociferously for quite a while.

'Are you sure about this, Bella?' Peter whispered in my ear, as they discussed the matter. 'It's going to be bad enough for you and your family as it is. Do you have any idea what on earth they're going to make of her?' As he said this he glanced round at them all again. The discussion was becoming more heated now. I got the impression Aja's idea was as new to them as it was to me. Perversely I found myself beginning to like her a great deal.

'It's nothing to do with me,' I said firmly. 'She's the real Isabella Wyndham-Brown. She's got a perfect right to meet her family. Besides, do you want to say no to that lot?'

I pointed to the blue men, with their funny-looking swords resting on their knees. Peter squinted at them briefly in the gloom of the tent before turning to me with a shrug.

'Frankly no, although I'm not sure she's

got the backing of everybody here for her little trip. Actually I don't think any of them want her to go,' he added.

The heated discussion had given way to yells and shouts, the gist of which in any language said quite clearly, 'You're doing nothing of the kind, young lady'. I stood up and beckoned Peter to follow me out of the tent.

'I think Aja will persuade them eventually,' I said, as we moved outside. It was dark now and cooler. A fresh breeze played over our faces as we moved over to where the horses were munching contentedly.

'Very likely. She is your sister, after all,' Peter said.

He moved closer to me and I turned towards him, fitting my body snugly into his as I put my arms around his neck. It occurred to me briefly that this was no way for Isabella Wyndham-Brown to behave, but since I was no longer her anyway, I didn't have anything to worry about, except possibly unpleasant comparisons to my mother. I ran my fingers through his hair and felt his lips come down hard on mine as his hands moved under the thin folds of my lace blouse and pressed firmly against my skin. A horse whinnied in protest as we pushed too hard against it.

'You know, perhaps we should be a little

346

more discreet,' he whispered. 'Your damned uncle is probably out there right now watching us and working out how he's going to have me killed.'

I laughed. 'Probably. I wonder what he's going to say when I tell him about Aja?'

He pulled back from me for a moment, a grin on his face.

'Whatever it is, promise me you'll do it when I'm there.'

I pulled him close to me once more, meaning to give him my solemn oath, but my words were lost in the still of the night.

15

We spent the next three months travelling
back up through Italy again, going slowly in
order to give Aja some time to acclimatize
herself to the weather and also the cultural
change. She was intrigued by our clothes
— 'Why do you wear dead animal bones
around your waist, Bella? It is uncomfortable
and undignified'; amused by the food
— 'This meat is bland and tasteless, Bella.
Can you not afford better cooks?'; and
disdainful of the architecture — 'That
building leans dangerously to one side, Bella.
If it falls, it will kill many people. I think the
tents of my people are much safer'. But she
was delighted by the art in Rome and we
spent a month there whilst she oohed and
aahed over the Sistine Chapel, *The Last
Supper* and *The Crucifixion*, although since
she wasn't a Christian, she was less impressed
by the sufferings of our Lord than by the
masterly brushstrokes. By the end of January
she understood a great deal more than I did
about chiaroscuro and sfumato. Kate took her
around the various museums, whilst I cajoled
her into the great fashion houses, dressing her

as befitted the daughter of an English aristocrat. In our own ways we enjoyed ourselves immensely.

Adam had had to leave us before we even arrived in Sicily. He had suffered no more than a bad headache in the end and by the time we returned to Algiers he was completely recovered. Whilst we were discussing the best way to proceed, a telegram arrived from the museum he worked for, instructing him to make his way to Egypt with all speed to examine some new tomb that had just been discovered there. Kate decided not to go with him. She insisted she needed to return to England and Adam concurred, the pair of them assuring me that they would only be parted for a few short weeks. I think they knew even then how little prepared I was for the fiasco that Aja's return would generate. Kate stayed with me throughout the coming months and was the best friend I could ever have wished for.

We decided in the end that Laurent and Peter would return ahead of us, in order to break the news as gently as possible to my various aunts and uncles. Laurent could also speak to his own family before he got to England so they could be warned to expect a visit from me soon. We did this partly because it seemed kinder to have someone explain all this in person; partly because Kate insisted they leave us when Adam did. It gradually dawned on me that with my new sullied parentage and Aja's murky upbringing among the nomads of Algeria, the Wyndham-Brown girls now needed every ounce of respectability it was possible to scrape up. Partly also because it became very clear early on that Aja and Laurent would never be friends. To be fair to him, he did his best and, as I knew, he could be very charming when he chose, but to Aja he was never going to be anything but a legionnaire and the Tuareg and the legionnaires were mortal enemies. So we waved goodbye to Adam one day as he departed for Cairo and Laurent and Peter the next as they took the first train to Italy and then up through Europe as quickly as they could.

I enjoyed our return journey very much, but became more nervous as we drew nearer to England. Realzing this, Kate wired her father and got him and Alice to come out to Paris to meet us two weeks after Christmas. There must have been a hastily convened Woodruffe family meeting as well and, showing more sensitivity in one hour than had probably been shown in five generations, it was decided that Harriet should accompany them. She was compassion itself, telling

Aja how excited they all were to meet her, how much they were looking forward to hearing her stories of life among the savages (luckily Aja did not hear her, as she was looking at photographs of Uncle Charles at the time — 'He is so like Mama, Bella. It is most unflattering') and constantly telling me to ignore anyone who said anything horrid about Papa and Agnès.

Alice Whitaker, however, wasn't quite so blinkered. One afternoon when Harriet and Kate had taken Aja riding in the Bois de Boulogne, we took tea together in the reception rooms at the Hotel d'Angleterre. At a table a little way away from us sat a group of English ladies. I did not pay much attention to them at first, although I was vaguely aware that they kept looking at us furtively and that occasionally there would be some undignified giggling. Alice ignored them for a while but eventually, even she could bear it no longer and with a gentle 'Do excuse me for one moment, my dear', she stood up gracefully and walked across to their table. I did not hear what she said, naturally, but, as she left them and returned to me, they all stood up rather shamefacedly and retired from the room.

'Friends of yours, Alice?' I enquired.

'No, my dear, just a few acquaintances.

You'd be quite bored by them.' Our eyes met as she sat down again.

'This is how it's going to be from now on, isn't it?' I said, my eyes following the now chastened group as they walked towards the door. One of the group turned back to stare at me, her eyes full of spite and contempt. I recoiled in shock and seeing this, Alice took my hands in hers.

'Yes, it is,' she said gravely. 'I wish it were not so, but already the news of your parents and of Aja and her mother has become the talk of the moment.'

'Shouldn't that be 'scandal'?' I said, trying to make light of it. Alice did not smile.

'Doubtless many will think so. And they will try to make you pay for your parents' indiscretions. But remember you have family and friends who love you, Bella. You must keep that in mind in the difficult months ahead.'

I nodded as the last lady left the room. No more was said between us of the incident, but if ever I had any doubts as to how different my life was going to be from now on, they were finally laid to rest forever.

16

London, April 1911

I climbed down from the carriage and paid the driver, before looking up at Peter's office building. The scruffy little sign he used was gone, leaving a square tidemark of soot in its place, but Laurent's car was still outside, guarded once again by a gang of little urchins, so I knew he hadn't left yet. I went straight up the stairs, my boots clattering on the bare wood as I manoeuvred past two women on their way down.

'Hello, Mabel,' I said, recognizing the taller of the two. 'Is Mr Bennett in his office?'

Mabel stared at me as she adjusted the feather boa, now more threadbare than ever, around her neck. 'Yeah, but you'd better be quick, darlin', 'e was packin' the last of 'is boxes when I saw 'im. You know 'e ain't open fer businesss anymore?'

'Yes, I know. I was just hoping to see him before he left. Had you gone to say goodbye to him?'

'Yeah. Bleedin' shame 'e's leavin',' she said, sounding genuinely sad at the thought. ''E

353

was a real soft touch fer a copper. Still,' she added, in a tone which suggested she'd get over her grief, 'at least I got a sov'reign outa that nice-lookin' Frenchie in there wiv 'im.' As she spoke she slipped a coin down her cleavage. This was obviously Mabel's preferred repository for storing small change. Then she looked more closely at me. ''Ere, I recognize you.'

'You were here the first day I came to see Mr Bennett,' I said.

'Nah, that ain't it. You look — ' Suddenly her face cleared as enlightenment dawned. 'You're that bird wiv' all the money. Only it weren't yours on account of your ma and pa — '

'Yes, that would be me,' I said, as Mabel and her companion looked at me more closely in the way many people did nowadays, as though they weren't sure I was to be pitied or reviled. The newspapers had a lot to answer for.

'An' there's a real one, an' all, ain't there?' Mabel's eyes glazed over for a moment. 'Cor it sounds really romantic.'

'Does it?' I was slightly surprised. I could think of many words to describe my current status, but romantic was not one which immediately leapt to mind.

'Oh yeah. Yer ma and pa fallin' in love like

354

that, 'im sweepin' 'er off 'er feet and takin' er away to foreign lands, all 'ot and strange, then dyin' an' leavin' you wiv loadsa money that wasn't really yours but the ovver little gel's and she's still over there livin' like a savage. It sounds lovely.' As Mabel spoke she waved her hand vaguely in front of her to indicate the colourful scene she was painting, her companion transported with her. For a moment I was transported too. Then Mabel turned back to look at me. 'Wodjer bring 'er back for, gel? You must be mad.'

I restrained the urge to laugh. It was a question, I suspect, that a lot of people wanted to ask me, but no one had had the courage to do so to my face before.

'Well,' I said, 'legally it is her money, after all.'

Mabel chortled. ''Oo cares abaht legally,' she said, showing a fine disdain for the backbone of our social system. 'Still, you ain't doin' too badly, I suppose,' she added, eyeing my black, ermine-edged coat.

I nodded. I might no longer be the possessor of a magnificent fortune but, as Mabel pointed out, I wasn't on the streets either. I had a lot to be thankful for.

'Yes. It was nice to see you again, Mabel.'

'You an' all, miss. Come on, Dais'. I wanna 'ave a look at that motor aht there. I ain't never seen a frog one before.' And she and her companion were gone, leaving me with a brief mental image of a car with webbed feet.

I climbed the rest of the stairs into Peter's office. It was cluttered with boxes, from which books and files overflowed along with some chipped cups and saucers. Peter was standing with his back to the window, packing another box on the battered old desk. He looked up and smiled when he saw me.

'Ah the Honourable Miss Wyndham-Brown.'

'Sadly no longer honourable, nor Wyndham-Brown either,' I replied. He nodded.

'So the lawyers had their way then?'

I sat down in the scruffy armchair.

'They've been threatening this for months, but in the end it was Uncle Guillaume who persuaded me to take my mother's name. Actually' — I grimaced — 'he and Aunt Augusta fought over it for nearly three hours last Sunday before he went back to Lisieux. She kept insisting I had every right to Papa's name and the Wyndham-Browns would not be dictated to by bureaucrats, and Uncle Guillaume was equally insistent that the Marivaux name was the only one by which I should be known. They were both most *formidable*,' I added in my best French accent. It was getting better slowly, but

Laurent still winced whenever I made a mistake, which was every other word apparently.

Peter smiled as he forced a thick book into a thin space. 'I must say the idea of you sitting there letting them fight over you like that seems quite unlikely.'

I let out a sigh as I took off my gloves. 'To be honest, I was feeling rather fragile and almost pathetically grateful that there were even two people in the world who weren't ashamed to claim me as their own. The Hargrieves' ball is next week and it's the first time ever since I came out that I've not been invited. That's the third one this season. Oh I know I should expect it,' I said, as he started to speak, 'but even so it hurts more than even I thought it would. And, of course, no one really seems to know what to make of Aja, so she doesn't get invited either. Not that she cares.' I sighed again.

Peter pushed a lid down on one box and picked up another from the floor and began filling it with papers.

'You shouldn't let it worry you, Bella.'

'I know. But last week Helen sent a note over saying she's terribly sorry, but she can't invite me to her soirée because there was a mistake over numbers and her table is full. But she's sure I understand.'

357

Peter put down the papers and came round to my side of the desk. he perched on the edge and took my hands.

'I thought you said the Woodruffes were rallying round you.'

'They are. For the most part. Harry's being an absolute trooper. She keeps taking me out to lunch and dinners and suppers all over the town and she holds on to my arm as though she thinks I'm going to run away and positively glowers at people who try to snub me. Maude Goodman tried to ignore us at the theatre last Tuesday and she forced her to come over and talk for ten minutes. It was quite amusing actually. Especially when one considers how much Harriet has always despised her and used to ignore her. But Helen and Edwin do have his career to consider. I can't blame them really, I suppose,' I ended forlornly.

'Rubbish. She's been your cousin for twenty-one years. Anyone worth her salt would say to the devil with what other people think. And as for that idiot of a husband of hers — he should be shot.'

I smiled bleakly. 'That's more or less what Harry said. So does this mean you won't be ignoring me if we should meet by accident in the street?'

He frowned. 'Do you expect me to take

358

that question seriously?'

I bit my lip. 'Actually, darling, I do. I'm still feeling a bit fragile.'

Peter took my face in his hands and kissed me. 'Bella, I couldn't care less what a bunch of toffee-nosed snobs think of you or your parents and as far as I'm concerned they can all go to hell. I'm on your side, remember?'

'I remember,' I said, feeling absurdly happier.

'Although since none of these people know I exist and wouldn't rate the opinion of a failed private detective anyway, I'm really not sure it's worth anything,' he continued, going back round the other side of the desk again and putting more papers in the box. I frowned.

'I thought you were going to wait one more month until you gave up.' He shook his head.

'No point. The rent ran out last week and anyway there was hardly anything coming in. Your aunt is the only one paying me at the moment and I feel a fraud taking that. There's no point delaying the inevitable.' He smiled grimly. 'Joe Connelly's offered me a job and since I don't have any choice, that's what I'm going to do.'

'I wish I could help,' I said, sighing, 'but — '

'I told you before: I wouldn't accept your

money anyway, Bella, even if you were still rich. And since you're not now, that's that. How is Aja?'

'Coping extremely well, under the circumstances. She's very sure of herself and she's absolutely revelling in all the legal complications over the money. Every time one of the lawyers comes up with a reason why she can't be accepted as the real Isabella Wyndham-Brown she produces another document that proves she is. She doles them out like sweeties. I think the lawyers will tire of the game before she does. Amelia taught her very well.' I laughed briefly. 'I suspect before she's finished, she'll not only have total control over the estate, but she'll have it before her twenty-fifth birthday too. And Uncle Charles absolutely adores her. He actually cried when he first set eyes on her. He said she's the very spit of M — Amelia.'

Peter looked at me. 'And how are you coping?'

I smiled. 'I'm glad for them all. Of course I am. How can I not be? And apart from Helen and one or two others I can't complain that they are treating me badly. Uncle Charles had a long talk with me last week. He was actually rather sweet really. Told me he'd always think of me as his niece too and I didn't ever have to worry about money whilst he was alive.

Considering what my parents did to his sister, that really is exceptionally decent of him. And Aja won't hear of me leaving Woodruffe. As far as she's concerned it's my home too.'

'I see.' Peter finished the last of the packing and sat down on the chair behind the desk. It was now late afternoon and sunshine was streaming through the windows. 'And what plans does she have when the money is sorted out?'

I shook my head. 'Who knows? I don't think she'll stay in England. She doesn't really approve much of us, to be honest. She told me last week she finds the English narrow-minded and intellectually dishonest. And, of course, Harry is beside herself with joy over the whole Tuareg culture. Did you know that they trace lineage through the female side of the family? When I left this afternoon, she was trying to persuade Aja to take her back to meet her family.'

There was a silence for a few minutes. Then Peter leaned forward, putting his elbows on the desk.

'Bella,' he said rather plaintively, 'how much longer have I got to put up with Marnie?'

'I thought you liked her, darling,' I said, trying to sound hurt, but in fact I knew this was coming. I'd seen Marnie only an hour before and she had been muttering darkly about Peter's habit of throwing his jacket on the back of the sofa and not on the coatstand when he returned home.

'I do like her. As much as I'd like any irritating, inquisitive old cockney lady, but if I'd wanted to have someone constantly tidying away my books and complaining about me not wiping my feet when I walked through the door and inviting hordes of other old crones into the house to drink tea and stare at me disapprovingly, I'd have gone back to live with my mother years ago. Surely Lady Faversham has found somewhere for her to go by now?'

'Not quite, darling, but it won't be long now,' I said, crossing my fingers behind my back.

This was another reason I'd encouraged Peter to leave us in Sicily. Angry though I was with Marnie in the aftermath of our adventures, she was still my responsibility and I knew she'd need protection from Uncle Charles. So I'd instructed Peter to leave Laurent to do all the explaining and go straight to Woodruffe Manor. I told him to take her to Aunt Augusta as I knew she'd always had a soft spot for the old wretch. As it turned out there was a good reason for this. Aunt Augusta, it transpired, had had her suspicions about me ever since I was a little girl, but being of a pragmatic mind, had said nothing to anyone. She and Marnie, apparently, had had an obscure, but enlightening conversation when I was twelve regarding my curiously strong resemblance to Great Aunt Evangeline, she of the disgraced French connection, and Marnie was instructed forthwith to discourage any interest I might show in France or any of its culture. Fortunately I never did show any interest in anything even vaguely intellectual, so Aunt Augusta grew complacent over the years, although I had recently realized, with rather bitter hindsight, why she was so concerned with my behaviour immediately after the Henry Fitzroy incident.

But I digress. Peter took Marnie to Aunt Augusta and explained everything to her and Aunt Augusta dispatched her to an inexpensive, but respectable apartment far away from Uncle Charles and his ire until I returned and we could decide what to do for the best. All went well at first, but by the time Aja and I came home, Marnie's conscience, which had been nagging away at her ever since Peter had explained about Aja, decided the only decent thing to do was to go back to Woodruffe Hall and throw herself on Aja's mercy. Luckily Aunt Augusta saw her coming up the drive and managed to hide her until Peter was summoned and ordered to convey her back to her lodgings with instructions not to let her out of his sight. I don't think he was particularly keen on guarding an obstreperous, if penitent old lady, but he knew how fond I was of her and since he had already had first-hand experience of Uncle Charles in full and righteous flow, he knew better than to let her return. Also Aunt Augusta promised to pay him handsomely and at that time he still had hopes that his business would improve. So Marnie was now installed in some very nice rooms in Bermondsey with instructions that she was to act as Peter's housekeeper until further notice, and Peter moved in, promising to put up with her ministrations in return for lodgings that were far superior to the ones he had hitherto enjoyed. The arrangement was working out well as far as I could see, although he had started muttering about being a kept man and Marnie was becoming very insistent on being allowed to visit Aja and make her confession. Aunt Augusta and I were still working on Uncle Charles, trying to downplay Marnie's role in all the duplicity, although it was hard going.

'I'm taking Aja to see her tomorrow,' I said, as he glared at me. 'I've managed to get her to understand how important it is that Uncle Charles not know of her whereabouts.'

'Is he still commissioning private detectives to find her?' Peter asked grumpily.

I cleared my throat. 'I don't think so, darling,' I lied.

Peter narrowed his eyes. 'Because there are only so many friendships in the business I can trade on to stop him finding her,' he said irritably. 'I've already fended off four as it is. And he's putting the price up, you know. It's only a matter of time before he finds her. And then what are you and Lady Faversham going to tell him?'

I sighed. 'I don't know,' I confessed. 'I'm hoping that when she finally meets Aja, she'll realize that everything turned out for the best and she's got nothing to feel guilty about really.'

'How could she possibly have got you both mixed up?' he asked me for the hundredth time. 'She was employed as Aja's nursemaid. Wasn't she supposed to dote on Aja and loathe you?'

'Well, you know as well as I what she says,' I replied. And despite his irritation, Peter nodded. Marnie had been startlingly frank when she'd explained the situation to Aunt Augusta and me.

'Little babies all look alike, Miss Bella,'

she'd said. 'An' add to that you was both little gels, 'ow was I supposed to know the difference? An' after yer pa got sick bad an' sent me off for 'elp, I was away for about three weeks. An' when I got back, worried sick 'cos I couldn't find no one to 'elp, Miss Agnes, 'er ladyship and one little baby was nowhere to be found an' I nat'rally assumed they was all dead and buried. Them 'eathens knew enough to bury the dead quick like. And there was yer pa, just breathing 'is last and you was lying in the cot with Miss Isabella's chris'ning shawl around you. What was I s'pposed to think? I was terrified I was gonna get sick meself and since you seemed all right, I just waited until I was sure 'is lordship was dead, grabbed you and scarpered quick. It never occurred to me you wasn't little Miss Isabella until you was about four or five and even then I couldn't be sure. I didn't remember much of yer ma, anyway. 'Er ladyship 'ired me when she was in Italy an' I joined 'er there. An' it was made pretty clear to me that if I wanted to keep my job I 'ad to ignore 'er — Miss Agnes that is — as much as possible. *An'* it was also made clear that I wasn't to mention 'is lordship's little liaison with anyone when we returned to England. I just thought I was keeping the spirit of my poor lady's dying wishes. After all, I thought they was all dead and you was little Miss Isabella. An' when it finally struck me you was more like Miss Agnes than 'er ladyship, what was I supposed to do? Go to Mr Charles and say 'Excuse me, sir, but I think I made a mistake. That little gel what you've been thinking is your dear sister's daughter, is really 'is lordship's little mistake with 'is fancy woman. Sorry about that.' I did the best I could under the circumstances, Miss Bella. I just feel dreadful about that poor little gel being left to be brought up by savages.'

She'd started crying then, and there was nothing Aunt Augusta and I could do but try to console her. 'After all, Bella dear,' as Aunt Augusta had said afterwards, 'crudely put though it is, she has a good point. What could one have done after all that time? One can only hope Charles will eventually see it that way.'

'So have you actually tried discussing it with Charles recently?' asked Peter, standing up and putting his jacket on. I nodded.

'I brought the subject up yesterday in fact.'

'And what did he say?'

''Don't talk to me of that wicked, immoral jezebel, Bella. When I find her, I will personally make sure the full might of the law is brought to bear on her for deceiving this family so wickedly for so long'.'

Peter raised an eyebrow drily. 'So he's not mellowing at all, then?'

'Not this week, Peter,' I admitted sadly. 'Please try and put up with her for a little while longer. I know she can be a mischievous old wretch, but I do love her and, despite what she did, if it wasn't for her I'd be dead. And I got to be brought up in luxury. She deserves my loyalty if nothing else.'

Peter sighed. 'Can't you point all this out to Charles?'

'I have,' I said. 'But he won't listen. And I feel guilty enough as it is, since I'm not actually his real niece, but the daughter of the woman who humiliated his sister. So I feel trying to force him to forgive Marnie on top of everything else is just too much to ask.'

Peter shrugged. 'He's going to find her sooner or later, Bella. You'd better resign yourself to that.'

'Yes I know, darling. I'm just hoping that when she finally meets Aja, she'll feel less horribly guilty.' I paused. 'Aja's terribly feudal when it comes to servants, you know.'

Peter laughed. 'Yes, I noticed that. She treats them more like slaves, doesn't she?'

I nodded. Aja had not endeared herself to the servants at Woodruffe Hall and I spent a lot of my time mollifying the staff and trying to act as a buffer between them and my half-sister. The many comments one heard about 'brown-skinned heathens' notwithstanding, Aja was as fair as I was, and apparently, among the Tuareg, the lighter the skin, the more noble one is considered. Consequently, Aja, with her mother's wealth to bolster her, had been brought up among the Tuareg like a little princess, with the best clothes and food, servants to minister to her every whim and her mother doting on her and giving her an education to which most western women did not have access. I think it was fair to say under the circumstances that she had not been deprived too terribly in Algeria and after meeting her and being exposed to her brisk way with servants, I was hoping Marnie would soon get over her own guilt.

Just then there was another clattering of boots on the stairs and Laurent appeared. He was wearing a long dusty overcoat, his motoring goggles perched on top of his cap.

'Bella, *ma petite*,' he said, pulling me towards him with the traditional dance of cheek kissing that the French seem to revel in. I had visited my Marivaux relatives in March and I don't think I have ever been embraced so much in my life. 'How wonderful you are here. I have just been

369

down to the excellent public house in this street and they deigned to sell me a bottle of whisky.' He pulled a small bottle from his coat pocket. 'I could not see Peter leave this place without a final salute. Will you join us?'

As he spoke Peter dug into one of the boxes and produced three rather chipped teacups.

'So,' said Laurent, sitting on the edge of the desk and pouring whisky into each cup. 'To what shall we drink? The end of an era? Or new beginnings?'

'Both would be appropriate,' I said, picking up a cup and chinking theirs each in turn. When we had all taken a sip, I put the cup down carefully. It didn't look like it would stand much handling. Peter meanwhile was looking rather distrustfully at Laurent.

'Did you know your uncle here has also offered me a job in his Paris office, Bella? Even though I explained to him I speak no French.'

Laurent beamed at us both expansively. 'I am becoming very fond of your young man, Bella. He shows great promise. There is no reason why I cannot find something for him to do in France. I have clients from all over the world.'

Peter took another sip from his cup. 'Yes. He also told me that if I lay another hand on you in his sight, he would have me killed. I'm still trying to work out if he was joking or not.'

Laurent's smile did not falter. 'Merely a *plaisanterie, mon chèr* Peter. Of course, I would not dream of harming you.'

'No, of course he wouldn't, Peter,' I added, patting Laurent's hand. 'But if you ever did feel threatened by Laurent, even slightly, just tell me. I'll deal with it.'

'Would you really, *ma belle*?' enquired Laurent, his eyes becoming momentarily darker, as they had done in the desert. 'What would you do?'

'I'd tell Uncle Guillaume of course. You won't believe this, Peter, but Laurent is actually frightened of his oldest brother. He hardly dare open his mouth when Guillaume is in the room.'

'I? Frightened by my brother?' Laurent frowned. 'You believe I am actually frightened by my brother?'

'Yes. And Uncle Sebastien and Uncle Bertrand too. Do you know,' I said, turning to Peter, 'he took me out for the afternoon when I was in Lisieux last month and brought me back later than he'd promised. Uncle Guillaume was absolutely livid. He shouted at Laurent for about half an hour afterwards.'

'I was just humouring him,' Laurent said,

but his eyes refused to make contact with mine.

'Rubbish. You tried to interrupt twice and he got even more angry. In the end you were practically grovelling on the floor.'

Laurent looked at me with narrowed eyes for a second, before finally conceding defeat.

'One would think I was still a little boy,' he said sulkily. '*And* it was I who found you. You would think they would give me a little credit for that at least. But no, whenever anything goes wrong it is always Laurent's fault. They are jealous. They have always been jealous of me.'

'I'm not surprised,' I retorted. 'Considering the way *Grandmère* dotes on you.' I had met and fallen in love with my grandmother instantly on my trip. She was a sweet, gentle soul who had gone out of her way to make me feel at home and cherished. But she spoiled her youngest son abominably; even I could see that.

Laurent shrugged, unconcerned by this accusation. 'Can I help it if *Maman* finds me adorable?'

Peter snorted. 'So that's Guillaume Marivaux, is it, Bella? Just make sure you spell it for me before you leave.'

Laurent smiled at him frostily. 'And how is life *chez Mademoiselle* Marnie?'

'Wonderful,' replied Peter. 'Although I think a little trip abroad would do her the world of good. Say France, for example. What do you think, Bella?'

I grinned, but before I could speak, Laurent picked up the teacup and swallowed the last of his drink. 'Not a chance, *mon vieux*. The old woman is your responsibility.' He stood up. 'So. I must be going. Might I take you somewhere, *chèrie?*' he asked, walking to the door. 'Or will you be remaining here?'

'I think I might stay a while, Laurent,' I said.

He sighed. 'That's what I was afraid of. Do not, I beg of you, tell Guillaume I permitted it. *Sois sage, ma petite*,' he said, as I followed him to the door and he kissed me again. Then he held out a hand to Peter who took it. 'Peter, let me know what you decide.' As Peter nodded, Laurent gave me one last smile and disappeared down the stairs.

We watched him from the window as he distributed coins to the gang of scruffy urchins he had employed as guards for his motor car, then roared off in a cloud of black smoke.

'Are you seriously considering working for him?' I asked, as I sat down again in the armchair. Peter shrugged.

'I don't know. Joe's job is only temporary; I don't think it will last for more than a few weeks. It's really just a bit of surveillance. I could do worse, I suppose. And I have to admit I am curious to see what sort of a business he runs. Especially after everything that Commissaire Fréret said.' He paused and looked up at me. 'Would you mind?'

'Not at all, darling. Although I confess I would worry about you. Somehow I don't think Laurent does anything as trivial as surveillance. But you know, I might be able to help you after all.'

'Bella, I've told you, I'm not taking any of your money,' he said in exasperation. 'You don't have enough of it nowadays to go around throwing it away. And besides — '

'No, listen, silly,' I said. 'I'm not proposing to give you my last penny, but I did come here this afternoon with something to show you. It's occurred to me I must still owe you something. Look,' I added, before he could interrupt. I picked up my handbag and opened it.

I pulled out a small blue and silver box and pressed the catch on the lid. The top sprang open.

'Ah,' said Peter. 'The Dragonsheart.'

He picked up the thin, delicate silver chain and held the slim blue diamond, encased in a silver filigree frame, up to the light by the window.

I took it from him. 'Look if you twist it this way, you can see the dragon. There, did you see?' I twirled it around under the last beams from the fading sun, until it was possible to see a crude but discernible figure of a tiny winged beast breathing a thin strand of blue fire from its mouth.

'It's very pretty,' he said at last. I raised an eyebrow.

'But — '

'Well, to be honest, I thought it would be heavier than that.'

'Peter, you're not a complete philistine after all.'

'What?'

I laughed. 'I'm sorry, darling, I couldn't resist that. You're quite right. After all the fuss the wretched thing has caused down the years, it really isn't very valuable at all.'

'Really?'

'No. That's why Papa's diary stopped mentioning it so abruptly. Well that and the fact that he'd just found out he'd got his wife's cousin pregnant. Laurent gave it to me just before you left us in Sicily and I had it valued when I returned to London. It is very pretty, you're right, and the craftsmanship of the frame increases its value, but the most I was offered for it was four hundred and fifty pounds.'

'You're joking! Only four hundred and fifty pounds? I thought you said — '

'I know. All I can think is that over the last few centuries the legend must have been more and more exaggerated and every time someone was told the story another hundred pounds or so was added to its value until in the end we had all convinced ourselves it was worth thousands of pounds. Poor Papa must have been devastated when he found out it was really worth so little. I think he really was going to give Mama — I mean Amelia — all the things he mentioned in his diary. Probably after all that time it was a nice feeling that he was the one with some money. And then he must have discovered that Agnès was pregnant and thought that at least he would be able to provide for her. That's why he insisted that she be spared the disgrace of being sent home. Aja said that Amelia laughed at him, but he really believed he had some money of his own at last. And then he must have found out that actually all he had was a rather handsome trinket. No wonder he had to sell his watch and the other things. You know, I realize that what he did was dreadfully wrong, Peter. And I do feel awful for poor Amelia. No one deserves the humiliation she endured. But even now I can't help feeling a little bit sorry for Papa. I don't think he was completely bad, you know.'

'People rarely are, Bella. It would be a lot easier if they were. But I wonder why he didn't just sell it off straight away. It would have been a lot easier and quicker than having to go round all the pawn-shops. Less humiliating for him, I'd imagine.'

'Oh, I think I can answer that,' I replied. I took a letter out of my handbag and gave it to him. 'Read this.'

He unfolded the slightly yellowed paper.

My darling Agnès

I hope that you will never have to read this letter, but the events of the last few days being what they are, I fear with a very real certainty that we will never see England again. Amelia grows ever more capricious and I realize now that I should never have agreed to us coming here in the first place. But here we are and here we must stay. Certainly I must do so, at least until the fever passes. I hope and pray that its course is mild and recovery is swift, but in the event that this is not the case and if for some terrible reason you find that you no longer have me to protect you, I pray you take our darling Angélique back to Algiers as fast as you can and throw yourself on the mercy of the consulate there. I can give you little hope of salvation in these circumstances, my love, but I pray that your family find it in their hearts to forgive us both for our transgressions and not lay the blame on our innocent baby daughter who even now enchants me so completely that I cannot bring myself to regret anything we have done. To this end I pray you take this key to Fortescue and Hopkins of Albermarle Street, London. There you will find the famous Bowood Dragonsheart diamond. It is not, alas, anywhere near as precious as family legend has always decreed, but it will help you for a while at least. Finally, might I lay one last burden on you? When you reach Europe, please go to the first British Consulate you can find and tell them of Amelia's whereabouts so that they may send someone to retrieve her. I know it is unfair of me to ask this, but I fear for the welfare of my little Isabella if Amelia is left to her own devices and although I know in my heart,

*and how it pains me to have to
acknowledge this that my two dear little
girls will never know or love each other,
at least I will know that they will both be
safe.*

*Keep this key safe, my love, it is all I
can give you,*

Robert

There was a long silence whilst Peter read
it. Finally he put it down and looked up at
me.

'Where did you get this? Did Laurent give
it to you?'

'No. Laurent knew nothing about it. Aja
gave it to me.'

'Aja?'

'Yes. A few days after we arrived in Rome.
Apparently her mother had found it amongst
some of the belongings she took with her
when she left In Salah with Aja and she gave
it to Amina with instructions to pass it on to
whichever member of her family came
looking for her if they ever did. Look, here's
the key.' I held up a little key that would have
doubtless fitted the strong box in Fortescue
and Hopkins. 'I think Papa must have
deposited the Dragonsheart there quickly
when he realized it wasn't the salvation he'd

hoped for, but was still a little nest egg for him to fall back on when he returned to England. Obviously Amelia wouldn't be helping him out any more. Poor Papa. He really was trying in the end.' I sighed.

Peter looked back at the letter. 'Do you really think Amelia just happened to find this in her belongings?'

I held out my hands. 'I really don't know. It's so hard to imagine how desperate things must have been for them all in the end. There is one thing though.'

'What?'

'That old woman, Amina. Do you remember her?'

Peter screwed up his face. 'The old crone sitting next to Aja in the tent?' He shook his head. 'Not really. She had her face covered in all that blue stuff Ishmail and his boys were wearing. Why?'

'Well, that's the thing, Peter,' I said, frowning myself now. 'I was telling Laurent all about this the other day and he said that was impossible. Apparently among the Tuareg only the men cover up their faces. The women are never veiled.'

'Really? How odd?' He put the letter down and looked at me. I stared back. 'Wait a minute. You don't think — that old woman — you think she's Amelia?'

'I really don't know. It was so hard to see anything in that gloomy tent and she had her face very well covered, but I'm sure her eyes were blue.'

'But why?' Peter said. 'What possible reason could she have for hiding from us?'

'I suppose for the same reason she hasn't ever wanted to come back home before. She just likes it there. And do you remember Aja's words when she told us her mother was dead? She said 'Amelia, Viscountess Bowood died many years ago'. Doesn't that sound a little too formal if you think about it? You know — this person died, but the real human underneath is still alive, but just living a different life?' I looked at him, but he was still frowning.

'What does Aja say?'

'I haven't asked her,' I admitted. 'I've tried a couple of times to bring the subject up, but she just evades all my questions.'

He thought about this. 'Well I suppose that in itself is an answer of sorts,' he said. 'So, what are you going to do with this?'

I didn't answer straight away, just looked at the Dragonsheart sparkling in the sun as he twirled it round on the chain.

'Well, I did think about giving it to Bertie at first, since it was once part of the Bowood inheritance,' I said. 'But then I thought, drat

381

it, why should I give it to anyone else? Papa
found it and he was entitled to do what he
liked with it. And he did give it to Agnes
— Mama — to help me. And frankly it's
worth so little anyway, I don't see what
difference it makes. Do you?' I must have
sounded a little guilty, because he smiled.

'Are you trying to salve a guilty conscience,
Miss Wyndham-Brown?'

'Miss Marivaux, actually,' I said rather
grumpily, then relented. 'And if you must
know, yes I am.'

He laughed again. 'Do what you like with
it, Bella,' he said, putting it back in the little
box. 'I don't think Bertie deserves to benefit
from your father's good luck in finding it and
I don't think Aja either needs nor cares about
it. He left it to your mother. And if that old
woman really was Amelia, you can be sure
she read this and knows all about it. So if
she's happy for you to have it, I wouldn't
worry about anyone else.'

I smiled. 'I'm so glad you said that.
Because this is what I think we should do
with it.'

'We?'

'Yes, we. You and me. I propose that I sell
this and give you the proceeds for your
business. I think you're a very good
investment and I'm hoping to see a good

return for my money in a few years' time. Besides,' I added, grinning at him. 'I rather like the idea of having you at my beck and call. It will make up for all the times you were horrible to me.'

He smiled. 'I was never horrible to you. I've always been the very soul of compassion and tenderness, even when you were behaving like a spoilt brat. But,' he added, moving round the desk and putting a finger to my lips before I could object, 'if you really want me at your beck and call all the time, there's a much simpler and cheaper way to achieve it.'

'Oh really? And what's that?'

'Marry me. I don't think Marivaux suits you anyway. You need a good Anglo-Saxon name.'

'Like Bennett?'

'Like Bennett,' he agreed, pulling me closer to him, his hands once more around my waist.

'Darling, do you really know what you're suggesting? After all, I am a spoiled brat.'

'I'll take the chance.' His lips brushed against my cheek.

'And I'm terribly extravagant. I'll probably spend all our money on hats and gloves.'

'Then I'll get used to eating hats and gloves.' Now his mouth had found my ears and the hollow of my throat.

'And I'm a dreadful housekeeper. I know nothing about cleaning things. Or cooking. Although — wait a minute, Marnie can do all that.'

He pulled back from the base of my neck. 'Marnie?'

'Marnie. She'll be in her element. She just loves cooking and cleaning and tidying and nagging at people.'

He sighed. 'I'm never going to be rid of Marnie, am I?'

'Darling, you'll get used to her. And I can't just abandon her, now can I?'

'I suppose not.' He moved back towards my neck again, then stopped. 'But she is absolutely not coming on honeymoon with us.'

'Of course not, darling.'

'And she's going to have a room a long way from ours. About three streets away if I have anything to do with it.'

'Um — ' I began, but he glared at me.

'We're not still talking about Marnie, are we?'

'Not at all, darling. I was just wondering . . .'

'What?'

'Does the door have a lock on it?'

There was a second's pause, then he began to laugh.

We do hope that you have enjoyed reading this large print book.

Did you know that all of our titles are available for purchase?

We publish a wide range of high quality large print books including:
**Romances, Mysteries, Classics
General Fiction
Non Fiction and Westerns**

Special interest titles available in large print are:
**The Little Oxford Dictionary
Music Book
Song Book
Hymn Book
Service Book**

Also available from us courtesy of Oxford University Press:
**Young Readers' Dictionary
(large print edition)
Young Readers' Thesaurus
(large print edition)**

For further information or a free brochure, please contact us at:
**Ulverscroft Large Print Books Ltd.,
The Green, Bradgate Road, Anstey,
Leicester, LE7 7FU, England.
Tel:** (00 44) 0116 236 4325
Fax: (00 44) 0116 234 0205

Other titles published by
The House of Ulverscroft:

THE SCARLET QUEEN

Jacqueline Webb

Kate Whitaker is the spoilt daughter of a Victorian Egyptologist; she enjoys playing tricks on her father's assistants on his desert digs. She anticipates amusing herself with her new prey, Adam Ellis. But Adam is made of sterner stuff and soon puts her in her place. Seven years later the pair meet again in London. Adam, now an archaeologist himself, accompanies Kate back to Egypt where her father is searching for an ancient fabled statue known as the Scarlet Queen. And when Kate discovers that she has a rival for Adam's love, her troubles are just beginning . . .